VIKTORIA LLOYD-BARLOW

All the Little Bird-Hearts

T0030618

ALGONQUIN BOOKS
OF CHAPEL HILL   2023

Published by
ALGONQUIN BOOKS OF CHAPEL HILL
Post Office Box 2225
Chapel Hill, North Carolina 27515-2225

an imprint of WORKMAN PUBLISHING
a division of HACHETTE BOOK GROUP, INC.
1290 Avenue of the Americas,
New York, NY 10104

Cataloging-in-Publication Data is available
from the Library of Congress.

ISBN 978-1-64375-661-5

10 9 8 7 6 5 4 3 2 1
First Edition

For my husband, SLB

fire can be mistaken for light

The Lake District

IT WAS ONLY THREE YEARS AGO THAT I SAW VITA FOR THE FIRST time. The day began as my days always did then, greeting a daughter for whom adolescence meant allowing me increasingly smaller glimpses of herself. I woke her before showering and dressing, then, predictably, had to wake her for a second time before going downstairs. I was in a long-standing white-food routine that summer, and my meals typically comprised various breakfasts: toast, cereal or crumpets. On days when food does not have to be dry, scrambled eggs or omelettes can also count as white. I cannot tell if it is a day on which an egg is a white food until I hold one in my hand. It is a small but real joy to me that as an adult I can decide, without explanation, whether eggs qualify as white, and therefore edible, on any given day. Without being told I am making a show of myself. That I am hysterical, attention-seeking and to be ignored until I eat something that is violently coloured.

Occasionally, and only in front of Dolly, I would

showily eat something that did not adhere to my assigned list of foods. *You can eat normally then; you can do what the rest of us do without a fuss.* My mother said this, often. I answered her silently when she was alive and I continue to do so now she is dead: *There is a cost, Mother, always a cost to such transgressions, and I am the one who pays.* I am the one whose throat and body burn when I politely swallow down food of the wrong colour; it is my arm that itches when a neighbour greets me by lightly placing a hand on my skin. I wear the marks of these encounters, these painful sensory interruptions.

In truth, though, the cost always felt less when it was my daughter for whom I performed. Because she is all that I have loved more than adherence to my routines. I was already afraid, then, of what was between us. I thought of it as a well-fed creature who was expanding rapidly, separating us further from one another every day. My response to Dolly's distance had always been to work harder on the illusion of normalcy. Whenever I was able, I concentrated on overriding my natural behaviours in front of her. In a white phase, I daringly added admittedly pale, yet non-white, pieces of food to my meals: chopped and peeled apples, pale green grapes, some poached salmon or chicken. During a period when fruit and pink yoghurt were all I found edible, I would make us a plate of cheese and biscuits to share in front of the television, and privately shudder as the dry crumbs spread out like fingers in my throat.

The year before Vita arrived, a cat had taken a liking to our garden. A taut, grey creature that stared fixedly into the distance whenever approached, he was as a little statesman, affronted by contact, but straining to remain polite. Despite this apparent disinterest in our company, he visited us regularly for a time, bringing the small dead bodies of mice and voles. These he placed carefully at our feet, before sitting in apparent reluctance next to us, his body tense and his little face turned away. At first, we tried to pat him, but although he did not move from his chosen position, he visibly shuddered at our touch, and, in his own unhappy way, he taught us to ignore him completely.

When I ate non-white items for my daughter, I held myself as tightly as the cat and, like him, I hoped the sacrifice would be appreciated wordlessly and without fuss. Dolly scrupulously refrained from direct comment on my attempts to challenge my style of specific eating. I chose, as I often did, to read her adolescent disinterest in me as discretion. In return, I resisted describing to her how alarming I found the vibrancy and textures in the broad range of foods that she favoured. I realise now that perhaps this gentleness between us was an imagining of my own; all the non-saying, the unspoken compromises, these felt like love to me. But I have come to see that my daughter does not find comfort in silence, that this is only what *I* find there. I know now that we are separate and unalike, in this way as in so many others. I should have remembered how quickly she came to hate that cat.

Shortly after I woke Dolly that morning for a second time, the door slammed, informing me that she had left for school and that I was now alone in the house. But voices from upstairs whispered insistently down to me in the hall. Her television had been left on, as it often was, to talk into the empty room like an elderly and confused guest. The set was a recent gift from her father, and the austere black boxiness of it was satisfyingly at odds with the otherwise girlish bedroom. These furnishings were her grandmother's choice many years ago, and the Laura Ashley frills had not been to Dolly's own, more sophisticated taste for some time. When she became a teenager, we planned to redecorate her room for her sixteenth birthday, and we had frequently discussed the various paint colours, or wallpapers and the curtains she might then choose. But our plans were made back when 1988 seemed implausibly far into the future, and the idea of my little daughter becoming a young woman was equally illusive. And that summer, when Vita entered our lives, Dolly was already sixteen and our redecorating conversation had been replaced by my silence as she wondered aloud about being off on a gap year or away at university within a couple of years, *How often will I actually return here?* she would ask. This, with a smile and one hand on her pointed Forrester chin, *how often would she actually return here? Because, you know, the travelling . . . and new friends and, well . . . a career, I expect.* When she said the word 'career', she gave a little intake of breath, the giggle of a child made to reference an embarrassing term in a biology class.

Dolly's conversation was often ungrammatical, lacking in clear subject or in structure, yet fraught with meaning. While she spoke in broken phrases about her future, her tone was especially light and lovely. Hers was a pretty song and I enjoyed the music but not the meaning; much of what my daughter said to me that summer met this description. Her conversation was a beautiful diversion, and I only felt the resultant wound later, when she was no longer there. The cheerfulness with which she spoke of leaving was as terrible to me as the sentiment itself.

Although I had entered Dolly's bedroom that morning with the intention of turning off the television, the factual nature of the discussion prevented me from doing so. An elderly professor was being interviewed by a jaunty woman in a brightly coloured dress, the pattern of which appeared to move and flicker independently, like interference on the screen. The professor was an expert on Victorian culture and apparently spent his summers on a cruise ship from where he gave lectures and sold signed books, one of which he was holding and occasionally managed to get into the shot.

The presenter in the studio was enthusiastic in a bright and uninformed manner, but conversation between them was complicated by their disparate locations. The satellite delay was not referenced or explained, and this created the appearance of hesitancy in the interviewee. In the immediate space after each query – *When did the British first start decorating a tree at Christmas? Why are Dickens's novels so long?* – the professor silently stared into the camera with his features resolutely unchanged. Once each question finally reached him, his expression was transformed, and his face became visibly animated. But his initial, blank expression and delayed answers were painfully reminiscent of my own daily interactions. It took me back to an embarrassed parent elbowing the back of my school blazer as I silently organised perfect sentences in my head but struggled to bring them to the surface, like a deft swimmer trapped underwater. Both strangers and acquaintances regularly repeat questions to me as I fail to respond within a time frame that I have no way of knowing. Their eyes fix on me still, as though their sternness will somehow extract the unvoiced words.

The professor's answers, when they finally came, were minutely crafted. I could pass undetected, I thought, in a place where conversation functioned in this extended period. The delayed conversational response and the accompanying discomfort were so familiar that I reached to turn the programme off. The professor stared impassively back as he faded with the picture, a lone face surrounded by the endless sea as he waited in silence for the words to land.

I began to tidy Dolly's bedroom, enjoying the reclaimed silence in my home. As I pulled open the curtains, the piercing early light flooded in and dazzled my view of the fields above us. We live in a scooped-out valley of a town. (Where orderly roads are buffeted by farmland on one side and then confronted on the other by the flat lake. The grey water spreads possessively along the length of our town and walls us in.) The street behind ours is met abruptly by farmland that slopes resolutely upwards and away from the town. I have always lived here, so I know the end of summer brings flames to those fields. I am drawn to watch after each harvest as the farm workers set child-sized fires to consume what is barren on the land. The smoke rushes down to the gardens below and it is rotten, but sweet with knowing. And every year, I repeat, '*Bruccia la terra, bruccia la terra . . .*', to myself. This is the way Italians describe the intensity with which Sicilians work their land: *burn the earth*. I whisper this as softly as a prayer, to make the fires seem good and pure. The post-harvest burnings taught me how fire can be mistaken for light and can call to you in the same way.

When my eyes acclimatised to the sunlight, I noticed a small, dark-haired woman lying on the lawn next door. The house was a holiday home, owned by Tom and his wife, who visited each summer and for occasional long weekends. Locals did not typically take to the summer people, whose numbers had increased in recent years, but

Tom was affable enough to remain outside this category. He had three children; all were so close together in age that for several years it had seemed he was bringing the same unchanged baby back and that the infants who toddled uncertainly behind him were the real newcomers. Tom's wife was fair-haired, and as soft-bodied and sweet-faced as a child herself. The woman in the garden was none of these things.

Her obliviousness to my gaze immediately moved me. She was on her back with her arms and legs spread out to a degree that looked unnatural, as though she had fallen from a real height or been positioned, unconscious, by someone else entirely. Here was the pleasure of observation without the ambiguity of eye contact, which costs but never confirms what you are being promised or refused. I once watched my baby daughter like this while she floated easily on her back across the screen of a scanning machine. *I have loved you longest*, I would tell Dolly when I felt sentimental, making my case in a contest that she did not, in any case, care to enter. *I knew you first*, I said, over and over to my daughter. *I watched you, loved you before you ever saw me*. I spoke first to her watchful baby face, and later, I addressed her composed woman face with the same tender and misplaced ownership. Her eyes remained unchanged with age; always, she was suspicious and scrupulous in equal measure.

The woman who would become my own Vita lay on Tom's green-striped lawn, as sweetly motionless in the sunshine as the fruit trees that surrounded her. The previous summer had been a long season, augmented as it was on either side by a warm spring and a gentle autumn; at its peak, the airlessness had confined us indoors in the manner of a belligerent father. The year of Vita, though, began as a demonstration of sunshine, a visual performance of summer without real heat. Those early days were memorably bright with a hazy quality of light promising a warmth it did not provide. On reflection, that time seems now like something of a dress rehearsal for what arrived later that year, for the explosion of heat that paced up and down our hazy streets, with a fixed grin and outstretched arms aflame.

Vita's arms were spread out horizontally and her hands were placed upwards, as though waiting for expected gifts. Her beautifully pinned-up hair and the inky neatness of her tailored clothes alarmed me. Such a formal appearance gave her position the suggestion of collapse or violence rather than intention. I ran downstairs and into my own garden, noisily slamming the French doors and then opening the creaky door of the shed, to check her response. Her head turned towards me, and as she opened her eyes, we looked directly at one another over the low wooden fence, the intimacy of her waking between us. Her lovely face, though, was serene, and she stood up to walk into her house entirely unselfconsciously, as though alone and unwatched.

Then my doorbell rang, and she was there. At my front door, sleepily blinking and stretching her arms behind her in the fake sunshine, fingers entwined behind her back. 'Mm . . .' she crooned softly to herself and then laughed as she saw me. 'I am not – yet – quite awake!' she said.

Kwaite. Awayk! I repeated silently to myself. *Kwaite. Awayk!*

I frequently mimic the pronunciation of others and have learned to keep this to myself where possible. I like to tap along with their syllables and trace both the emphasis and the softness. The sharpness of Vita's vowels was that of a foreign speaker with an immaculate and studied accent. I listen to dialogue intently; since childhood, this practice has protected me from eyes that are always seeking mine in greetings or conversation. Facial expressions typically tell me nothing more than what is being said. The manner of speaking – the tone, the points of hesitation, the emphases – these are what talk to me.

'Hello! *I* am Vita,' said the fragrant little woman who stood on my doorstep.

Duh-duh! DUHHH dee dee-dee, I imitated silently, searching for patterns that might suggest another county – or country – of origin, or a social position. It helps enormously to use my fingers in the style of a conductor when I listen to conversation, but I have found this can distract and perturb the speaker. At an initial introduction, the speaker typically emphasises first the greeting and then their name, but Vita's deliberate pause on the personal pronoun gave her the air of an awaited celebrity – *Here I am at last!*

My former father-in-law has a long-standing, and often referenced, friendship with a local and mildly celebrated actor. I met the man several times at their house, and on each occasion he greeted me as if for the first time and with a fixed routine: he dipped his head and looked up modestly before announcing his name with a small and twisted smile, as if we were simply playing at formalities, because no one needed to be informed of who he was. Vita, though, was not congratulating herself. The excited tone of her introduction felt like an acknowledgement of something between us; her accented 'I' seemed to include me. It was as though I had been expecting her, or, at least, had been aware of her existence, shared some familiarity with her.

It is always the duty of the established resident to make friendly overtures. If the existing neighbour does not extend an invitation, the newcomer must observe formal practices in any passing interactions and not request or offer personal information. My reference on this subject was a much-consulted book acquired when I was a teenager, with the aim of demystifying some of the ongoing social puzzles in which I found myself. *Etiquette for Ladies; A Guide to Social Activity* was written in 1959 by Edith Ogilvy, an aged and prolific author of romance novels and a daytime wearer of diamonds and cerise chiffon. Edith was at once socially punctilious and acceptably eccentric, an elusive balance and one that I still hoped to achieve myself. The late Lady Ogilvy married twice, and both husbands afforded her aristocratic titles and a glamorous lifestyle. These happy circumstances were frequently referenced in her writing and in the accompanying photographs. Her concerns, therefore, tended towards the rarefied – the management of staff at one's country house and the appropriateness of address for visiting dignitaries, for example – but the social advice was generally sound. Edith committed a whole chapter to neighbours and new acquaintances. However, her writing did not mention the possibility of you watching a stranger sleep before they awoke and appeared at your front door without invitation.

'I saw you and couldn't wait to introduce myself. I wanted to meet you. My husband says I am so impatient to make friends I don't give anyone the chance to actually invite us anywhere!' giggled Vita. Her laugh was loud and unapologetic, and she did not cover her mouth or try to swallow her amusement, as people do, but instead opened her mouth wider, displaying shiny little teeth.

Calm down, calm down, quiet, quiet, quiet, I had always been cautioned as a child when I made any noise. *Speak up, repeat that, say that again*, I have been told regularly since adolescence, but Vita's admission of eagerness over etiquette removed all blame from me for this back-to-front introduction, and I was grateful. Her accent carried the considered precision of a moneyed life, of tennis lessons, private education and summers spent abroad. The tone was self-assured and soothing; that of a guest ordering drinks from an inexperienced barman. I realised that, far from being foreign, Vita had the most English accent I had ever heard. Her pronunciation was so clipped and perfect that even I, who make a practice of detecting incongruities, thought at first that it must be a deliberate and carefully executed performance, a parody. But her voice came cleanly and effortlessly to her.

'Why are you in Tom's house? Are you a friend of his?' I asked.

Her slim elegance made her appear younger from a distance, but close up, I could tell she was considerably older than me. Her gently lined face placed her perhaps in her mid-to-late fifties, with sharp eyes and the kind of skin whose upkeep requires regular and carefully oiled exposure to sunshine. *She will not keep that colour in our town much past August. Nor will she have much opportunity to show off a tan here, covered as we mostly are in coats and scarves.* I told myself this in my mother's voice, but even as I silently scolded Vita, I knew that this woman would be tanned all year round, and that she would find plenty of occasions that demanded the kind of clothes that celebrated her sun-touched skin. There was a glittery sheen to Vita's body that I have never seen on anyone else. I do not expect to know another Vita. She was a person-shaped precious stone, something mined and brought up to the surface to live among the pebbles, a shiny reminder of our comparative dullness. Where I am pale and insubstantial, Vita was dark and deliberately formed, as real as a piece of marble. And as cold under your hand. I am a stutter of a person, a glitch that flickers; I am the air blurred by the summer sun.

'Tom? Oh, yes, Tom! He is a good friend of ours. Sweet, *sweet* man, isn't he? Sweet. And what is your name?'

Her unexpected presence on my doorstep that day was an awkwardness and I mentally leafed through the files of first meetings in my head. Although Vita was watching me, there was not that familiar tick-tock of waiting; she seemed entirely without curiosity or concern. Her steady gaze was without expectation, and this was both new and pacifying. Eventually, I introduced myself, trying to repeat the pattern of her initial greeting: *Duh-duh! DUHHH dee dee-dee*.

'Hello! *I* am Sunday.' As I said my name, I stepped backwards to create space between us. I am constantly reversing away from people; the whole world is a revolving series of rooms I have walked into by mistake. And I am never allowed enough time to settle, but am instead called out into another room, which demands another, unknown set of behaviours. Sometimes I back myself flat against a wall while escaping from an acquaintance and then I move sideways instead, crab-like and rigid-jointed. *Say how do you do and never, never, say pleased to meet you*, Edith invisibly prompted. 'How do you do?'

Vita replied: 'You're Sunday? Fantastic, darling! Fantastic. How do *you* do?' She was all approval, as if we had agreed to make up names and my choice pleased her.

I did not ask Vita to explain her implication of complicity regarding my name; long ago, I tempered the part of me that expects people to be clear. But accepting confusion means living alone down the rabbit hole. It means I must cling tightly to whatever realism and facts can be confirmed, to the accents and voice patterns that speak truthfully. It means a cartoonish life where the impossible and unscientific must not be queried, however peculiar they seem. The owner of my local post office does not greet me with the cheerful 'Hello' that he uses with other customers. When I visit his shop on overcast days, he asks, 'What have you done with the sun?' He speaks sharply and without humour, as if I am withholding something material that rightly belongs to him. His other greetings for me include querying why I brought rain, or snow, or wind; it is me, rather than the seasons, who he holds accountable for every change in the temperature. His preferred and commonly employed rejoinder is the equally nonsensical, 'Bring summer with you tomorrow, all right, love?' and this is reserved for goodbyes. The man thanks me for pleasant weather in the polite and routine tone of someone handed their change.

I have perfected a sound like an exhalation for people who talk like this: *Ha!* This effectively indicates that I am both amused by and understand their point. It is the answer to all social riddles that cannot be solved by stating the alternative option: 'That's interesting.' People like this observation, too, but both responses must only be made during the silences between their statements and not spoken during their speech, even if they are repeating themselves. Do not reference their repetition or correct them, however factually wrong they are. People, too, like eye contact. But not too much. I have a system for this, as I do for many of the social situations in which I find myself. I hold the person's gaze for five seconds and then away for six, then back on for five. If I am unable to reach five seconds, I try instead for three before allowing myself to look away.

People do not like you to fidget, or tap your fingers, or to move much at all; they prefer stillness. And smiles. Edith Ogilvy insisted: *A smile can lift even the plainest face into attractiveness. If one cannot be beautiful, one must still endeavour to look kind and happy. A smile will bring social success, while a sulky countenance, however pretty, will inevitably fail to secure friends and new acquaintances.*

But the impending relief is what I focus on when you are speaking, and I frown back at you in concentration. So many rules and reminders that I can hardly hear a word you say.

On my doorstep, Vita took my move away from her as an invitation and walked inside, exclaiming on the similarity of our homes. She patted my wrist as she passed me, and the navy fabric of her suit was surprisingly soft against my skin. Her surety was something like perfume and I breathed it in. She commented favourably on the uniformly white walls that run throughout my house, but it was in the non-possessive manner with which one approves a passing view or a glimpsed artefact. I knew, already, of course, that her own home, wherever it was, would be riotous with colour of all kinds, as well as visitors, pictures, clutter, noise. Edith Ogilvy was stern about interiors being natural and unpretentious, while retaining an air of comfort. *To achieve good taste, residents should avoid ostentatious displays in their homes, such as obviously new or novel items, or photographs whose objective is only to demonstrate social connections.* I have succeeded in this last directive, at least.

My house and Tom's are lone twins on the quiet street, two early Victorian buildings huddled together amongst a collection of mid-twentieth-century semi-detached family homes. Tom's, the first to be built and positioned at the far end of the cul-de-sac, enjoys the most private position. The builder of our two houses went bankrupt before he could realise his plans to replicate the solid red-brick houses, with their elaborate porches, along the street. The two detached Victorian buildings, with their square and serious lines, then, are incompatible with the smaller rendered houses surrounding them, and this shared difference affords our homes an air of considered solidarity against their subsequent neighbours. The feeling I have for my home is painful; that of a spouse who has married above themselves and whose love is frequently interspersed with the cold panic of possible desertion. A house is something I could not have acquired for myself, and I think, often, of the parallel life I might have had, housed in a disapproving institution, or homeless and unwashed on the streets, frightening myself and others. My parents' hard-working and modest lifestyle meant they paid off the mortgage some years before they reached their tenth wedding anniversary, an accomplishment that astounds me when I consider my own paltry income.

Vita and I entered my kitchen, which still features the turquoise cupboards with amber crackled glass that my father fitted when I was a child.

'What a beautiful colour!' she said, stroking the units without self-consciousness, and as I might have done myself.

But it was already too late for me to change what I had planned to say. On meeting for the first time socially, I have found that people typically ask where you live and what your job is. Vita already knew where I lived, therefore I had prepared a line that described my work at the farm. I certainly had not expected this topic deviation into interior décor, and it takes time and considerable effort for me to adjust my conversation or focus. I do not envy other people's ability to adapt; I find it alarming. Their minds are like caught fish, shining and struggling and engaged in a perpetual and pointless circular motion. Those like me swim on, unaffected by the change in currents around them.

'I work at a farm. In the greenhouses.' It was involuntary speech; once I had said what I planned, I would be able to continue along her route of conversation. But I knew she would find the timing of this information peculiar, so I deliberately said it quietly, almost to myself. Then I spoke again, more loudly: 'My father built those cupboards himself. They have been here since I was a child.'

The freestanding units remain an incongruous burst of colour in my white, white house. My mother had no interest in interiors. The thing she loved was the water waiting outside and gently swaying; it was one road away and visible from her bedroom window. Whenever my father asked her what colour she wanted any room painted, she always chose white.

If he continued to ask, she would say, 'You choose, then, Walter,' and go silent on him.

He could not bear her silences. So, he decorated according to her first answer, and we had a white house, with all furniture and fittings chosen and arranged by him. He worked in silence to build the turquoise kitchen, while my then eight-year-old sister and I, just one year younger, watched him from the hall for hours at a time. We reported his movements to one another in a formal, hushed tone, as if we were anthropologists examining a strange and ancient ritual for context. *He is drawing on the wall with a pencil, he is holding a hammer, careful, he just saw me!*

Vita nodded approvingly at my father's décor; she was also enthusiastically counting the collective characteristics of our two houses. The architect and builder responsible had apparently been keen on embellishment, and Vita noted each twinned flourish, each elaborate archway and fireplace that corresponded with those in Tom's house. She was apparently pleased rather than disappointed by the reproduction of her temporary home; she told me this while she looked around and patted my arm distractedly, as casual as an intimate friend. I offered Vita a chair at the small table but not a drink. *Etiquette for Ladies cautioned that it is bad form to attempt entirely new practices when hosting an unfamiliar guest. The host ought to give the visitor a flavour of one's own habits rather than adopting pretentious ways which are then impossible to keep up.* Lady Ogilvy despised pretentiousness even more than bad manners. In my imagination, Edith's gauzy pink frills rose and resettled around her soft body (*physical exertion is generally an undesirable practice for ladies, excepting social activities, e.g., tennis or croquet*) as she lectured on the danger of showiness, warning against this above all else. She was also strict on the topics one might discuss with new neighbours: *I recommend one talks about the local area, the shops and the houses and so on. Never comment on the personal*

traits, behaviours, or habits of existing neighbours: such
conversation is in very poor taste.

I told Vita the story of our matching houses and the
builder who was bankrupted by optimism. I had always
imagined an earnest man with a flimsy moustache, aspiring
to house his community and shamed by his failure.
She made the closed-mouth exhalation that Dolly often
used. It was an indication that the subject was too predictably comic to justify the effort that regular laughing
requires.

'But I find it very sad. Don't you think so?' I said.

Vita did not pause before replying: 'Sad? No! I think
he was an idiot like me! I think of a new way to make
millions every day too. Luckily, my husband points out
the holes in all my great plans.' She pronounced 'my' as
'may' and 'husband' with an extended soft 's' like a hiss:
may husss-bind. I tried this out silently to myself: *Lucki
-lay may huss-bind* . . . while she continued to talk. 'Our
builder would never have gone bankrupt if he was married
to Rols. And we'd be in a street of houses exactly like our
two. Instead, we are the special ones. I prefer it this way,
don't you, Sunday?'

Both the use of my name and my inclusion as one of
her 'special ones' diminished all my sympathy with the
hopeful, thin-moustached man who built my home and,
in doing so, lost everything he had. His loss became a gift
of exclusivity to us.

'Rols does houses. It's his thing. He's awfully clever at
it. Too good, in fact, because our townhouse sold the day
it went on the market. Foreign buyers: you know.' She
mouthed the last sentence in a stage whisper, showing her
teeth.

I tried this unfamiliar new phrase out in silence while

looking away from her: *Foreign buyers: you know.* I spoke as she had, holding my mouth away from my teeth as if the words themselves were unsavoury. *Foreign buyers: you know.*

'And even his unfinished properties are all reserved. But lovely Tom stepped in before we were *completely* homeless. *So* sweet of him. His wife's having another baby, you know. Another one! She is on bed rest this time. *Complications.*' She said this word in the same confidential and toothy way she had referred to the foreign buyers. 'So, they won't be up here this summer.' She turned down her mouth in an exaggeratedly sad face as if emoting the information in an interpretive performance. *Look! This is how I feel about Tom's wife being on bedrest and unable to visit her second home. See?* Then, just as quickly, she was smiling again. '*That's* why he lent us the house.' A silence fell between us. 'Do *you* have children?' she asked eventually. Her attention flickered around the room as though seeking evidence of any offspring; her yellow eyes resembled the glossy, black-centred discs used on expensive dolls. It was easy to imagine those eyes, round and unblinking, multiplied in the neat rows of a storeroom.

'I have one daughter. She is sixteen, though.' When I said this, Vita's doll-eyes altered, softening or sharpening; all I saw was a noticeable shift. The faces of new people are particularly unknowable and disorientating. What is readable in their expression is often unhelpful, something like recognising the nationality of a foreign speaker yet not understanding the language itself.

'She's a grown-up then. Thank fuck for that!' Her clipped vowels softened the profanity, which she pronounced 'fack'. Hearing a person swear still made me nervous then; in my experience, such language typically preceded some argument or fight. When Vita swore, though, the disparity between tone and content afforded a necessary distance, a kind of aural relief. She used coarse language with a casual ease that made the words fall away like discarded cigarettes, collecting at her feet but never touching her. 'Our house in town was surrounded by children! And our friends were always reproducing. Even my best friend just . . .' As she trailed off, she became entirely still for the first time and closed her eyes. Then her eyes opened again, and she was there, her glittering smile almost, but not quite, undimmed. 'This will be a return to the world of grown-ups, Sunday. At last!'

'You don't . . . ?' I spoke in response and trailed off as I remembered the personal nature of this question. Edith would not approve of such a direct query at a first meeting, where conversation ought to remain general. Motherhood was on the long, long list of Things You Must Never Ask About, along with everything else I have ever wanted to know. *How tall are you?* I want to know this of every stranger I pass. *Can you drive a car? Have you considered the effects of Italian unification on the South? Do you like to take the bus? And this book? Do you like this book?* I do not let these words out but swallow them back down daily; they crawl around like ants inside me, tickling, biting and unspent. Quietness is regarded as strange, but it is less demanding to people than questions are. I have not arrived at the formula for the number of questions one can ask; I do know that mine are always too many. And that one question is not satisfying to either party.

'Have children?' finished Vita. 'No thank you, darling. It looks bloody exhausting!' *Blood-day*, I tried out to myself, smiling. *Blood-day*. That was a good one, although *fack* remained my favourite.

'You're married, though.' I would have known this even if she hadn't already mentioned her husband. Whenever she spoke, her hands, with their glinting rings, danced impatiently as if hurrying her own speech along. In Vita's exuberant presence, I thought, I might be able to do the speech conducting with my fingers after all.

'Yes. And you?' She merged the last two words into one, extending the final syllable, and it sounded like *anddieu*? I used my three middle fingers to follow her words as she spoke, tapping them out on my leg and finishing on a light upward note, which registered in my hands as a gentle kind of interest and not a call to conform.

'No. Not any more,' I said. *Notanymore*. I pronounced it this way on purpose because I liked the way her blended words had sounded. Mine, though, came out harsh and the consonants made a rat-tat sound, rather than the appealing French style of her pronunciation. Vita's face, though, became obviously softer and incurious in response to my tone. Married women are often interested in my divorce and probe anxiously for details, as if I might reveal one of my mistakes and, in doing so, arm them against my own fate. But Vita was too socially graceful to push me for gossip.

'Rols never wanted children,' she continued, smoothly moving us both away from the disturbing subject of my former marriage. She looked fixedly towards the window with a brief and brilliant smile, as if at the request of an unseen photographer there. 'He insisted very early on. He couldn't share me with a child, he always said. He's sentimental like that. Although I don't think he is quite so certain any more.' She looked down and studied her engagement ring, turning the large stone upwards so it flashed blankly. I waited, but she did not clarify whether her husband's possible alteration impacted either his desire to remain childless or his sentimentality towards her.

She returned to watching me closely, and I concentrated on refraining from mouthing her words back to myself. I considered what I wanted to say, which was that I imagined life could be very fulfilling without motherhood. Vita settled into her chair and shrugged lightly in the silence, as though displacing a small and unthreatening insect. There was a loosely tied bow below her throat, the thin fabric of a blouse that could only be glimpsed under her suit jacket, and she rearranged the limp ends of this with one hand in a soothing, patting gesture.

Her fingers were small and her hands like those of a child, despite the burgundy-painted nails that shone darkly each time she gesticulated, which was often. I do not as a rule like to touch people, but I wanted to close my hand over Vita's little hand just then, to gently still her fingers as they danced across her chest. Later, I did, and her skin was cold, as I knew it would be. I knew things about Vita in the instinctive way that people like you know about one another. I believed it was preternatural, until I realised it is the same way I know precisely how soil or plants will feel in my hands before I touch them. These things that I accurately discerned about Vita were not, as it emerged, the important ones. But still, what I did know of her came to me with an effortlessness that mimicked love.

'Rollo works in town. He's there now.' She spoke with the acquired indifference of a raffle winner, as though her husband's persistent absence was too much good fortune to claim as intentional. 'We used to work together more, but I got old, and he didn't. Men don't, do they?'

Well, yes, they do, I thought, irritably. That makes no sense.

And for once, my confusion must have been evident, because she continued, as if in explanation, 'They have choices for longer than us, that's all. Rols could still have a houseful of children.' She gestured airily around her as if we were already surrounded by these ghostly and un-realised offspring. 'And I cannot.' She pressed her hands together, closing the subject, and smiled brightly. 'What is your daughter called?'

'Dolly.' I could not, cannot still, pronounce her name without smiling.

'I *love* that name,' Vita cooed. 'So pretty! Mine sounds like a great old nanna . . .'

I knew that her expanded pronunciation of *nan-na*, with the upward inflection at the end, was an affectation, that she would have naturally used the word, *grand-mother*, each syllable as tight and distinct as a swimmer's breath. I knew because my own speech is also porous and mimics other people's accents. The thing that exists between me and language, between me and other people, is flimsy and shifting. Vita had gently lengthened her vowels, perhaps to blur the difference between us. I pre-ferred the sound of her real voice; Vita spoke like a Mitford sister, or a white-gloved débutante captured distantly on black-and-white film. I imagined myself telling Dolly about our new neighbour after work that evening. I would say, 'Vita doesn't speak, she *trills*. Actually *trills*. Like a small bird.'

Vita was still talking. '. . . And if I chose my own name, that is exactly what I would choose. Dolly.' She looked out to the garden as though seriously considering this, her parallel name. *Door-lay*. I never tired of hearing her say my daughter's name. Not even when she called her *Doorls*. Not even at the very end. I expect I would still like to hear her say that.

'It's a shortened name, in fact. Dolly's full name is Dolores, after my sister. My sister, Dolores.' I repeated the name in the hope that she might then say it too.

As Dolly was named for her aunt, so my mother had been named for her late paternal grandmother, Marina. The oldest of seven siblings who all saw her as a supplementary parent and struggled to pronounce her full name, she was only ever known as Ma. I said nothing of this to Vita. I did not care to hear her say my mother's name.

'Your sister? How lovely, and I expect they are very close? Does she live locally?' she asked.

'She isn't . . . didn't . . . Well, my sister isn't . . . here . . . any more. Nor are my parents, in fact. It is just Dolly and me . . .' Again, I trailed away, immediately sorry to have begun this and begrudging the fact that it would bring questions, exclamations of regret and, most uncomfortably, attempts at solace. 'Historically,' I said, as though I was a teacher replying to a student query, 'in Southern Italy, families believed in the rebirth of the soul to the extent that a baby would automatically be given the name of the most recently departed close relative or sibling. So, parents might give several of their offspring the same name, consecutively reusing the name of the child they had just lost. And that surviving child is favoured, because it has the soul of many and must be loved for all the others, too.'

Vita listened to me patiently. Then, when I finally fell silent, she echoed my last line back to me. '. . . And must be loved for all the others, too? Yes, that makes sense.'

She leaned towards me and looked at my face, closely and entirely without self-consciousness. I began to feel that I had crossed some invisible social boundary that I should not have, had stepped off the path and on to the forbidden grass. I looked away from her and out towards my garden. But when she spoke again, it was with the deftness of a mother tightening her hold on a stumbling child. 'Well, how lovely to give your daughter a family name then, darling. It's entirely the right thing. And I can already tell that you love Dolly enough for them both.'

With this assurance, she gifted me a sureness that was then entirely unknown to me. It did not bring the blanketing comfort I had expected of certainty, but rather, it whispered to something sleeping inside me. Something that had only ever been asleep.

the shining fish

THE MORNING AFTER OUR FIRST MEETING AND SHORTLY AFTER Dolly left for school, Vita appeared at my door again. This time she was dressed in pyjamas. She did not reintroduce herself or apologise for the early visit. She moved easily, elegantly, through my hallway and into the kitchen, as if these visits were a routine between us. Her conversation was without preamble or introduction; she talked as if we were already in the middle of an ongoing discussion. It had been a long time since I had desired, or even allowed myself to believe in, the possibility of closeness with anyone. But I wanted it then, could feel the want beating like an excited little creature within me, rapid and rhythmic as a too-small heart.

'Do you have milk? We have absolutely *nothing* in our fridge except wine. I am a *terrible* housewife. Rols always says he would *starve* in town without all the *friends and restaurants*.' When she said 'friends and restaurants', she placed a hand on the outer side of each eye in a shielding motion and looked downwards, shaking her head slowly. It was as though she was emoting shame for a distant audience. Vita was extravagant and theatrical in all her expressions, and I appreciated that then. Her smile remained brilliant as she looked up at me winningly, hands still half-covering her large eyes. 'What *will* he do up here?'

'There is a café in town. And a Chinese. There's a Chinese that does takeaways. You'll like that,' I said, intending to soothe her as I would have done with Dolly.

I repeated her phrasing silently to myself: *no-thing* in our fridge; *ter-rible* housewife; *s-tarve* without *friends*. It was unclear, as yet, how this seemingly random stressing on such words related to the content of her conversation. I naturally speak in a monotone, and Dolly sometimes imitated this, using an exaggeratedly robotic voice, which made us both laugh. 'Good. Mor.Ning. Moth.Er,' she would say in response to my flat greetings, her arms and legs moving stiffly as though she were fashioned of metal.

Vita's claim to an empty fridge and wifely failure was not self-deprecating but congratulatory. I knew this because when I checked her face, she was smiling broadly, thrilled that she did not function like the other women on our street. Vita's face was open; she had the perfect combination of facial symmetry and a profound lack of interest in pleasing people. These factors made her face as seemingly easy to read as that of a child. This appearance of naturalness was, in fact, a construct, but a beautiful one. Her conversation, too, was appealing; I had not considered that our inability as wives might be celebrated. Edith Ogilvy believed that *being a wife is the highest and most esteemed privilege of womanhood*, although this had not been true for me. Vita sat at the kitchen table, leaning casually against the back of her chair as if she had been visiting me like this for years.

I did not know, then, that one could ask a neighbour to provide anything, especially if the lack of the item had been a matter of poor planning rather than emergency. Certainly, Edith's book had never mentioned this. Vita yawned loudly as she watched me open the oversized white fridge that Dolly's grandfather had gifted us the previous Christmas. He had been replacing the older-style display units in the shop with clear-fronted, square models that were edged in silver metal. I had been pleased with the gift, as I do not like to make such expensive purchases. I still have a considerable sum in my account, but I cannot earn such amounts of money myself. That summer, my inheritance was exactly half what it had originally been, and I still cannot tell when I would run out of money if I lived more extravagantly. I live now, as I did then, on the presumption that I have just enough. But that restraint was never the case where Dolly was concerned.

I handed my visitor a cold bottle of milk and she placed both hands around it, in that grateful and covetous way people sometimes have when given warm tea. She was not going home. She had the requested item, but she was still there, still talking. I sat down opposite her at the small Formica table that is one of the many relics from my parents' marriage. I do not drink tea or coffee; Dolly had made those things for herself since she was very young. Vita would have to wait until she got back to her own house if that was what she wanted. She was wearing an Alice band and a pair of blue-striped pyjamas that had the navy initials 'RJB' monogrammed neatly over one breast. The fabric was of the thin summer sort that makes little effort to conceal what it apparently covers. I could see her chest rising and falling through the light fabric as she spoke, could see her small breasts shift, unfettered and soft.

I had never had a visitor in nightwear before, and was unsure whether her outfit would be on Edith's list of Things That Must Not Be Mentioned, so I carefully did not. But when Vita casually compared her own dishevelled appearance to my plain and practical work uniform, it was me who blushed, as though my carefully observed omission was something more like a lie or a secret I was keeping. Vita had a scar that covered most of her hand, a silvery-pink covering like fish scales, which caught the light as her fingers moved across the bottle.

I remembered, as I often do, the fish that used to cover this kitchen when my parents were alive. The fish that were laid across every counter, opened up like trusting patients. During the tourist season, my father had taken holidaymakers out on his boat early each morning, and he brought the catches back to my mother to be prepared for the wives or landladies of these men to cook. Ma liked to watch for my father's boat from her bedroom window, an early return reassuring her that the tourists were already satisfied.

Our little house had smelled permanently of the lake and the shining fish that shivered in my parents' hands each day. Ma, self-taught, filleted and skinned as expertly as the local women knitted and sewed; her fingers came to know knives as theirs knew needles. Bones as delicate and white as baby teeth regularly littered our kitchen, as though it were the scene of a recent tragedy.

'My parents caught fish,' I told Vita. 'My father was a fisherman here.'

'My father used to fish!' She said this excitedly, as if the activity were a rare and surprising one, a peculiar quirk the two shared. 'He liked shooting best, though. Did yours?'

'No. He just fished,' I replied. But she was already talking again, explaining her own shooting triumphs.

As Vita spoke, I looked at the pearl-pink scar on the back of her hand; it made her seem fragile and breakable to me. My mind is an electrical and involuntary force. Everything touches many, many other things, and these points of intersection are the only way in which the world can be properly understood. I already knew that when I described Vita's visit to Dolly, she would lose patience if I talked about the peculiar shine of this scar and its relation to my parents' fish; if I cited this pinkness as evidence of both our new neighbour's frailty and her obvious need of us. My daughter was a pragmatist who did not allow this kind of talk. She warned me often that I focused on the wrong details. She wanted facts, and not stories, so that was what I tried to collect and bring home to her each evening. I never knew, though, which of these answers would be deemed allowable and which would mean my daughter sighed and disappeared upstairs to her room.

My focus on apparently incongruous details embarrassed Dolly, and her refusal to discuss such things was her way of training me to refrain from it. Like a husband who frowns and kicks his wife under the dining table when she accepts a second drink. Or when she talks about Sicilian rituals. My husband was one of those men. And he smiled handsomely throughout, which was somehow worse and certainly more effective than the kick. At least, the beautiful and undimmed smile was the part of this that successfully silenced me.

I needed to understand Vita's scar because she seemed impenetrable and yet something had marked her. I could not, cannot, conceive of her breaking; cannot imagine the force that would dare to smash open her skin enough to leave such a mark. When I think of Vita now, it is still the scar that comes to me first and before the other parts of which she is composed. It is such disparities that reveal a person and not, as my daughter believes, the things that all concur agreeably with one another. The scar told me more about Vita than the clipped accent, the confidence and the pretty face ever could. And I need to collect clues about people, where Dolly does not. I spend hours alone putting social evidence together in silence: what did that sentence mean? Why did he speak quickly; was that anger or was he in a rush?

Such investigation rarely comes to anything knowable, but I remain convinced there is a universal code to be broken, a pattern to be understood. Sometimes I imagine how it would feel to access the effortless communication that Dolly and Vita enjoy. Oh! I would say, shocked at the ease of conversation. I see! I know what they mean, understand what they all want. What would it be to live without the laborious work of translation, to hear and instantly know what you have heard?

What I had assumed was a headband was, in fact, a green silk sleep mask pushed up into Vita's dark hair, holding it back from her face. Her hair fell past her shoulders in sleek and precisely trained 'S' shapes, rather than curls, giving her the appearance of a guest at a formal event, despite the pyjamas. The sleep mask was somehow more intimate than her thin nightwear; it was an item so private that perhaps only her husband and I had ever seen it, I thought. She took the top off the milk and drank straight from the bottle for some time. She was obviously making no attempt to drink quietly and swallowed audibly several times. I had not seen a woman behave in such a natural and unguarded way since Dolores. My sister, too, had met her own needs in an open and obvious manner, not attempting to conceal the satisfaction of addressing her hunger, her thirst, or the itch that she scratched while moaning lightly in relief. I watched Vita with fascination as she put the half-emptied bottle back on the table, her upper lip ringed in white. *Calling attention to a person's soiled appearance is correct,* Edith reminded me, *if this can be done discreetly, with sympathy and without drawing the notice of others.*

'You have a . . . erm,' I looked at the wall behind her and made a repeated circular motion around my own mouth.

'Moustache?' she said. 'Does it suit me?' When I looked back at her, she was wide-eyed and smiling, and her hands were spread out to frame her face in a film-star pose. She blinked exaggeratedly and made no attempt to wipe the milk away. Then she abruptly adopted her usual expression, already bored by the pretence of her beauty as a debatable subject rather than fact. Her loveliness was so evident that I felt sure it could hold no interest for her. I liked her face enormously; it pleased me in the way that my ex-husband's looks once had.

'Your hair is marvellous,' she announced, looking back at me unflinchingly while I gazed at her. 'Is it your real colour?' As I began to speak, she held up a hand in warning. 'No, let me guess, darling, I am good at this.' She peered closely at my face. 'It is yours, isn't it?'

I nodded.

She leaned across the table to take a piece of my hair in her hand; with her elbows on the surface, she held the strands up to her face for inspection, as if considering it for purchase. 'I could already tell from your eyelashes. This is really pretty.' I enjoyed the way she pronounced 'really pretty'; it emphasised the softened 'r' and sharp vowels of her speech. The words seemed newly exotic, and I mouthed them to myself in silence: *wah-ly pwe-tay, wah-ly pwe-tay wah-ly pwe-tay.* 'Gorgeous,' she continued. 'Is your daughter's hair this colour?'

I nodded again. Dolly's fair hair was the one feature of mine that she was happy to possess.

I had always thought of our hair as colourless and unfinished; it is more silver than blond, with the cold blue undertones of my mother's hair. Dolly was always proud of the pale and unusual colouring that our family carried. I had dreaded her beginning school and learning that silver hair and pale eyes were not universally perceived as the gifts she assumed they were. But her classmates apparently agreed with her self-evaluation; it was if there had been a convention held somewhere in the few years between my leaving school and Dolly entering the world. At this event, it had been decided in concrete and binding terms that our colouring was to be considered not only entirely acceptable, but a qualifier of status and beauty. My daughter is like that: her people all come to believe whatever it is that she does herself and they do not know why they never object. She is entirely herself and that is enough to draw people to her.

'And does Dolly look like you?' Vita continued.

I imagined my daughter's smooth and unreadable expression, like that of her father: an unfixed thing, engendered to please. Our house still has many photos of her, and it pleases me that our (admittedly rare) visitors confuse the pictures of Dolly and my sister for the same girl. My purse was on the table, and I handed Vita the most recent photo from a selection that I kept in there. That I still keep in there. The picture had been taken two years before, and Dolly was pink-cheeked and radiant, even in the grey tones of her school uniform and with her hair pulled sternly back from her face. She was looking off to the side, and not so much smiling as laughing at something or someone unseen behind the camera. A private joke, not for the onlooker.

'No,' I replied. By this, I meant to be clear that Vita should not judge Dolly by her mother, a point often made explicitly by my in-laws. 'She is very clever. She's going to go to university. She's hoping to take maths. At Cambridge.'

I was not supposed to discuss this potential destination with anybody except Dolly's grandparents, but I could not help saying it to Vita. Such magical ideas seemed suddenly possible in her presence. I imagined that girls in her world would routinely go to university; they would also attend parties in dresses with huge skirts and travel with smart luggage, and they would know, as such girls do, that only good things could ever happen to them.

'Marvellous! So pretty. And *clever*.' Vita pronounced the last word with an excitable lowering of her voice, as if it had exotic and improper connotations. 'Does she get that from you?'

'No. I left school before the exams. I was on my own and I wasn't . . . I'm not as quick as Dolly.'

'*I* was at Cambridge. *History of art*, darling.' Vita's voice was higher and thinner than it had been, and she gave a flat little laugh.

I laughed politely along with her – *ha!* – as if we both agreed that the place and subject of her education was, indeed, an amusing admission. Vita looked at me intensely and frowned, which made thin cracks in the milk that was now set drily around her mouth. I stopped laughing.

If I had the luxury of referring to my own degree, I would not laugh about it. When Dolly and I talked about her future at university, it was always in tones of reverence – on my own part, at least. I typically pretend that education is not something I want for myself. It is not difficult to conjure the reasons I cannot go: the people, the noise, the choreography of daily relationships, the academic community, and then, the inevitable expulsion from all that. Sometimes, though, the books and the possibilities there seem bigger and more important than all this. The way I felt about university was the same painful feeling I had for Dolly's father, the King. It was the fury of unmet wanting, the wanting to possess something not meant for me. I am compelled to covet these beautiful things, but not built to withstand their effects.

'. . . But, of course, Rols did maths, too,' continued Vita, with a now measured smile. 'We met at university, in fact. He was nineteen and I was twenty-eight. I was a *mature student*.' She said this phrase in a slow voice that was not her own, and laughed at the apparent ridiculousness of such a title.

'Why?' I said.

She smiled. 'Why?'

'Why weren't you nineteen too?'

She sighed, and for a moment was silent. 'I was engaged before, you see, darling. For a long time . . . and it didn't work out. I was quite *distraught*.' She grimaced only as she said the last word, and it was the fleeting expression of pain easily resolved. As if she had briefly felt the pinch of a small and invisible hand. She smiled broadly as she continued. 'Daddy said I should go to Europe to recuperate; we have family in France and Holland. But I had a cousin already at Cambridge and

35

somehow, I ended up there instead. So, there I was, a *mature student*.' Again, she used a different intonation to pronounce this phrase. 'And Rols wasn't. Not at all. He even missed his finals to go to the races, which he never admits. I'll tell him to have a word with Dolly when they meet. He loves maths, all that, can go on about it for *ages*. Poor Dolly! What *am* I letting her in for?' She stopped smiling and managed to look serious, despite the milk still settled on her mouth. One of her hands went up to smooth her hair and settled on her chest. She patted her pyjama top as if feeling for something lost, seeming to remember how she was dressed, and she sighed heavily, as though exhausted. Gesturing to her outfit again, she made a gentle and hopeless little motion with her long fingers. 'I honestly haven't unpacked *anything*, Sunday. I simply don't *want* to. It isn't *in* me to do it. Even my clothes. All I have is the suit I arrived in. Which needs cleaning.' She paused thoughtfully here, as if considering who was responsible for cleaning her suit. 'Rols chose to come to Tom's . . . we were actually offered a place in the South of France . . . but here we are, so I told him *he* can do all the unpacking.' For a moment, it was like speaking to Dolly, whom I frequently watched talking herself into petulance and then out again. 'We've only brought clothes and a few of our favourite pieces, our paintings; everything else is in storage. Although now I've seen Tom's interiors, well . . . The removal man was so sweet; he actually offered to stay on and unpack for me yesterday.'

Yes, I thought, of course you would want to stay in the company of this woman. You would naturally try to remain near her, even when you were no longer being paid for your assistance.

'But I said no,' she continued, confidingly lowering her voice. 'I am *not* going to make it easy for Rols, darling. I am going to the shops today to get new stuff. I will just keep buying whatever I want until he arrives and unpacks.' She sat up, rubbing her hands together and smiling right at me, a portrait of childlike excitement.

'When will he be here?'

'Hopefully not until I've got a *lot* of new clothes, darling.' She was unsmiling, her eyebrows were straight dark lines, and the thin line of milk still framed her top lip. Her short red mouth was triangular with a gentle overbite, and I imagined, correctly as it transpired, that this would become something suggestive in photographs. It gave her a bird-like appearance, this sharp, curved-bone beak of a mouth.

Having Vita's full attention was like returning to the lake, like being immersed in that cold body of water for which my town is named and for which tourists come with their cameras and picnics. The lake in which I had once regularly swum until it flowed, invisible and uninvited, through my family. I had known the lake-water as only a swimmer could. First, the tiny shocks alerted you to the sudden drop in temperature, and then, when the water had numbed your body so much that you did not know any more if you were cold or burning, the body finally acclimatised, feeling seeping back into your limbs with the warm comfort of morphine. A man once approached my sister and me as we stood on the shore one morning preparing for an early morning swim. As he crossed the beach, he stumbled on the pebbles, but his gaze remained fixed on us, as if he had been sent with a specific task. He warned us that we must not swim during that initial cold-water shock, but ought to float instead until our bodies accepted the temperature. We nodded, and he walked away without further comment. The stranger was like that, abrupt and professional; a policeman alerting a motorist to a broken brake light.

And with Vita, I found the stillness he'd recommended, this surrender to the shock, came naturally to me. I was engulfed by her. I was held up weightlessly within her gaze, exactly as I had once floated in the cold, dark lake with my sister. It was a sensation like safety.

But Vita was still talking: '. . . to come with me? I suppose you're, um, *working*?' Vita said 'working' as if it was a foreign and unfamiliar word that required concentration for correct pronunciation.

'Yes. But I would rather work than go shopping with you.'

Her gaze was still fixed on me, but she remained silent for a time, and I noticed the break in her pattern of speech. So far, she had only taken brief pauses in her speech when she specifically wanted a response, and her words were like early fireworks: -tuh -tuh -tuh -tuh -tuh -tuh -tuh – silence -tuh -tuh -tuh -tuh -tuh -tuh -tuh -tuh – silence. I wondered if anyone had ever refused this charming woman anything before.

Then she smiled and clapped her hands together like a starlet in a silent film. 'Oh, I fucking *love* that. I love honest people, darling. It's so much easier to say what you think, isn't it? I bet there isn't much of that here, though, is there? Everyone in these little towns is so polite. Inside their little houses. *So* concerned with what other people think.' She opened her eyes very wide, and her mouth became a distressed 'O', her hands framing her cheeks. Then she laughed and patted my leg, her palm curling around my knee. 'We aren't like that, though, are we, Sunday?' Removing her hand, she placed it back around the milk, with a smaller and more private smile. 'I bet the neighbours here aren't like us.'

She did not wait for an answer, which was fortunate because Edith's book made it clear that criticism of one's neighbours was an unacceptable practice. Instead, she drained the rest of the milk from the bottle, placing it back down on the table empty and placing both palms up in evidence of completion like a partygoer downing a shot. No, I thought, the neighbours were not like me and Vita. Not like *us*. We were different from them, and the same as one another. I had never known a person who delighted in, or even admitted to, any similarity with me. Before Vita, I had believed I was something ancient and unfinished. But if Vita values *our* eccentricities, I thought, I could prize them, too. It was like discovering that you are not the very last one of your own people.

She stood up and directed her lovely, milky-edged smile at me again. There was a formal handbag next to her that I had not noticed before. She had set it on a chair of its own, rather than on the floor, as if it were a beloved pet. In one easy gesture, she pulled the bag close to her chest and began to stroke the soft-looking leather fondly.

'Right,' she said. 'I'm going shopping, then. Rols left his stupid car behind for me. I hate it, but he says it's the only thing in the world that he loves as much as me. Have a good day at *work*.' The final word was pronounced with an emphasis and a knowing look, as if my occupation was a polite fiction between us, an agreed euphemism between old friends for something quite improper.

I saw Vita to the door and then watched from the doorway as she went to her husband's red car and opened the boot. I already hated the stupid car, too. She pulled a pair of flat laced shoes and a thin pink sweater from the back and sat down immediately on the pavement to put them on over her pyjamas. She inhabited her body with the unselfconscious practicality of a toddler. Dolly always said it was unacceptable to go out in nightwear, even if I put a coat over it, and even it was just a quick errand. It looked fine to me. It actually looked very good. Standing up, Vita waved cheerfully at me, obviously expecting to find me still watching her from my doorway. I did not go back inside until her car was out of sight.

Despite my interest in Vita, I knew even she could not make shopping a leisure activity for me. The airlessness of clothing stores alerts me to the fire exits, but renders other women docile as domestic pets. The overhead lighting forces their dazzled eyes downward to the racks, which are carefully positioned for ease of contact. Their soft little hands stroke the clothes as they consider them, but I find their subsequent rejection or acceptance of a piece entirely incomprehensible. So, too, is the pleasure and possessiveness with which they watch the cashier bag their new items before they leave, holding their purchases as close as a prized secret.

At fifteen, looking for an outfit for my sister's funeral, I had become transfixed by another shopper, a slight and dark-haired woman. Her mode of selection consisted of stroking random items in quick, fluttery movements, then stepping backwards to stare blankly at them in silent contemplation. I followed her through the displays, touching each item she had touched, then moving away to look intensely back at them. Eventually, the woman settled on a busily patterned blouse and moved briskly towards the cashier. The fabric featured tiny cockerels wearing jaunty green hats and dancing alongside tilted Martini glasses; each cocktail was topped with an olive speared through its red pimento heart. I placed my palm expectantly against an identical top on the rail and closed my eyes. But it lay smooth and dead in my hand, cool against the relentless hot breath of the store. Still, I bought the ugly blouse and wore it to the funeral of my sister and then to those of both my parents the following year. This was the first of my four acts of faith; the King would be next, then there would be motherhood. Vita would be my very last.

winter bees

VITA NEVER ASKED ABOUT DOLLY'S FATHER AGAIN AFTER THAT first meeting between us, and this was, I think, to her credit. She knew already that further reference to him would have pained me and so she did not enquire more. She was instantly incurious when she met resistance in conversation, and she seemed to sense such resistance almost before it properly surfaced. This social delicacy is, I think, a practice of her class, because I am used to fending off anxious enquiries from local wives about my unmarried status. Vita's discretion would certainly have met Edith Ogilvy's detailed instructions for *gracious behaviours in the unfortunate event of divorce*.

I was grateful for that. I had long kept a few impersonal lines ready to cover any queries about the end of my marriage: *it was a long time ago; I am used to being on my own; it's over now, anyway;* and I have not said more than this to anyone, ever. And even Vita did not merit a telling of the whole story. She, of all people, was not to know the damage that was done to me. I had been lost in my daughter's father, was overwhelmed by him at eighteen.

And I have not yet recovered myself. If I had not already been odd when I met him, if I had belonged to people who cared for me and who were troubled by my decline, his influence would have been sympathetically described as an enchantment. But he is a charming and beloved man. The onlookers to our romance were from his side alone; the story told of our marriage, therefore, is that I am defective; that even a man like the King could not shape me into a wife.

We met shortly after his family moved to the town of the tiny fires. His parents inherited the largest farm in the area, and they opened a shop for their own produce, a pleasingly rustic enterprise housed in a huge barn. It was popular with both locals and tourists, and it was there I first met Alex, home on his summer break from university. Alex's parents told me that I was the only person to reply to the handwritten advert on their counter, and they gave me the position in the greenhouses without interview.

When I had been working at the farm for three years, Alex finally finished university and moved back to the farm. In the evenings after work, I replayed all the pretty things he said to me in the greenhouses. It was once traditional in Southern Italy that a man calling on the girl he loved would not take a seat unless offered a chair specifically by her. This was a symbolic offer; a sign that the suitor was being considered as a future husband. When Alex came to the greenhouse to visit me, he sat on one of the sturdy wooden worktops. I generally stood as I worked, but when I was handling young plants, I sat in a chair to remind myself to work slowly and conjure the gentleness they required. The wood of my chair was glassy with age, like a rock polished into smoothness by the lake. I kept it unseen, tucked under a work surface at the back of the greenhouse when Alex was home. I did not offer my chair to him, and he did not seek it.

I studied the conversations that I overheard him having with the customers when I brought plants into the backroom to be marked for sale, and I privately renamed him the King. I am unable to address him by his real name. I came to dislike it, due to people's careless overuse. They littered their sentences with it – *Alex-Alex-Alex-Alex* – wanting both his attention and the feel, the claim, of his name in their mouths. When I confessed the King's nickname to him, he laughed delightedly, without a moment of self-doubt. He even played up to his name in our early years together. Arriving home after work, he would announce in a borrowed, stern voice: 'The King is here! Where are my subjects?' And our daughter would shriek with excitement at the very sound of him. It is telling that this game was the way they communicated best; he in someone else's voice and she rushing to greet this performance of himself. And I laughed along, back then, as I would not now.

The King was a film that I watched alone each night. At the end of his post-university summer, I brought some plants into the shop. As he arranged them on the table, he spoke to me, without looking up.

'I've decided to go travelling. I'm leaving next month.'

He had a confessional and defensive manner, as though revoking an earlier promise. The remaining grains of soil were warm on my unwashed palms, and I closed my fingers, concentrating on the sensation. The King was still speaking, but I could no longer process his words. He touched my shoulder without any pressure, as though theatrically demonstrating the act of restraint for an observer. He was watching me expectantly and I replied, still engrossed in the heat of the earth on my hands.

'No,' I said, unsure whether I was rejecting his plan to leave or the peculiarly weightless sensation of his hand on my shoulder.

'No?'

'No.' And I left the shop with the good soil still buzzing softly on my skin. It whispered into my hands and my head with the gentle menace of winter bees, drunk on sleep.

He followed me. The King had never followed a girl; they came to him. They waited for him, as bovine and broken as patients in a dentist's waiting room, their cheeks flushed with something that was not, yet, pain. He pursued me because I was the only thing he ever had to ask for, because he had not known want before.

And the King never did go travelling. I remind myself of this now, when I see him marching possessively around his parents' farm, hand in hand with his beautiful second wife. Instead, a little under a year later, I gave birth to our daughter. And, like the good Sicilian I wished I were, I named her for the aunt she would never know, for the girl drowned on land. For my love, Dolores.

The elderly neighbours of my childhood kept a Larsen trap; a magpie held in a cage that allowed others of his kind to enter but not to escape. Arthur and Fran considered this type of bird a garden pest due to its appetite for more vulnerable peers and their eggs. They kept the original magpie for many years, and even named him like a domestic pet: Robert. The bird called passing friends to their deaths daily; his exuberant song seemed to be in collusion with his owners rather than the call of a fellow inmate. The music was made no less beautiful by its intent, but his little heart was hard in his blue-black chest. Arthur and Fran strangled the captured magpies in a weekly cull that culminated in a bonfire of tiny corpses. Sometimes my parents went next door on these evenings, and the four of them would stand motionless, staring into the fire, unflinching even as the flames occasionally caught on something, and sparks flew at their heads.

When I was fourteen, Arthur had a fatal heart attack. Fran released the magpie on the day of the funeral. My parents were in the garden; black-suited and quiet, they whispered together about whether they should go and check on her. Later, my father, his voice low and concerned, told my sister and I how they had heard Fran crying, shaking the Larsen trap and shooing Robert away when he would not fly, but tried instead to go back inside. She let the garden grow wild without Arthur, only occasionally acquiescing to my father's offers to mow the lawn for her. He would call over the fence and she would shrug nonchalantly back from her plastic garden chair. Without looking up at my father, she would gesture minutely around her with the cigarette that was permanently in her hand – *if you like* – as if granting him a favour.

The empty cage had been secured shut and a magpie often sat on the delicately criss-crossed roof, darkly hunched over in affront, like a drinker at an abandoned bar. Only Fran could have known with certainty if that regular visitor was their own, adopted bird. This magpie was always alone and wore bald patches of attack across his head and wings. If it was Robert, he seemed to have lost his bird-ways during his time as gaoler and perhaps retained a taste for captivity.

The wanting with which girls looked at the King's lovely face as he called, and the effortless way he

46

enthralled them, was the trickery of the magpie. The magpie in the Larsen trap, too, must have shone as the birds considered him from the sky. It was only afterwards, when pressed close against him in the confines of his little cage, that they could realise that what they had mistaken for brilliance was simply the undisturbed grease of his flightless wings.

talk louder, talk normal

DUE TO VITA'S UNEXPECTED VISIT FOR MILK, I MISSED THE FIRST bus and was uncharacteristically late to the farm. I have always chosen to work longer hours than those set for the job. The greenhouses are marvellously silent, unattended by anyone but me and occasionally David, who is himself a quiet person. When I work, the dark and silky soil still satisfies my hands with a quality like gravity, the reassuring and even weight of a sought embrace. My hands are never at rest. Uneven brick, glossy plants and cold car doors all call out to be touched as I walk down a street. In shop queues, tinny music is muted by the darkly curling hair of a woman in front of me; it invites me to trace its squirming descent down her thick wool coat. I typically spend my time in public with my hands curled in fists against the silent requests made of them by all those things that I cannot touch. The call is most compelling when I am overwhelmed by lights and noise. I was born with this intolerance of noise and light, and an accompanying greed for touch and smell. Working with plants does much to temporarily aid my sensory imbalance.

My condition does not accompany me into the green-houses but waits at the door. When I am alone or at work, he sleeps outside with his dark head low on his paws; he resents the lack of challenge in the greenhouse environment, where no one speaks in riddles or looks at me oddly. Here is a magical space without social context or burdens. But in the company of others, the animal is fixed to my side. He is a smiling partner whose iron hand on me looks like affection, yet functions as a reminder of who I really am. The wolf-husband's wiry whiskers graze my skin as he whispers into my ear, *talk about Italy go on go on don't look at their eyes oh no don't they don't like it at all look at the floor, the wall and isn't that music loud Sunday and aren't those lights too, too bright . . . ?*

Sicilian folklore is rife with such wolves. A woman is cautioned that on specific nights, such as Christmas Eve, she is not to allow her husband into the house on his first knock, but to wait for his third. It is said that one woman, roused late from her sleep and confused, answered the door on her husband's second knock. He reportedly ate her, for he was still a werewolf. He had not performed the third knock, which would have made him human once again. I would have survived as a Sicilian wife, for I can follow rules as clear as these. But I was married to an English King, and so the wolf consumed me on my own doorstep.

I was still opening all the greenhouse doors when David arrived to do a morning with me. He was only working a half-day on the farm as his parents had arranged to take him out for lunch. It was his twenty-fifth birthday the following day and they wanted to celebrate with him on their way to the airport for a fortnight in Italy. Despite my obsession with the place, I have never actually visited, and I was hoping to learn the details of where exactly they would be staying and what they planned to see, none of which David had been able to tell me. When they returned, their youngest son would no longer be living with them, but would be settled in a cottage rented from the King's parents by an assortment of young farm workers. It was the first time David's parents had been to the farm; their smart black car pulled up on the concrete yard outside the greenhouse at exactly 1 p.m. It is difficult to keep a black car clean on the country roads round here, and I grudgingly admired this badge of persistence on their part.

David is, still, often late by at least ten minutes, and this should bother me, would bother me if he were anyone else. But I like the way he arrives; he comes in quietly, and unless I happen to notice him, he begins his work without any announcement. When the King or Vita enter a room, it is with a flourish and an expectation of acknowledgement, magicians with bright smiles and a rabbit in one gloved hand: *tah-dah!* When I was married to the King, he would start when he saw me: *Why are you always creeping around? Can't you walk into a room like a normal person?* My mother had frequently asked me the same thing. In the same voice. It was unnerving to be critiqued daily by a different version of the same person, as if the second one was endorsing the disapproval of the first.

That morning, I looked up from my own planting to admire the immaculate line of greenery behind David and his skilled and careful hands.

When I waved, he raised a thumb back, made the half circle across his chest – *Good morning*. He signed, as he generally does, in an amused and easy manner, as if the greeting is just one of many pleasant things on his mind.

If someone spoke as David signs, people would describe their accent as lilting and melodic, like that of Mr Lloyd, a Welshman in his fifties, who is a regular at the farm shop. When Mr Lloyd talks, in his calm and musical way, about seasonal vegetables and the agricultural implications of the predicted rainfall, it sounds as though he is singing. I like to close my eyes when he speaks, and I think that perhaps I could come to love Mr Lloyd. He often has to repeat himself when we talk because I focus on the lovely sound and do not hear the intention. Mr Lloyd is very accommodating with my requests for repetition. He politely informs the other customers if he thinks they are speaking too quietly or not clearly enough to me.

My signing is aloof and clipped in the way of my speech, and whenever I ask David for correction, he points out this over-formality in his gentle and smiling way.

That is how I speak! The same in signing as speaking! I finally responded crossly one day. *Dolly tells me. I don't need you to do it too.*

He looked seriously back at me. *I know how you speak. I can* – here he touched one eye with two fingers and pointed them back at me – *see. I can see you, Sunday. I can still see you.*

Still cross, I made a tight fist and pointed a thumb towards my forehead. *I know!* I turned back to the plants I had been working on.

David knocked abruptly on his counter, and I looked up. He was untroubled as always by my mood and wore his usual broad smile.

Luckily, you sign much better than you speak. He

signed this cheerfully in the way of someone unconsciously moving to the sound of a distant song; the actions were light and loosely made, gently formed as mine were not.

David can lip-read and speak clearly because he was hearing for several years, he explained to me once. He contracted meningitis at the age of five, and when he awoke in hospital, it was to a new version of his life: everything looked the same as before, but there was no accompanying sound. The staff and his parents would open his door, move around his room, and pour water in a glass, all in silence, like ghosts. When they leaned down to his bed to speak to him, their mouths moving more quickly than he remembered, he finally realised that the new noiselessness was not a trick, because their voices, too, were broken.

'Talk louder!' he commanded. 'Talk normal!' And as he spoke, he found that his own voice no longer worked – to his ears, at least.

He explained all this one morning in the greenhouse, after an argument with his parents, they would prefer him not to work on the farm but to go to university, as his two brothers did. David remained suspicious of them and of their intentions, wary as if he were still the child who believed that they alone were withholding the sensation of sound from him.

His parents did not learn sign language, and still insist that he lip-reads and speaks with them. When he was younger and keen to sign in the new language he had learned, his parents sometimes made him sit on his hands during conversation to prevent him from signing. My mother had enforced this rule in our house, too, so that I would not flick or clap my hands, and later on, when she had almost eradicated the public enactment of that behaviour, so I did not pull reflexively at my own hair – in her presence, at least. I understand that David prefers to sign, rather than to speak in a voice that he cannot hear and does not even know himself, now that it no longer belongs to a five-year-old child, but to a man. It suits us both to work in silence and sign to one another across planted rows in the large greenhouses.

David still works with me most mornings and on the farm in the afternoons. During harvest time, he is needed in the fields more and often cannot come to the greenhouses for weeks at a time. I miss his quiet company during these periods.

On that particular morning, his parents entered the greenhouse, announcing themselves with loud greetings. 'Hallo! Hallo! Here we are!'

I flinched at the overt noise of them both, realising that I had expected David's childhood version of the couple, had expected them to move their mouths as if speaking, but to maintain a deliberate and mocking silence. I found myself watching their faces intently. David had inherited the most appealing qualities of them both. He had his mother's round, brown eyes, rather than his father's pale and fixed gaze; he had the generous and easy smile of the latter, rather than the accusatory little mouth and chin of his mother. Silver-haired and dressed in navy and beige, the couple could have accurately been cast as glamorous retirees advertising expensive holidays or private health-care. David's mother wore a sharp-ended necklace that spread itself out above her collarbone like a watchful pet. She and her husband strode towards me with their hands identically extended, and I held up my soil-covered palms in a warning. They instantly stopped walking and waved back at me from some distance instead.

David was already washing his hands at the little sink by the entrance. His father went to him and patted him hard on the back. The sink is set low on the wall, as if for children, and David must stoop a little to use it. The two of us often conjure nonsensical and colourful reasons for the sink's position, such as the greenhouse historically being run by a crew of tiny people. His rounded shoulders and softened knees that day, though, looked more like a surrender than an adaptation solely for his height.

'Where are you going on holiday?' I asked them, raising my voice so it would carry across the greenhouse to where they stood. I signed pointedly at the same time, although David could not see me.

'Italy! We're going to Italy!' they replied in one voice, both smiling.

'I know. Where are you going in Italy?' I said. This time, I only signed a few of the words as I spoke: *Where, you, Italy?*

'We are going to . . . Lake Como!' It was David's father who spoke, and his intonation was that of a man making a celebratory toast. His wife watched him closely as if he had said something very accomplished.

I shrugged. 'Ah, well.' I was no longer signing along at all. It was not the South, but they looked happy about it. I thought about telling them some of the history of Sicily. Then I looked up at their expectant faces again, and I returned to the planting.

'We are very excited,' said David's mother.

I said nothing, but carried on with my work. What could be said to someone who was excited to visit the Italian Lakes in the North, but chose not to go to the South of that country? I regretted their mistake, but it was theirs to live with.

'Come on, David,' said his handsome parents in their large voices. 'Let's go.' But neither moved, and they remained side by side and facing me as if by prior agreement. A speaking person might naturally gesture towards the door, the car, at this point. These two, however, seemed to hold their arms and hands deliberately still. And David was behind their frozen backs and could not know what they had said. They spoke to me, collusively: 'He is always running late, isn't he?'

They looked at me expectantly, so I said, 'Ha!' and returned to my plants. I did not like these people, with their television outfits and their refusal to include their son in conversation. Finally, they both turned away from me, and David put one outstretched hand up as he followed them out to their car. I waved brightly back at him.

He smiled tightly and made a large circle across his chest: *Sorry*.

I noticed for the first time how smartly dressed he was. His shirt had a navy checked pattern and was so uncreased it must have been new; David did not iron. His trousers were of the same deep blue, a colour too determinedly dark and even to have been part of his usual faded work wardrobe. These obvious efforts made me like his parents still less.

I smiled at him, signing back exaggeratedly so he would not miss it – *It's fine* – before I went back to my work.

When I returned home that afternoon, the house was quiet, and I immediately knew Dolly was not there. The bones of our house are most relaxed in summer, and the wooden front door opened smoothly. During winter, the entrances and windows swell up unhappily like a person made puffy with water retention, an Alice in shrinking shoes and tightening rings. Doors must be wrestled open, then, and cold breathes through the ill-fitting sash windows, whose dimensions appear to have been decided on without recourse to the existing surrounds. I stroked the warm brick of the porch and went inside, going upstairs to shower before Dolly got home. From my bedroom window, I could see a fluffy white shape, motionless on the grass in Vita's garden as she had been herself the day before. I assumed it was an abandoned toy of some sort, until it jumped up and ran inside as if escaping an invisible pursuer. It was a small dog with a pointed face and an impressively long coat.

I left the French doors open in the warm evening as I prepared dinner and baked David's birthday cake. This is a tradition that I adhere to still, as he is so pleased with the outcome, regardless of what I produce. I did not make cakes for my daughter's birthdays, because they did not compare to the impressive creations her grandparents ordered from the local bakery each year. On her sixth birthday, Dolly looked at the cake I had made for her and told me not to bother any more. I think, now, that I should have persisted.

As I mixed the buttercream for David's cake, I listened to Vita talking in her garden. At first, I assumed that her husband must have arrived home, because she spoke in a conversational tone. But it soon transpired from the subject matter, a lesson on spoiled rugs and naughty pets, that she was talking to the little dog. Vita, though, did not use a voice reserved for babies and pets; she talked seriously and without pause, her distinctive speech rising into a question before she answered each query herself.

I heard Dolly arrive home, waited for her to announce her own arrival to the empty hall and then called her into the kitchen. She was lovely that summer. I picture her often as she was that day, in her school uniform, with her pale hair loosely tied up away from her face and a bag of revision books on her arm. She rarely wore make-up, then, and had a plainer way of dressing than her friends, which, coupled with the lack of cosmetics, made her look even younger. I flattered myself that this individuality was the influence of my own unfussy appearance rather than the extended demands of school study, revision and exams.

'Dolly, you're late. How was it today?' I put my arms around her and felt her stiffen, surrendering briefly to my embrace rather than returning it.

'Yeah, fine. No surprises. You know. Exams. Can we eat now? I've got to revise. Is that cake for tea?' Unconsciously, she loosely made the sign for *cake*, placing one open clawed hand over the top of the other. We rarely signed with one another by then, but I found it touching when she occasionally did so, even unintentionally, as she reverted to it only with words concerning childhood subjects: *cuddle, mum, cake, goodnight, love*.

When Dolly was little and the King was at work, she and I often slipped into an easy silence together. We enjoyed communicating through gestures we learned from a library book on sign language, and could agree on an activity or a lunchtime choice with our hands alone. Instead of telling Dolly that we were going to buy her new Wellington boots as I put on her coat and gloves, I would sign. I preferred to kneel down and show her with my hands. *We are going on the bus. To get you boots.* Then I would continue: *For the rain. The storms. Puddles.*

And Dolly would sign back, hopefully: *Ice cream, Mummy? Chocolate! I love ice cream! You love ice cream!*

The frequently colonised Sicilians, I knew, had once used a sign language that was unique to the locals. This signing apparently developed to meet an historic need for private communications in the presence of foreign oppressors. The King did not allow the quiet knowing of each other; he did not want us to keep private thoughts from him. But he soon discovered that our thoughts were not what he wanted anyway.

If our young daughter became silent, as I routinely do, he would provoke her into speaking by withholding the things she loved best until she acquiesced and asked him for their return. Both Dolly and I visibly stiffened at the sound of her father's over-used phrase: 'Use your words. If you want it, use your words.' He did not, of course, want her to use her words; he wanted to hear her speak like him. Most of all, he wanted to know that she would not become lost in my own sweet silence. I recognised his approach as one people tried with me as a child. Among Dolly's greatest treasures were the soft white bunny she had received for her fourth birthday, her bumble-bee-striped gloves and a large-headed doll with oversized eyes, the same too-bright blue as her own. The King regularly kept such favourites out of her reach until she finally surrendered her attempted silences and became less like me.

Our places were already set, and I served the food, laying Dolly's plate before her. She sat at the table in her queenly and expectant manner. Dinner had been ready an hour before, when she was expected home. It had been kept warm ever since, and it was dry and curling now, like a sea creature left out in the sun.

'It's David's birthday cake. I'll bring you some home tomorrow . . .' I began, but she was already talking again. I put the cake into a tin and sat down opposite her.

'Great,' she said, looking down at her dinner. 'White food. Again. Yum.'

Now that we were sitting together, I noticed that the dinner was indeed very white, or at least cream-coloured. But it was a Thursday, and so we were eating rice and fish. Typically, I served salad or greens alongside it, but the more preoccupied I was, the whiter our meals became. It is a natural point of return and only Dolly's disgust ever drew my attention to this habit. I offered to grill her fish, so it would brown.

'That's still white food,' she said. 'It's just burned white food.' But she began to eat, although without interest.

'I met the neighbour again this morning,' I told her. Dolly's face remained blank as she continued to regard her plate resignedly. 'You know, Vita,' I continued.

'Who?'

'Vita.' I nodded my head towards next door, encouragingly. 'Remember, I told you she'd moved in. Haven't you seen her yet? That's their red car out the front.'

'Nope.' She got up and took a bottle of tomato ketchup from the fridge.

'Well, she told me that her husband took maths too, and he could talk to you about it sometime.'

'Ooh, Mum. The thrill.' Despite her flat tone, she smiled at me. Dolly's face, her mood, was what determined how I felt at any time, and when she smiled, I too felt happy. I thought how tired she must have been, after another afternoon of exams and all the months of revision. She squeezed the sauce all over her food and gave a little exhalation of satisfaction at the bright red addition to her plate. 'Ahh. It's not white any more.' But she stopped eating her then-pinkish dinner soon afterwards and opened the freezer. 'Revision!' she said, emphasising the final syllable like a farewell as she left the room with a box of vanilla ice cream in her hand.

'Well, that ice cream is white, anyway,' I said a moment later, raising my voice so she could catch it. 'And you couldn't possibly eat all that,' I finished. But she did not hear me, was already upstairs, and I was talking to myself in an empty kitchen.

The next morning, when I opened the cake tin at work to present David with his birthday cake, we found that there was a large slice already cut out of it.

I frowned, and David raised his eyebrows, signed *Dolly* by rocking an invisible baby in his arms. I did not sign my daughter's name in this way, as he knew.

I pointedly spelled her name out on my fingers: *Yes, you are right. It must have been D-O-L-L-Y.*

He looked at the cake, at the careful icing and the cyclical face with the large missing section. *D-O-L-L-Y has good taste. Can't blame her for that.* This time, he signed each letter of her name and we smiled at each other. David's face is good for reading; he wants to be under-stood, unlike Dolly's father or her grandparents, with their fleeting and changeable expressions. We signed several repetitions of 'Happy Birthday' to each other, as we always did, in large gestures and in perfect synchronicity, as if performing a dance routine that we had devised together.

He insisted that we each had a slice of cake at break and again at lunchtime. It was a deep, two-layered vanilla sponge, thickly covered in white frosting, and he still had a lot to take home with him. Dolly's piece had not made much difference after all. But I did not take any home as I had promised her.

Dolly was revising with friends and did not plan to be home until later that night, so I ate a bowl of milky cereal alone before preparing her a cold chicken salad and putting it into the fridge. The doorbell rang while I was clearing away the salad remnants. Phyllis, an elderly and outdoorsy woman who lives at the end of our street, was standing on the doorstep expectantly. She was my court-appointed guardian, at her own request, for the two years following my parents' death until I turned eighteen. Her brief daily visits meant I was able to stay on in my family home rather than being assigned to the care system. Phyllis, in fact, proved a better fit for me than my own mother had been. Her eccentricity and the upkeep of her smallholding left her little time to worry about the way I lived, but she always made herself available when necessary to help me with practical tasks, with arranging doctor's appointments and paying bills. She had a confidence, too, in my abilities, which she spoke of often and especially in the company of others, such as the court-appointed social worker. Phyllis's faith in this regard was apparently undimmed by my slow progress and regular confusion, which remained a private matter between us, at her firm request. I recognised, even then, what an enormous commitment she had undertaken. I think we were both relieved to be released from the arrangement on my eighteenth birthday, although I still had to remind her several times that she was no longer obliged to visit me or to enquire into my needs and general wellbeing. Eventually I read aloud the entire letter that officially released her from her commitment to me and she nodded back. She, too, had received the letter, she told me in a quiet voice. My reading it to her directly, though, seemed to help her adhere to our imposed release from one another, for she stopped the daily visits and, when she did come, she no longer asked if she might come into the house, but remained on the doorstep.

Phyllis delivers home-grown vegetables and pastel-coloured eggs from her own hens along the street each week, and that day it was our turn. A thin plastic bag containing carrots, tomatoes and a box of eggs were placed into my hands gently and with a knowing smile, as if we both knew that I had been waiting for this and was now satisfied at last. The gift always comes with a modest disclaimer: *I couldn't use them, couldn't see them go to waste.* Phyllis could not reasonably eat all the vegetables she grows, or the eggs that her brood produces; she has at least fifteen hens and has lived alone since being widowed many years ago.

I had no need of the vegetables or the eggs as, when Dolly was still at home, my in-laws always let me use the farm shop without charge. I was scrupulous about using this familial benefit fairly and regularly cautioned my daughter to do the same. She sometimes took friends there to fill their schoolbags with home-made biscuits, heavily frosted cakes and expensive chocolates, which could add up to more than my modest weekly shop. The King and I avoided a financial settlement or maintenance in our divorce; the house was mine and he had little in his own name at the time. His parents had been generous with my daughter and me, supporting Dolly, particularly, in ways that their son might have otherwise. I knew this grocery provision would change, though, when she eventually left home for university. Richard had begun to prepare me for this, in his peculiar rhetorical way, when I saw him in the shop. *You won't be shopping much when it's just you, will you? I expect you'll want to use the supermarket when Dolly's gone, won't you?* And it seemed – seems – right that I should be independent of them when their granddaughter no longer lives with me.

'Thanks, Phyllis,' I said. 'It's kind of you.' There was no point in repeating the fact that the farm let me have all the fresh produce we needed. I had tried to convince her of this several times, but she remained determined to bring me eggs, and it was quicker, anyway, to accept them than to protest. I began to close the door with the bag of produce in my other hand.

'. . . met them?' I only heard the end of Phyllis's question.

'Sorry?' I opened the door again.

'I said, have you met them yet – the new neighbours?' she repeated carefully, gesturing towards Vita's house.

I am the same as the customers who used the King's name, just to hold something sweet and thrilling in their mouths. Like children with chocolate. I wanted to say 'Vita' repeatedly until it was no longer exciting but natural, until I could casually possess a little of her.

'Her mouth speaks of that which fills her heart,' my mother used to warn us. This line had been a family dinner favourite with her during my silent periods. For Ma, such quietness evidenced that my heart was empty, while within the bosom of my talkative sister beat an organ full of filial love. And perhaps this is what Ma intuited when she spoke of my empty heart, that there was no place for her within it. She did not know I would have a little daughter with a tendency to fall unexpectedly and sweetly asleep, at my breast, at mealtimes and during conversations or games, as if in sudden collapse. A child who could fall asleep even while opening presents; her snoring gently blowing the ripped paper up and down beside her face. Dolly's habitual surrender to sleep was what broke something hard within me, this damage to my heart that I never want fixed. These daily infant acts of faith rushed like water into the empty heart my mother assigned me. She, herself, knew all about housing vacant chambers where love should be. Even my father knew that my mother's heart contained only lake-water, running cold and lonely inside her. His was a different kind of bird-heart; it was full and loving, but available solely to his wife.

On my doorstep, Phyllis was waiting patiently for me to reply.

'Yes, I have met her,' I told her. 'Vita. She is . . .' And I paused, because I found that I didn't really know anything about her, even though I had spoken to her more in the last two days than I had with anyone else for some time. A fact appeared. 'She went to Cambridge University. History of art.' I said this like a proud parent.

Dolly appeared behind Phyllis and patted the older woman as she slipped past us both into the house. 'Phyllis!' she said warmly, her voice carrying as she went down the hallway. 'I hope you've brought us some of your delicious eggs!'

Phyllis blinked happily at the compliment. 'Lovely girl, your Dolly, really lovely girl. And so like you. Still can't see her father in her. Not at all.' Phyllis is one of the rare few who is oblivious to the King's charm and is unafraid to say so.

She pointedly watched Dolly disappear down the hallway before continuing, as if our conversation was confidential and potentially disturbing. 'I've been round there, of course, next door, with the eggs, you know, but there's been no one in. For. Days. Even when the sports car is outside.' She widened her eyes and frowned at this, as if puzzled by such absence, and the lines already etched into her sharp little face deepened. 'I remember when Fran and Arthur lived there, do you? Lovely couple, they were. But, of course, it's all different now. It's all different.' She made a small, helpless gesture with upturned palms and her arms fluttered limply down to her side. Our street was, in fact, entirely unchanged. Many of the residents remained from my childhood, and photographs my parents took in the early years of their marriage evidence the same trees, the same neat hedging and private driveways that surrounded us then. 'I even heard they are selling Lakeside. With all them children in it!'

Lakeside was the local children's home, an austere but lovely building on the edge of the town. I might once have been an infant resident there myself if my mother had got her wish, and, later on, if Phyllis had not offered to stand with me as she had. Her phrasing implied that the home would be sold with the children included as part of the exchange. I assumed this suggestion was a tactic to continue the conversation, for Phyllis has always loved to talk.

'No. I'm sure that is not right, Phyllis,' I said, preparing to close the door again.

But she hadn't finished yet. 'I had to kill Florence, you know,' she said conversationally.

Reluctantly, I opened the door. *Ha* would not cover this admission. 'Yes, OK,' I said.

'She turned into an egg-eater, and I couldn't stop her. And then Mary started, and the others would have copied them too. I stopped Mary by filling the eggs with mustard water, but Florence had got a taste for them. She wouldn't stop.'

'So you killed her?' I said. It did not seem possible that Phyllis had killed one of her chickens, whom she carried around her front garden like infants and introduced by name to anyone passing, regardless of their interest.

'I strangled her, and I will do Mary, too, if she starts again.' Phyllis clenched her bony fingers as if in memory. The tension caused a protrusion of the veins across the paper-thin skin on the back of her hands, giving her the claws of her own large avian family. She looked even more pointy-faced than usual, as if expecting I would disapprove of what she had done. I had not decided, yet, how I felt about her and her new, chicken-killing ways.

'Well, yes. You will,' I said, as nonsensical as my weather-fixated postmaster, and I finally closed the front door.

Dolly called to me from the sofa where she was sitting with a can of cola and her salad. 'Did you really make this, Mum? It's coloured food!' She wanted me to watch a television programme with her. It was a period drama, a poorly made series, but it made both of us laugh, and this fact itself was a rare enough occurrence for us to watch it together. The younger members of the cast kept becoming too popular for the show and finding more worthy jobs, so the death rate was high. Previously unheard-of characters would be referenced in conversation one week – *My sister lives on the coast and is married to a vicar* . . . – and then invariably appeared in the next episode, following an unexpected personal tragedy. The heroine was a young woman with a lovely face who permanently wore heavy eye make-up, even when she woke up in the morning and despite the nineteenth-century setting. She was also fond of making the observation: *Papa would not allow that in his house.* Dolly and

I joined our little fingers in a miniature handshake whenever this statement was repeated, and we said it to each other gravely at every opportunity: in cafés with grubby tables, when I had messy hair, when she came home late, or I overcooked the dinner, or dressed inappropriately.

As we sat companionably on the sofa, Dolly put her legs up across my lap. She was tall, much taller than me, and her long legs were both familiar and foreign to me. I focused on the reassuring weight of her and traced the shape of her sharp-boned feet in my hands. I once knew those feet, that body, more closely than my own, for I had carried and fed her when she was soft and round. I had bathed and dressed her and placed her carefully in her cot each night with the reverence of a priest performing a practised and holy ritual.

The baby, though, had changed into the elfin creature who was my daughter for several years. The child who staggered around like a tiny drunk and regarded me as a perfect extension of herself. Who met the strange new discoveries of each day, from pancakes to traffic lights, with a derisory laugh and a sideways look at me, as if to confirm that she and I alone knew the ridiculousness of such things. In those early years, we watched in fascination every morning as the schoolteacher who lived opposite locked his door and then aggressively tried to get back in without his key. We often shared a plate of toast while we observed him, occasionally motioning with the little triangles to emphasise important points. *He looks smart. Is that a new briefcase?* we asked one another at these morning meetings. *Has he had a haircut? It won't do. It's far too short.* At the shops, we studied the habits and preferences of our neighbours and discussed the merits or strangeness of their purchases, sometimes in authoritative and unchecked voices, sometimes in the shared silence of sign language.

And now that daughter was, once more, a new person. In only two more years, she would doubtless be different again and living away at university. She discarded the versions of herself with an ease I could not share. I wished her unchanged and unchanging, and solemnly mine in all that once-tiny perfection. For we had formed each other once, and out of nothing. And I remained constant while she regularly transformed, dancing further out of reach with each alteration. I came to understand, just then, why Phyllis had killed her beloved Florence, why she might still kill Mary. And I would accept her eggs gratefully next time she called, and listen to her talk on the doorstep for as long as she liked.

the untraceable heart

A WEEK AFTER VITA MOVED IN, I RETURNED HOME FROM WORK to see her sitting on her own front step. She wore a man's tweed blazer over a red dress that became full-skirted tulle at the waistline. Her hair was glossy and darker than I remembered, and as I approached her, I realised it was actually wet. She was holding a cigarette delicately, as if about to discard it, and regarding her small bare toes with some concentration. I liked her little brown feet. I stood quietly while deciding whether to interrupt this reverie. But she looked up before I could speak, and her slight frown cleared instantly, replaced by a wide smile.

'You!' she said, as if this were my name. As if I was the only person to whom this title could possibly belong. 'I hoped I would see You today. Come! And sit.' She patted the stone surface beside her, and I dutifully sat down. She shifted slightly and the tulle arranged itself prettily across my work trousers, as if the fabric were animate and colluding in Vita's insistence on beauty. She flicked her finished cigarette butt away, rolling her finger along her thumb. Her spread hand remained in position for a moment afterwards, pointing at the discarded object.

'Why are you dressed up?' I asked.

Vita looked down at her dress, as if to remind herself what she was wearing. She touched her wet hair thoughtfully. 'I'm not. Rols finally brought back the dry-cleaning. And I just got out of the shower, and this was hanging up. It was this or a tennis dress. Do you play tennis?'

'No. You are, though. You are dressed up,' I corrected her.

She wriggled her shoulders and spread out her skirt extravagantly with both hands as if in agreement.

We watched in silence as one of the Fraser girls parked opposite us and unloaded several small children from her car before taking them into her mother's house.

'Who are they?' asked Vita. But she was already standing before I could answer; her move created a little explosion of sparkly fabric and unfolding petticoat beneath her brown jacket. 'I'm just going in for my ciggies. Stay there. Wait for me. Or would you like to come in?'

'No. I would not,' I told her. Dolly had mislaid her key the day before and I needed to see her arrive home to let her in. I put my hands flat against either side of the tweedy jacket; one of my palms touched the satin lining and the other rested on the rougher wool. It was not unpleasant. 'Is this your husband's coat?'

She nodded, and when I let go of the fabric, she jumped easily up the front step and disappeared inside.

While Vita was inside, I considered what to tell her about the Frasers. I know too much about the people who live here. Perhaps they know too much about me also. The Frasers' house is next to Mr Atkinson on one side and Phyllis on the other. There are five Fraser daughters, all evidently carefully planned. When Dolly was younger, we had found them a pleasingly symmetrical group, with one head height between each of them, from the smallest up to their mother. The girls had attended a school in the next town and did not mix with the local children, perhaps preferring, or perhaps simply being restricted to, the company of one another. Mr Fraser was rarely seen, but his wife and their daughters could regularly be observed, leaving their home and moving along the path in pairs. The pavement along our road is only wide enough at any point for two people to walk comfortably side by side. Mrs Fraser typically took up the front, along with her eldest daughter, and then they paired off by age with the youngest two at the back, holding hands. When the father joined them, he walked alone in front of them. The mother and girls dressed similarly, in long coats and wide skirts. The only allowance made for any disparity in their ages was their shoes. The pair leading the group wore noticeable heels, the following two wore heels of a lower height, and the very youngest wore shoes that were sensible and flat-soled. The parading habits of this family put me in mind of a story I had favoured as a child, in which a group of farm animals decided to behave as people. The animals dressed carefully and behaved in ways they perceived to be human. There was much narrative attention paid to the animals' new habits and modes of dress, and yet they were at their least convincingly human when they were acting for show, rather than on their instincts. The individual charms of the Fraser girls, the little skips and the unruly plaits, became increasingly subdued over time as each gradually morphed into the older girl in front of her, and eventually, of course, into the mother herself.

The youngest girl was the one for whom I harboured hope the longest. She had a heart-breaking way of being always cheerfully out of time with her family line, a frequently unbuttoned coat and a poorly hidden absence of gloves. The child had a tendency to stop and become immovably distracted by the feeling of either rain or sunshine on her neck, by the various domestic pets on our road, and, on one occasion, by a pornographic magazine, which had apparently escaped from the bin outside the house of Mr Atkinson. He was indisputably the most respectable and senior resident of our street, and when anyone spoke of him, they did so in their best voices. Phyllis had her own version of talking 'well-to-do', as she phrased it, and she referred to him as 'the man what lives next to all them lovely young girls', as if his choice of house was itself something seedy and suspect that she was alert to.

Then Vita was back beside me, with a cigarette already lit in one hand and the box in the other. Her lovely face was all concentration as she inhaled and then exhaled with a little shudder, staring into the distance, as if trying to process something unfathomable. She inhaled again deeply and nodded towards the Frasers' house to remind me of her earlier question.

'What would you like to know?' I asked Vita. 'That is one of the Fraser girls. There are five. I can't tell them apart, except for the youngest one.' But I should not have been concerned about Vita wanting more information. She crafted conversation by herself and from nothing. She gently carried me along on her words, and I could have loved her for that alone.

'Five? *Five?*' she laughed as she exhaled smoke, and the sound was pure amusement. 'Tom has . . . what, four now?

I can't imagine being responsible for one other person, but four . . . five? The idea of five coats, five pairs of shoes, even . . . If I had to find five pairs of gloves before I could leave the house, well, I wouldn't leave the house. I suppose that's the problem: I *would* leave the house. On my own.' She giggled to herself and put her forehead to her raised knees, as though hiding from the possibility of these conjured children. Then she turned and looked directly at me, her cheek pressed against the red net of her skirt. 'Did you ever think about having more children? After Dolly?'

'I didn't think about having Dolly,' I said, and she patted my arm, the smoke from her cigarette travelling in a neat vertical stream up to my face. I turned away from the smoke and she waved her other hand to clear it. 'But she came along and then I found I did want her. Very much. Painfully so, in fact.'

'Was it like that immediately? As soon as you gave birth?' Vita's cheeks were flushed, and the questions did not come in her usual, nonchalant way, but spilled out as if from an overfull cupboard.

'I think so, yes.'

After four hours of labour with Dolly, the invisible forces that had been making my womb painfully contract came to an abrupt halt. It was like being at the centre of a storm that suddenly stopped swirling around you. But it was not met by sunshine, or the certainty of a black night-time sky; there was just an eerie silence and the shame of exposure. The adrenaline that had been blanketing me crept away from my bed to hold the hand of another woman, and the ache of my labouring immediately made itself known to my bones like hard blows. The nurses were unable to locate the baby's heartbeat. They mentioned the missing heart to one another with a querying note in their voices, as if one of them might suddenly recall having misplaced such an object and then return it.

'Well,' said the senior nurse, placing a possessive hand on my eerily still stomach, which had been hard as bone throughout the contractions and was now soft and watery once more. She was a tall woman with cold, searching fingers. Her thin, arched eyebrows, wide eyes, and round mouth all served to suggest a state of constant surprise. I supposed such a persistent expression of shock was often inappropriate to a situation, as were my own, overly restrained features. It could not be helpful either, I thought, to appear as fixedly amazed as the nurse when the resemblance between her child and her husband was commented upon, or when she received the news of a friend's engagement.

But occasionally, her face must have suited an occasion, and my labour provided such an example. She ran her hands over my now-relaxed stomach and tilted her head to one side like a big-eyed bird. 'You don't see that every day,' she said, pulling down a clipboard from the bed headboard to write on it briefly. She shook her smooth head in brief and rapid twitches. 'No, you don't.'

She left me alone for half an hour, during which time the King came to the hospital to look in on me and my underperforming body. His visit was brief, and he left with the explanation that he would return after supper. His mother, apparently, had warned him that first babies arrived slowly; that my labour would take days and not hours. While he was away, the nurse with the bird-head returned, this time with a short and smiling man. He frowned when she told him about the untraceable heart

74

and gestured that she ought to attach her stethoscope to my rounded stomach. She demonstrated, with large theatrical movements, how the baby's heartbeat could not be detected. I imagined the doctor would look from the nurse's incredulous expression to my own impenetrable face and then doubt my investment in my unborn child.

'It is a new one,' said the nurse, considering her stethoscope, 'but it did work fine on my last lady.'

The doctor looked at his watch and then put his palms up as if to discourage further conversation. 'Caesarean.' He said this to the nurse in the manner of a guest ordering from a familiar but disappointing menu. As he left, he patted my shoulder absently. The receipt of his demand did not encourage any quickening of activity among the nurses, but rather induced loud sighs among them and a general slowing of pace, as though a predicted crisis had already passed.

The anaesthetist congratulated me on the complete loss of feeling in my lower body as I lay on the table in the operating theatre. I felt that the drugs were shrinking me, transforming me in minutes from a large pregnant body into only a torso and arms. Two nurses wheeled a large frame into the operating theatre and, without speaking, they efficiently clipped a green sheet over it to screen the lower part of my body. Once the installation of the sheet was approved, this being agreed between the two of them with a look and a silent nod, the women stood back in a synchronised manner, as if staging a magic trick.

The untraceable heart was discussed with only mild interest during the procedure. My nurse spoke to a young woman dressed in office clothing: 'There's a code for stillborn on the top left. See?'

The woman looked at the page and nodded. 'Oh, yes. I see.' Then she reached over to me and touched my shoulder. 'Excuse me. This is your first birth, isn't it?' I nodded politely and she made a consoling face; her mouth exaggeratedly turned down. She wrote something down and looked up at the nurse, who smiled approvingly back at her. I could imagine the nurse telling her husband at dinner: *We had this lovely young girl in today for training. I took her under my wing, you know, Reg, like I do. I can't help myself.* And Reg would listen with his small bird-head tilted, exactly as his wife did. He would blink his black eyes at her in solemn agreement – *you are kind* – while she shook her sharp-boned shoulders in a fluttery and modest way, as if displacing drops of rainwater.

The little man who had visited my room to announce this operation reached inside my midsection while in unhappy conversation with the anaesthetist positioned at my head. After much tutting, he lifted a tiny person out and held her aloft above the green sheet, as though in celebration. The baby did not cry immediately, but first gasped loudly as if outraged, interrupted in an important task.

'It is a girl. You have a daughter.' The man's voice was unexpectedly formal, not that of someone whose hands were about to tidily rearrange my insides. I appreciated the briefness of the doctor's announcement, the absence of description. I imagined him as a medical student, practising these moments alone and holding a towel-wrapped bundle, before the reality became part of his daily life. At the beginning of his career, he would have deliberately employed a quavering note of importance into his pronouncement as he held up the baby like a prize that he had won himself. Gradually, he had learned that there was more spectacle created by his underperforming at this life-altering moment, like an actor schooled to speak more softly at moments of high tension. 'There you are. All back in one piece,' he told me moments later, a phrase at once reassuring and alarming.

After the baby was checked and washed, she was placed on my chest. She fixed her brilliant gaze on me and gave a single perfunctory cry. I had not known that protectiveness could be both furious and tender. That a first sighting could feel as familiar as a reunion. I was sorry that my heart was beating so fast and so loud that it would surely disturb her. My peculiar half-awake body went into shock while I was still holding the serene baby. I started to shake, violently. I shook like an earthquake. I shook as though I wanted to bring down the whole building. I watched as my rubbery anaesthetised legs flailed as if powered by someone else. The bird-nurse immediately took the baby from my arms. She did so without a word or a glance at me; her silence and speed were as sharp as any reprimand. I had long puzzled over motherhood, for I had not been mothered myself. My mind had never conjured anything like this.

'And when does that intense new-mother feeling change?' asked Vita.

I did not have to consider how to express my feelings about Dolly. I was a devoted student, and she was my specialist subject. 'It's the same now. The difference is that she doesn't want to see it on me any more. But I feel the same about her as I did then.' And for the first time, I felt sad for my own mother, for whom I had not provided that other-worldly immediate enchantment that Dolly, and apparently Dolores, each had. 'It's easier to love one, I expect. My parents didn't want children at all. And they had two of us.'

Our parents had been scrupulously honest, and in their candour, also uncharacteristically modern, in telling my sister and I about their original intention to remain childless. Although we would have known, anyway, that their love was already portioned out: our father had Ma and she had the Lakes. Perhaps they did not tell us of their own accord. It is the sort of question Dolores, herself as real and fleshy as a warm infant should be, would have asked them without concern for her continued existence. Had I dared to query the degree to which I had been a wanted child, the answer would inevitably have rendered me even less substantial.

My father acclimatised to late parenthood with less difficulty than my mother, and featured in our lives as a distant but not unkind relative. He was often surprised when he came upon us in his house; he would visibly start when faced with these tiny intruders sitting non-chalantly on his chairs and eating biscuits taken from his cupboards. Then, he would raise a polite smile of acknow-ledgement, as though expressing recognition to reassure both himself and his uninvited visitors. 'Oh. Yes, there you are,' he would say benignly, to give the impression that he had not forgotten his children, but had instead been actively looking for us. And with this, he would walk briskly away, as though he had other small people to discover in the rest of his house.

Vita was watching me in that close and considering way that she and Dolly shared. She ran one hand thoughtfully up and down my arm. Her cigarette was now in her other hand, and she held this carefully away, as if in demonstration of her gentleness with me.

'Perhaps your parents simply loved you differently than your sister.' Her tone was soft and clear, and she lingered over the last vowel as if in thought: *sis-taaaar*. When she continued, though, her voice was sliced through with the sharpness of confidence. 'People do that, even in families, you know. You are so funny, Sunday.' She grinned collusively at me, as if we had accepted my humour as an established fact some time ago. 'And so lucky. With Dolly, I mean. I would have loved a girl if I had had children. But Rols . . .' She covered her face briefly with both hands, the cigarette obediently trailing smoke up and away from her. 'I think I might have liked . . . not a big gang like Tom has, or . . .' She pointed her cigarette accusingly towards the Fraser house of girls without looking away from me. 'But just one. Of my own. Like you have. Rols always sold it as romantic, that we couldn't share each other with a child.' She drew on her cigarette, hard and noisily, like someone taking a necessary deep breath.

'Well,' I said, 'that does sound romantic.' I could not imagine the King ever making such a claim about me.

Vita made a brief choking sound as she exhaled; it was almost a laugh. Almost. She spoke in a small, clipped voice that was not her own. 'Except, you see, I haven't had him entirely to myself.' Then she shook her head and spoke again, sounding like herself this time. 'It's worked out for the best, I'm sure. And, anyway, I might have had a boy! Boys, eugh!' She inhaled on the cigarette in a rapid gasp, then raised her chin and blew out a little cloud of smoke. 'It's bad enough living with a grown-up one, right? Rols is fun, but I miss my girlfriends *ter-rib-ly*.' She extended the last word for extra emphasis and pulled a theatrically sad face, putting her head to one side and turning the corners of her mouth down. I reminded myself this was only a demonstration but still felt a mirrored grief tremble up inside me. 'I've told him I will need to go back to town for some weekends while we're up here. Otherwise, I will be missed. I really will.' She smiled brightly. 'And, of course, now I've got you right next door, too. I dreamed about you last night, you know. We were out there' – she nodded towards the garden behind – 'sunbathing together. Oh, I *love* sunbathing. Do you?'

'I hate sun. And light. Oh, I *hate* it.' I was practising to see if I could catch the same intonations as her, but even when I copied her sentence structure, it sounded off. 'I will never sunbathe with you.'

Vita did not laugh this time, as I had expected she would, but instead asked me, in my own blunt tone: 'And what do you like, Sunday? What do you dream about?'

But I could not tell her about my dreams, for they were small and unbeautiful, and Vita was interested only in loveliness. I did not tell her that I often woke in the night, breathless and tight-chested, convinced that I had left my baby daughter behind somewhere. In my dreams, an infant Dolly walked uncertainly down long roads, with her arms outstretched, but was always physically blocked from reaching me by the teenage version of herself. By the time I met Vita, I existed already in a form of maternal grieving, a refusal to accept that I had somehow lost my greatest love while still living alongside her.

For, as a teenager, Dolly had naturally begun to observe me and my oddities, which alternately amused and concerned her, the latter becoming more common as she approached independence. It was like living with a former lover who no longer remembered you as such, but be-haved as a lodger, parading his preferred girlfriends past you with a friendly wink. As if you had both agreed on the separation. Any mention of your recent intimate past would be received with a polite and distracted tolerance, as if you were unstable and must not be corrected, even when you were wrong.

'I like your dress, Vita,' I said. 'Although I would not wear it. It will keep you safe.'

'Will it, darling?' she said. Her lips thinned as she inhaled on her cigarette, and I watched the fine lines rush to gather around her mouth and then dash away fearfully as she exhaled. 'How?'

'The colour. Coral protects against *il malocchio*, against the jealous one. But if you don't have coral, then you can wear red, like this.' I lightly pressed on the piece of her tulle skirt that rested on my trousers and immediately withdrew my hand; although it appeared soft, it scratched like wire. 'When Dolly was little, I kept a red ribbon tied on her pram. For the same thing, the Evil Eye. You should probably wear more red.' A lot of people would envy someone like Vita. I supposed *il malocchio* must be trained on her wherever she was.

'I like red.' She flicked away her second cigarette, again holding her hand in position momentarily after it had landed on the path. The pose put me in mind of an archer whose elbow remained high over his spent bow while he waited to see if he had hit his target.

'Good. You need to.'

We sat together in companionable silence until I finally had to go and prepare dinner for Dolly's return.

a carefully constructed toy

I DID NOT SEE VITA FOR SEVERAL DAYS AFTER OUR ENCOUNTER on her front step and I found myself thinking of her often. Whenever I left the house, I did so deliberately loudly, and, on my return, I walked slowly up the path that ran parallel with hers, allowing time for her to appear. I wondered what it would take to conjure her up to sit and smoke on her front step, to get her out on the street again.

I constantly imagined her: lying on her back on the grass, fast asleep in the warm sunshine; laughing cheerfully at our bankrupted builder; sitting at my table in pyjamas with her mouth ringed in milk; sitting on the pavement and fitting shoes on to her bare feet with the sweet focus of a child; the feel of her tulle skirt in my hand. Late one night, as if I had summoned her through recalling these visions, Vita knocked on my door.

'I'm lonely,' she said when I let her in. I was barefoot in pyjamas, and she was wearing a long dress and heavy jewellery at her throat and earlobes. There were no hellos, just a bald announcement of her feelings and intentions. It was like communicating with a child. 'I don't like being alone in the house and Rols isn't coming back for days. I haven't spoken to anyone. For hours! I want to be in here with you.'

How easy Vita was to understand. This bluntness, then, was what she meant when she sat in my kitchen with milk around her mouth and gravely informed me that we were alike. If everyone talked in this way, instead of telling riddles about weather control and chicken killing, I would not need to endlessly translate. Dolly was already in bed; she had only two exams left and now wandered the house disconsolately on the evenings she was home, which were rare. She had begun to remind me of my father when he had circled the same house possessively and equally unsure of what he was looking for; my daughter now found my continued presence as inexplicable as he once had.

Vita was not talkative that night, but quiet and practical. She put her hands on my shoulders for support as she stepped delicately out of her high-heeled shoes, which she left in the hallway. Then she sent me back into the front room with maternal bossiness: 'Go and find something to watch. I'll make some food.'

I could hear her searching familiarly through my kitchen cupboards before bringing a plate of toast and marmalade into the front room. It was the first time in years that I had watched television with anyone except Dolly, and we stayed up for hours. We ate together and laughed at programmes that were not supposed to be funny. Sometimes we just laughed because the other one was laughing. Vita fell suddenly and sweetly asleep, exactly as Dolly had as a small child, and I gently put a blanket over her so that she could sleep undisturbed. When I awoke on the sofa a few hours later, she was gone. In historic Sicily, men who woke in the night to find their wives gone would know they had married a witch, a 'strange woman', and so a *maga* would be employed to provide a solution to his spousal predicament. Sometimes the cure killed not only the witch but also the real woman inside.

I think it was the cold that woke me briefly that night, the particular kind of sudden cold that reveals itself in summer between midnight and the sun coming out. The soft blanket was still spread out on the sofa next to me where Vita had been. I was shivering lightly as I crawled underneath the cover like a loyal pet, and Dolly found me asleep there in the morning, with the leftover toast on the tray.

After a long week without any more visits from Vita, I arrived home one evening to find a letter addressed to her among my own. I did not understand why the letter pleased me until I realised it brought me a reason to see her. I stood at her door for some minutes and then she was there, already talking animatedly as if we were in mid-conversation. When I passed the large envelope to her with the beginning of my prepared explanation, she placed it on her hall table without interest. I remain childishly convinced that all post contains life-changing news; therefore, the sight of my mail brings enormous anxiety and excitement. While I appreciate this is an excessive response, the visceral effect that letters have on me is undiminished, and each morning brings the potential for drama. The King used to leave his post unopened for hours, sometimes days, as Dolly does, until I reminded him about it, and then he would hold up his hand in dismissal. *You open it, then*, he would say. *Just don't tell me about it*. But I thought it was illegal to open someone else's mail, and I did not, although I would have liked to.

'You,' she said, and again she made the word sound like an intimate address to which blushing with pleasure was a reasonable response. 'You are a much better wife than I am. You bring my post, keep me supplied with milk, and you listen to me talk nonsense all night until I fall asleep. I am going to call you Wife.' This intention was announced with some gravity, as though it were an honour being bestowed, so I did not laugh, did not say, *Ha!* She kissed me efficiently on both cheeks and walked away up the hall, still talking as her voice faded. 'I've never met a Sunday before. I think it . . .'

I remained in the open doorway of Vita's house, awaiting an invitation.

'Wife! Come in!' she shouted.

I closed the front door gently behind me, and it seemed she was already relaying a story to me about a 'bossy little person' she had recently encountered at the farm shop. '. . . And the man kept asking me what I wanted. Really, he was just telling me what he thought, but *as if* it was a question. He said, "You'll be wanting steak, won't you? I expect you will." No thank you, I said to him. And he said, "Men always like beef best, though, don't they? I expect you're a lovely cook, aren't you? Yes, you will be. I can tell." No, I told him, I am, in fact, *horrendous* in the kitchen, and all I ever cook is lamb chops. But my husband doesn't mind, because apparently I make up for it *hugely* in the bedroom.' When she said the word 'hugely', she extended the first vowel, making a whistling sound. I attempted this effect as I followed her obediently down the hallway. *Huuuuge-lay*.

She was still complaining cheerfully when we entered her kitchen. Some moving boxes were still visible, but the house looked cosy, and Tom's pieces of furniture were obviously good. The fluffy white dog appeared at her feet and looked up at her with eyes as shiny as plastic. She picked him up with one hand and clasped him to her chest, where he remained, motionless and rigid, as if with self-consciousness. The dog was small and appealing to such a degree that responding to him was shaming, like falling for an obvious deception. He was as pleasing and ridiculous as a carefully constructed toy. A board of men in lab coats might have compiled data on the most appealing canine traits and subsequently created the formula to produce this creature.

Vita was still talking. '. . . And this man blushed and finally stopped asking bloody questions. He said, "Right. I'll just wrap up some lamb chops for you, then."' She laughed, amused at his embarrassment.

How fortunate she was to remain a bystander. I absorb other people's emotions; they are greedily encompassing, like children who will not let you finish a conversation. They dance showily at your feet, costumed performers who refuse to be ignored. *But I am here!* they say, *And you must feel what I feel.* And the shame, the fear, whatever it is, leaks from them into my body, causing my own cheeks to flush and chasing my heart to beat faster, as they click their fingers theatrically in demonstration. *One-two, one-two, one-two. Like this, like this*, they say.

The little dog had been entirely still in Vita's hand, but he shook lightly against the rising of her chest as she laughed. He blinked sadly and stared past me and into the distance.

'That's where I work. At the farm. Not in the shop. Well, sometimes in the shop,' I told her. Bunny and Richard are openly opposed to me spending time with customers, but occasionally it becomes very busy, and they are forced to relent. When this happens, one of them comes to collect me from the greenhouse, typically Bunny. She brings me a clean towel from the shop cupboard and watches me while I wash my hands and smooth down my hair at the sink; it is as though she is supervising an unhygienic toddler.

'Oh, *that's* where you work. You might know him then. He's a smallish man, one of those country types, cords and tweed and . . . all that, darling. Quite handsome I expect, in his day.'

'That's Richard. He's my . . .' Who was he to me now? He wasn't my father-in-law any more, but we remain something like family. 'He's Dolly's granddad. They are the Forresters. Dolly is one of them. She is a Forrester.'

A once-popular Sicilian insult accused unimpressive people of having fish-blood in them, and I know that whatever once ran in the veins of my family, whatever is in my own body, is something different from the King's people. Dolly is the only family I have left, but in every way that finally forms a person, she is a Forrester. My daughter is not *sangu du mi sangu*; she is not the *blood of my blood*. My family die from minor infections and drown in dry beds; these are deaths that Bunny and Richard would not understand. *Forresters*, they often said, when encouraging Dolly to improve her times tables or when announcing a new acquisition of land, *Forresters Do Not Give Up. Forresters Get Things Done.* The sign on their farm shop reads: 'Forresters' Specialist Farm Shop'. I once asked Bunny about that; what exactly did they specialise in? And she smiled and told me patiently, 'Everything, Sunday. Forresters are specialists in everything they do.' My daughter, too, spoke of herself in the third person and made the proud Forrester family claims.

'Oh, great. I've only just found you and already I've offended your people. Sunday, I am sorry. You do know he thinks I'm mad? Or at least sexually deviant?' Her face had a familiar look. It was an expression of acknowledged but appealing unruliness: Dolly in a new dress and covered in mud; Dolly coming home late on a school night or found smoking in the garden on the morning of a French exam.

The telephone rang, and Vita picked it up instantly in a practised manner. Of course, her telephone rang all day.

She said, briskly, 'Hello?' Then, 'Darling! Can't talk, I've got Sunday here.' Pause. She smiled broadly at me. 'I mean, Wife. I've got Wife here.' She laughed at his response and then said curtly: 'Yes. Later. Bye!' She nodded at the telephone. 'Rols. He'll be home tomorrow.' All family offence acknowledged, and apologies apparently dispensed, her expression changed again into something soft. Without warning, Vita handed me the little dog like a parcel that I was there to collect.

'Now, Wife, you sit there with Beast,' she said fussily, indicating a wooden chair at the small table. 'He doesn't like being held standing up; he's too small and the height frightens him. What shall I get you to drink? Tea?'

Beast was frozen in my arms, and I sat down at the table, but he continued to hold himself rigid as though playing dead. His fluffiness disguised his thin frame, and the peculiar little skeleton was easy to trace through his fur. His protruding ribs, like a set of infant's toes, were discernible against my fingers, and I put him down gently on the floor. His initial contact with the wooden floor was soundless, his body too light to make any noise. The only audible sound as he walked away was a light clip of his claws on the wood, the rhythmic tip-tap of a practised secretary typing with long nails.

'No, thanks, I'm OK,' I said. 'I don't drink anything hot or . . . anything that is not fizzy.'

'So you drink champagne and lemonade? I can offer you either of those.' She laughed; it was a short and musical sound.

'Well, yes. I do. And . . . tonic water.' I was ridiculous. It was the inevitability of these moments, these declarations I had to make, that made company so alarming.

'Marvellous. I'll make us cocktails, then. Fizzy ones.'

Vita moved happily around the kitchen, taking various bottles out of boxes. Her silence and the profile of her face reminded me of my first sighting of her, asleep in the garden. In a voice loud enough to carry above the noise, I asked her where Rollo worked and how long he had been away for.

'Can't talk, darling! Concentrating!' she said.

When she finally placed blueish drinks on the table, it was with some satisfaction. I raised the glass to my lips, and tiny bubbles escaped into the air and on to my face like small, uncertain fingers.

'Hold on. Wait!' Vita said. She held up the flat palm of one hand in a command and left the table to rummage in another huge box, this one marked 'ENTERTAINING' in thickly drawn capital letters. She returned, smiling, with miniature yellow and pink paper umbrellas, and dropped one in each of our glasses. 'Found them! Cheers! We'll toast to you and Dolly coming for supper on Friday. Rols will be home, and he can't wait to meet you both. You will come?'

a private home

DOLLY'S FINAL GCSE EXAM TOOK PLACE THE FOLLOWING DAY; she spent the rest of the week either out celebrating or involved in excited phone calls with her classmates. At home on Friday evening, she changed into a favourite green dress and flat brown sandals. She was lovely, and I kissed her delightedly while I told her so, not caring that this would make her cross. The dress was very short, but so plain that the length of it was naive and sweet, like a childish outfit outgrown but sentimentally favoured. None of her clothes were patterned, and this had been the case since she was of an age to choose her own outfits. Since Dolly was small, whenever I wore any piece that was not a single colour, she typically raised her hands and blinked theatrically as if blinded. My own wardrobe has, therefore, come to resemble my daughter's singly coloured pieces, which is, I suppose, a style of some kind. I had chosen a black skirt and a loose white blouse, which must have been appropriate because Dolly did not comment. We were expected for 8 p.m., and so we left home just one minute before this. *Arriving early is just as rude as being late*, Edith warned gravely from the pages of her book. *Be prompt, but do not impose on your host with a premature entrance.*

'For an 8 p.m. invitation at a private home,' I reminded Dolly as we approached the front door, 'guests must be prepared to leave at 10.30 p.m. We will announce our preparations for going at this time and then allow the host to agree, or to persuade us to remain for a short time if that is his preference. OK?'

Dolly nodded and, on their doorstep, she asked, 'And what is the penalty if we do not observe *Etiquette for Ladies*, Mum?' She had seen me refer to the book often, and occasionally she read passages aloud to me in a censorious tone, pointing her finger threateningly as she did so, until we were both laughing so much that she could not continue. 'Is it *very* serious?' She smiled, then, and pulled the knocker loudly.

Vita's glossily red front door was opened by a tall man. His smart suit was at odds with a leanness that made him appear boyish and even younger, perhaps, than he really was. He touched his already smooth, dark hair before extending his hand to hold first my hand and then my daughter's. As he leaned towards us, a powdery smell rose from him and filled the hallway. It was the impersonal, soapy fragrance of an infant with a scrupulous caretaker. The smell of a man with shiny pink fingernails, ironed pyjamas and an insistence on pure silk ties and monogrammed handkerchiefs. I blushed as I remembered Vita the morning she had come to my house for milk; the initialled pyjamas had been his. How peculiar to have seen this stranger's nightwear before we had even met. He wore a thin moustache in the imagined style of my Victorian builder and thin-rimmed round glasses. He had an open and lovely face with a gentle expression.

'Sunday and Dolly, how do you do? I am Rollo.' He used the same inflection as his wife, the same inference that he was the one we had been expecting, waiting for. 'How lovely that you were both able to come. Please.'

And he made a sweeping elegant gesture behind him into the long hallway. Dolly immediately understood and moved down the hall towards the kitchen door. Rollo was waiting for me to pass him, too, and I filed obediently into line between them both like a child flanked by her parents.

I heard Vita before I reached the kitchen. 'You're Dolly!' she said loudly. Then, 'Oh, you are *gorgeous*! Are you really only sixteen?'

I winced to myself, did not need to see my daughter's response to know that this kind of exclamation embarrassed and annoyed her. But I moved round the open door to see the two of them in a friendly embrace. They were laughing, and Vita, who was considerably shorter than my daughter, was reaching around Dolly's middle and pretending to extend the length of her green cotton dress.

She tutted in comic disapproval. 'You girls with your minidresses! Mind you, even this old thing would be a mini on you, wouldn't it?' She gestured at her own, exotic outfit. Vita was wearing a long kaftan in a thin, silky fabric. It was something another woman might wear over her bikini on a foreign beach and, indeed, the strappy outline of her dark underwear was faintly visible through the material. However, paired with Vita's centre-parted black hair, tanned skin, and various pieces of thin, gold jewellery, it became a special evening dress.

'I think you look lovely,' said Dolly in a serious, quiet voice that I had not heard her use before. And they laughed and talked in lowered voices, which I could not quite make out. I heard Dolly say something about celebrating and knew she must be talking about the end of her exams.

After looking forward to introducing the two of them, hearing them giggle together made me feel uncomfortable, as if I were the newcomer myself. I had wanted a little of the glitter from each of them to fall on me as I stood between them and they listened to my introduction in silence.

Dolly had her back to me, and Vita looked up to see me first. 'Wife!' she said. 'You look so pretty. Dolly is so like you.' Her voice and gaze were both unusually serious, and I moved forward to receive her kisses, already forgetting that I'd missed her introduction to my daughter. 'Come on, I'll show you round the house. Or have you already seen it all? With Tom?'

'I've been here before, but it was a long time ago. Before Tom.' I thought uncomfortably of Fran and Arthur, who had lived here for so long. I still could not really imagine the house belonged to anyone but them.

Vita's eyes narrowed as she looked closely at me. Can she tell I do not want to talk about this? I wondered. And, apparently, she could, for she took my arm and Dolly followed us on a tour of Tom's house. Vita gave all the rooms extravagant titles: . . . *and here is the parlour . . . the bedchamber . . . the lavatoire . . .* like an estate agent overselling something ugly. We both found her charming; we both laughed along. I think, now, that she was laughing at Tom's relatively modest house. At my house. Our homes have identical first-floor layouts, but Vita's bedrooms were beautiful, carefully furnished by Tom's wife, while ours, with the exception of Dolly's room, have always been the functional but impersonal rooms of an economy guest house. Tom's house has the worn glamour of an ancestral holiday home. The soft furnishings were once obviously richly coloured, but were now faded, as if they had been out in the sun for many summers, along with their leisurely owners. The gilt corners of chairs, picture frames and mirrors were also gentled with age into a restrained and black-speckled gold.

'I want this painting. It is so pretty. Tom has some lovely art, doesn't he?' said Dolly, when we were standing in Vita and Rollo's bedroom. The picture my daughter coveted hung opposite the bed; it showed an early twentieth-century couple in wedding clothes. The new bride gazed inscrutably down at her bouquet of orchids, while her husband looked at her profile, his delicate face earnest and puzzled. I had already chosen my favourite of the many paintings around the house. It hung in the guest room and depicted a contemplative mother whose brood of plump children sat around her feet as though in organised restraint, their soft, dimpled hands all poised as if ready to reach out and still her.

'It's mine. *Ours*,' Vita corrected herself. 'All the paintings are ours. We only brought our best paintings. They are too big for the house, but we didn't want to leave them in storage. Luckily, Tom's walls were covered in photographs of the children, so we just swapped them with ours . . .' Dolly was still looking at the painting. 'Are you interested in art, Dolly? I must take you to my in-laws' place; they have a small Canaletto, and we have friends who own a beautiful Panini.'

'Gosh,' I said, carefully copying their shared, wide-eyed expressions. We stood together in a rare moment of silence in the bedroom, as though all processing our admiration for these painters. *Canaletto*, *Panini*, I pronounced silently, tapping into the air with my fingers. 'Italians? And would they be from the South or the North? Whereabouts?'

Dolly laughed, and Vita made a satisfied little sigh, as though she had expected my response. 'Oh, Sunday, I do love you,' she said. And she reached out with her easy touch to take my arm.

Painted subjects are easier to read than their physical counterparts. One can watch them for as long as required with no thought of committing excessive or inadequate eye contact. In such pictures, clues of intent, which in real life are easy to miss, are instead deliberately sprinkled throughout. In real life, the details I am drawn to are often secondary, and these often mislead. That evening, when I looked at Vita, I saw her pretty hair, her little wrists wrapped in gold chains, and her welcoming smile. I did not notice the grip of her hand on my daughter's arm or the intensity of her gaze when they spoke to one another. Of course, in a painting, the artist intends all the uncomfortable truth he has put there, somewhere within the beautiful image, to be read. In life, the opposite is more often true.

Downstairs, Rollo was waiting for us in the dining area that runs off the kitchen. This room was built over one long-ago summer by Arthur, and remains the sole architectural difference of our homes. Rollo appeared in the double doorway between the rooms with a flute of champagne for each of us. We did not keep wine at home, because we did not entertain, and I had never seen Dolly drink anything alcoholic. I expected Rollo to ask my permission before he gave her a drink. But he did not, and she took the glass from him graciously, and as though pre-dinner champagne were a nightly habit of ours also.

Rollo raised his own glass, and at my side, Vita did the same. 'To our new friends,' he said, and his voice was low and serious. 'Vee tells me that you only drink champagne, Sunday. Very sensible, considering what I have been served in some private houses.' He patted his hair again, in the gentle and comforting manner his wife used with her little dog. He spoke as if my avoidance of still drinks was the calculated ploy of a sociable wine connoisseur. Any drink that is not sparkling runs down my throat insidiously, spreading rather than making itself known as fizziness does. The finest wine Rollo has ever tasted would still make me gag unless I consciously took it in careful, tiny sips.

'To Wife, Dolly and champagne! And to the end of exams. And the end of school!' said Vita, laughing.

Dolly and I clinked our glasses with each of theirs and then with each other. We each made identical little turns, in our revolving pairs, without moving our feet; it was like a polite dance in which one does not show favourites. Dolly had two high points of colour on her cheeks as she looked at Vita. I touched my own face and wondered if I looked like that when I was in Vita's company. The room was quiet for a moment and, as we regarded each other, carefully dressed, and engaging in unfamiliar rituals, I considered what it was we were promising. And to whom. My glass was delicate and thin-stemmed, but it was made of crystal and weighed heavily in my hand. At last, Rollo asked Dolly a question about her exams, and suddenly the three of them were exchanging stories about revision and test strategies. I listened to them talk; they were excitable and quick to laugh at one another and at themselves.

The table was set formally, with several sets of different-sized cutlery, multiple glasses and tall candles in silver holders. I had imagined Vita entertaining in a more relaxed way, with the pride she took in being non-domestic. But there were two low vases of cut flowers and a heavy white tablecloth and napkins. There were even stiff place cards for the four of us, small and carefully written in green ink, with a large outline of our first initial and then a name underneath. My card was opposite Dolly's, and it confusingly read 'S' and, underneath, 'Wife'. I hoped that Vita had written the cards; I did not want to think of a man claiming me as a wife ever again, even in humour. Even in Mr Lloyd's sweet and lyrical voice.

'Vita,' said Dolly admiringly, and it was rather brave, I thought, to use an adult's first name so casually. 'The table looks lovely.'

We sat down at the table and Rollo poured more champagne, while Vita brought us prawn cocktail in wide glasses. It was beautifully presented: lettuce and seafood drowned in a pale pink sauce dusted with specks of paprika, with one large prawn wrapped over the top of each glass like a question mark. I had read Edith Ogilvy's chapter on cutlery; I was confident about which pieces to use with each course. Each of the others, including Dolly, smoothly picked up the knife and fork at the outside of their place settings, and I felt as though we had all passed a secret test.

'This is really good,' I told Vita. 'How did you make the sauce?' The starter was all green and pink pastels, soft, creamy-tasting food with no sharpness.

'Oh, it's not me,' she said cheerfully. 'I don't cook. Rols made most of this himself. He unpacked a lot of boxes, today, too. Didn't you, darling?'

'*Most* of this?' He raised an eyebrow at her and smiled. 'And what exactly have you prepared, Vee?' He never used her full name. Instead, he called her 'Vee' and 'Queenie', softly and with a smile, as if these were private and loving jokes between them. I could not, though, imagine this formal and precisely moustached man interesting my Vita, who was excitable and loud, who delighted in and drew attention to her own blunders. Then she moved over to him and leaned close to tell him something. They looked as natural and relaxed as if they had spent their whole lives together, with both everything and nothing left between them.

'What were you doing today?' I asked her, surprised at Rollo's domestic industry.

Vita leaned forward to me and covered my hand with her own.

And, as she spoke, she gave a resigned shrug. 'I *always* take a nap and a long bath before dinner. It's a habit now, and I don't see any point in changing it.'

'You will discover, Sunday, that it is not for us to question Vita's methods.' Rollo laughed as he spoke, but his wife's face remained serious. 'How was the tour, Sunday?' he asked me. 'You and Dolly must have spent time over here, I expect? With Tom and his family.'

'We don't know Tom like that. We know who he is, but we don't socialise,' I said.

'Isn't it funny, Rols?' said Vita. 'We always know everyone, don't we?' She said this with a distant bewilderment, as if referring to something beyond their control, to an interesting yet naturally occurring phenomenon. 'Am I *terribly* nosy, do you think?'

'You? Queenie, *you* are a complete horror.' He paused and smiled softly at her as if he had just expressed a sentiment of love. She did not hear him; she was already distracted and laughing with Dolly.

'What I really admire about Tom,' Rollo continued, 'is his commitment to charity. He is a good friend of Ed Taylor, actually. Did a fundraiser last year at the bank. You know, for Lakeview. He's hosted a few before for different causes, but this one was fantastic. Great fun. Do you know Ed? Runs Lakeview?'

In Vita and Rollo's world, I was to learn, people were all expected to know each other. Their whole social circle was connected. They went to school or university together; they holidayed, partied and hunted in the same fashionable places; and always, always, there were distant family members keen to introduce them to someone useful. I had not considered, before meeting Vita, that acquaintances could be more beneficial than injurious. I had not properly understood, then, that people could be played like instruments to produce whatever sound you demanded of them.

I nodded non-committally to Rollo's query, but he was satisfied enough with this to continue. 'Ed is marvellous, isn't he? He takes in all the kids the other places don't want; he runs Lakeview more traditionally than the new children's homes. It's all therapy and first names in residential care now, according to Ed. He's more conservative, of course. And he and his wife are very, very good to those children.'

My sole experience of Edward Taylor was attending a talk he had given at the town hall the previous December, titled 'Lakeview: A History'. Leading up to the event, there had been local rumours that he would be announcing his early retirement that night due to a minor administrative misdemeanour. Whatever the truth of these whispers, the suggestion cleverly aligned that evening's attendees with him as we felt ourselves protectively taking the side of a hardworking man against an ungrateful council. He was charming, with the formal bearing and authoritative voice of an aristocrat, tall and dressed in a well-fitting dark suit. It was easy to imagine Rollo and Mr Taylor as brothers, never mind peers or acquaintances. The hall was full on the night he addressed our town. Lakeview housed an unknown and private community, who were schooled on site and rarely seen outside the grounds. Rumours about the residents were persistent and often creative, so locals were naturally curious about the children.

The council officer in charge of the home, a small, sweating man in a pale yellow shirt, sat on the stage, along with a young and gentle-looking woman who was briefly introduced as the children's home's economics and physical education teacher. They both watched Mr Taylor's back gravely as he strode around the stage. 'Freemasons!' whispered a man seated next to me, as if I had asked him a question pertaining to the subject. His wife pressed his elbow and shook her head disparagingly at him. I smiled politely and stared ahead, but he continued to mouth the word at me, raising his eyebrows at me and nodding theatrically towards the stage, as if encouraging me to intervene with this new information.

Mr Taylor had spoken about Lakeview and the importance of charity in a Christian community. He did not speak about the teenage girl who had drowned in the lake six months before and had subsequently been named in the local paper as a resident of the home. He told us that the resident children were educated on site purely because the local schools were reluctant to take them. As he said this, he spread out his arms in an encompassing gesture, and we all shrank back from the association. Many of the audience were parents whose children attended those unwelcoming schools. They began to fidget at this point, the fathers adjusting their ties and the mothers pursing their mouths and tapping their shiny earrings. Their movements gave them an impression of restlessness, and Mr Taylor responded with increasingly tragic stories about those he called 'our children'. *Our* children, as if the town was an unwieldy and careless couple who had accidently left dozens of their offspring behind like forgotten parcels with Mr Taylor, his officer in charge and the sweet-faced teacher. Mr Taylor told a lot of terrible stories about the lives that the children at the home had suffered before they had come to him. A few were orphaned, some were neglected or abused, and some, he said, looking gravely at his audience, were Very Bad, but they were all, each and every one of them, Very Sad Children. And they all needed our help and our support, he told us, his face brightening handsomely with an expression of encouragement.

Mr Taylor had large, clear features, which lent themselves to the stage, and he emoted effortlessly as though it were his true profession. His expressive face was like a loyal choir that repeated and reinforced all that he told us. The officer and the teacher, too, frowned knowingly along with the tragedies of which Mr Taylor spoke, and nodded to the happier tales, as though they also knew all these stories first-hand. The commitment and oneness between the three figures gave their performance the gravity of a sermon.

Afterwards, the sweet-faced teacher served tea and coffee in little green cups and encouraged us to look at the photographs that were displayed on two large boards behind a tray of thickly cut biscuits. Phyllis was already there, looking with interest at the display. These biscuits, announced the young woman, had been made *especially* for us by the Lakeview children that afternoon. She told us this in the manner of someone bestowing a valuable gift. However, after she spoke, some people discreetly put their biscuits back down on the serving plate, untouched. I was pleased to see that Phyllis remained unwaveringly committed to her own free tea and biscuits. The teacher had the gentle and resigned expression of a model advertising home appliances, and she featured in one of the larger photographs, drowsy-eyed and bare-legged in a miniskirt, along with a brief personal history that stated she had once been a child resident of the home herself. At thirty years old, she had a bedroom of her own at Lakeview and had never lived anywhere else. The images traced the history of the children's home in black and white, and were accompanied by brief lines of explanatory and misspelled text. There were also photos of some of the children, these presumably selected due to their appeal, for theirs were beautiful faces, despite their wary and sometimes resentful stares.

We learned from the display that the home was first built for a group of doctors and optimistically called The Lakeview Clinic, although it was too far away to provide any views of the water. The evergreen trees across the front of the property that now entirely screened the home were evidenced in photographs as the neat and boxy plantings they had once been. Lakeview is several streets away from my home, at the end of a long row of terraced houses that back on to the railway line. It is an enormous red-brick building, with a pillared rectangle in the centre symmetrically flanked by two smaller but still sizeable wings. There is an austerity to the building, with no relief provided by the decorative elements that Victorian builders seemed to favour in the rest of our town. I imagined the man who built my house would have looked unfavourably on the simple and unfettered lines of Lakeview, whose grandeur was of proportion rather than architectural flourish. When the huge city hospital was built in the early part of the century, the council bought the local clinic and opened it as a children's home. The clinic sign was repainted to include the home's Latin motto. This transformation was shown in a photograph taken at the opening ceremony of the home, which also displayed what were then the still glossy wrought-iron fencing and gates expected by those wealthy patients. '*In pulvere vinces*', the repainted sign read, and this was translated below: 'In dust we win'. The same elaborate black script announced that it was 'Lakeview Community Home with Education' and a line of smaller writing alluded to the names of the director and the officer in charge.

At the end of the evening, people left the large meeting room to be confronted with a wooden donation box on a table in the narrow hallway. Everyone put money into it as they passed through to the exit. Some of the women tapped their husband's arms through the thick sleeves of winter coats, encouraging them to donate more, and then discreetly put more money in from their own purses when they passed the box themselves. We were all thinking of those Very Sad Children, with their tragic stories, and hoping our modest donations might improve their Christmas that year.

I did not tell Rollo about the town hall speech. I felt small and intrusive talking about the home and the people inside it as if I knew them when I really did not. All I knew was the stories told by Mr Taylor that night, alongside the collection of photographs. It was an evening of sadness made tolerable by beauty, of lives carefully curated to incite sympathy and, most of all, donations.

I listened as Rollo talked about his admiration for both Tom and Ed, and in that moment the three of them somehow became one impressive man, a force of strength, kindness and charitable compassion. And Vita and Dolly studied him so carefully when he spoke that I watched their admiring faces instead of his, and I deliberately thought what I imagined they were thinking: here is a good man.

The main course was hare, which Rollo had brought up from London, where it had apparently been marinating in wine for a whole week. It was extremely dark and rich, with a gravy as black as treacle. I wondered what Dolly would think of this food, but she smiled politely when Vita placed it on the table and looked entirely unmoved as the hare was spooned generously on to her plate. I was unsure, myself, about this strong-tasting meat, but I ate small bites of it and drank after each one. The accompanying greens were buttery, salty and served in individual earthenware dishes. This was the opposite of the pale, bland food I favour when anxious or out of routine.

'Do you like hare?' asked Vita. 'We love it, don't we, Rols? It's our absolute favourite. That's why we made it for you.' She smiled brightly at her husband, who seemed to blush under her gaze as much as Dolly and I did. 'Why *Rols* made it for you.'

'Well, I've never eaten game before, Vita. I don't . . .' I began uncertainly, but Dolly spoke over me.

'It's really very good,' Dolly said politely, as I should have done. 'You must give my mum the recipe, Rols. Were you at work today?'

'Yes.' Rollo smiled. 'I've been in town all week.'

Vita and her husband both referred to London this way, as if it was not a city, but actually the sole town in the country. As if our homes were not also in a town made up of streets of houses and roads and shops, pavements and street lighting, but were instead nestled alone together in a quaint hamlet. When they went back to the city, they told me they were going 'into town'. If they went out here, they named the place they were going to instead: 'I'm going to the dentist' or, 'We are off to the grocer's'.

'We're at the end of a project and I'm just popping in and out when they need me,' continued Rollo. 'It is rather an exciting one. Beautiful proportions.' He leaned back and eyed Dolly carefully, as if considering whether to tell her more, and then evidently decided he would. 'It was a factory building with warehouse space upstairs, and it is turning into some rather fantastic apartments. I would happily live in one myself if they weren't all reserved. I mean, if they were ready now, we might have moved into one instead of coming to Tom's. We actually would have, Vee, wouldn't we?' He said this as though their acquiescence to live in a place was the ultimate evidence of quality.

'Mm . . . possibly we would.' Vita frowned as she spoke, tilting her head and raising one hand to her chin as if in consideration. The pose left her in picturesque disarray; the unlaced kaftan slipped off one shoulder and the elaborate gold earrings made a light tinkling sound before settling back determinedly against her neck.

Instead of adjusting her neckline, she leaned forward, displacing it further and exposing the thin strap of whatever she wore underneath. The gold chains layered heavily around her throat seemed suddenly more conspicuous and immoderate against the obvious flimsiness of the underwear. 'Or perhaps living up here will turn me into a country wife!'

We all laughed agreeably at the ridiculousness of Vita conforming to either part of this title, and she smiled, leaning back into her seat and clasping her hands together in modest pleasure, a performer at the end of a well-received show.

'So, are you a builder?' Dolly asked Rollo, who was still watching Vita.

He turned visibly away from his wife to fix his attention entirely on Dolly, who unconsciously drew back a little as she looked up at him. My daughter did not typically retreat as she did just then, but Rollo's charm was not like that of his wife or Dolly, or the King; it did not reveal itself all at once, but in devastating little pieces. Sometimes he let you forget all about it, blinking awkwardly behind his round glasses and allowing Vita alone to be the entertainment. And then, occasionally, he would focus on one of us with an intensity that left the recipient dazzled. He could even have this effect on Vita.

Rollo put down his cutlery and gestured with both hands as he spoke, turning his palms upwards and then down as if making a complicated point. 'Not exactly a builder. We renovate. Mostly we turn commercial buildings into residential. There is a lot of scope for that in town and Vee has a great eye. Sometimes we make apartments, sometimes houses.' He pronounced 'houses' with a peculiar vowel emphasis; he actually said 'haices' so it would rhyme with 'faces'. I repeated this silently to myself several times – *haices, haices, haices* – then looked at Dolly and Vita, who had both been listening to Rollo with entirely serious faces as though he were announcing a political development on the evening news. 'In fact, an opportunity has come up here. Lakeview? I didn't say earlier, did I, but it's coming on to the market. The children all have new places to go to, so I could be in very soon. I'm hoping to buy it directly from the council before it goes to auction. It would be a good project to keep me busy here.' He looked at Vita. 'To keep *us* busy here.'

'He is being modest,' Vita told us. 'Rols is *famous* for his houses.' *Rahls is fay-mousse for his haices*, I repeated back to myself in silence. 'At first, I used to help out, but now it's really his thing. I just choose the wallpaper.' She frowned. 'But, Rols, I thought you had already bought the place?'

Rollo touched the side of his nose and raised one eyebrow to give his wife a meaningful look.

'Steady on, Vee! I'll talk all about it when it's signed off. With all of you. In the meantime, we are enjoying our little holiday up here. Of course, we have known Tom forever. He's enormous fun,' said Rollo. Vita smiled warmly in agreement at Tom's name, like a child hearing a mention of Christmas, and her husband looked softly back at her. They were alone together for a brief moment, remembering whoever they were when Dolly and I were not there. What was it to be part of such a casual and intimate exchange?

'We could even buy a place up here, couldn't we, darling?' Rollo said to her.

I nodded and replied firmly, 'Yes.' As if the three of them were just waiting for me to confirm their future housing plans. And, after a moment of silence, they all laughed, and I joined in. Vita put her hand possessively over mine again and it seemed that the four of us had been together for years.

While Dolly and Vita discussed the quality of the only local clothes shop, Rollo asked me about the large house at the top corner of our street, a striking mid-century building with an impressive protruding wraparound window. The window offers a sweeping view that incorporates both directions of the road, and must be as revealing as it is panoramic. Rollo leaned towards me and laid an arm along the back of my chair in a pose of absorption, and I told him how a quiet couple once lived in that house for several years with their teenage son. The boy was tall and thin with a friendly smile, and he attended a local private school, whose morning bus left later than ours, leaving him time to stand in his window and watch us pass his house on the way to the bus stop. He liked to stand at his bedroom window naked and watch people's faces as they saw him, his smile remaining fixed and serene. At night, he would stand in darkness until passersby drew parallel with his window. Then he would light a lamp to reveal himself, his bony ribs and chest darkly shadowed, while the area below his waist was efficiently highlighted as if in an operating theatre.

At this point, Vita left the table to go to the kitchen, and Dolly moved to help her. Rollo stood up but remained at the table. This was something he did whenever any of us left or entered a room. Every time he moved, a light waft of his soapy smell resettled around us, and I found myself pausing to appreciate the unchanging quality of the fragrance, as I do in the greenhouse when working on a good plant. The smell of a person usually changes over the course of a few hours. When Dolly, for example, had come in from our garden earlier, she was warm, and her skin and perfume together had a discernible sharpness. But then, as she sat still and chatted to me, the edge of the heat on her had softened and the smell of her shifted too, becoming cool and sweet. When Vita had greeted me that evening with a close embrace, she had covered me in a musky, amber-based perfume, and I knew that when I kissed her goodbye later, the warmth of the house, the candles, the alcohol and the coffee would all have combined and become a new fragrance on her skin. The unchanging quality of Rollo's smell was appealing; it gave him a fixedness that I admired. The permanence of people in any sense is a rare and pleasing thing. The more symmetrical a person's face is, the less likely they are to smell unpleasant to those of the opposite sex. Having a symmetrical face is apparently an indication of superiority in sperm count or egg production. Dolly's father, of course, smelled of nothing; after a summer day working on the farm, his sweat was as odourless as fresh water. I imagined the King and his new wife, with her heart-shaped face and childishly dimpled cheeks, would prove as fertile as their herds of reproducing cattle.

When Rollo was seated again, I stood up and watched in fascination as he immediately copied me. But then, rather than following the others into the kitchen, I sat back down. Rollo, too, sat down, without querying my move, and placed both elbows on the table. His action informed the now familiar soapiness of him; it resettled comfortingly around us both like scented dust motes. He laced his fingers together and placed them thoughtfully under his chin, his fingertips just grazing his jawline.

'And the naked boy?' he said, straightening out one finger to point at me.

'For three years, my sister and I passed him daily on our school journey,' I told Rollo. 'And we always wondered, what had come to him first, the exposing window or the compulsion? Perhaps he was once a typical teenager but found the huge window called him to perform. Or had his parents deliberately chosen that house as a gift for their exhibitionist child?' I explained how I was unnerved by his exposure, while Dolores found his nakedness an amusing diversion, an alternative and unthreatening view on our school journey.

But I did not tell Rollo how once, on a hot summer day, my sister stopped in front of the boy's window to unbutton her school shirt. At thirteen, her chest was still undeveloped, and she did not wear the small white bra that our mother had bought her. When Ma insisted Dolores wear it underneath her school shirt, she did so without comment, but then casually removed the bra while we sat at the bus stop, without pausing in conversation or attempting to conceal what she was doing. Once news of this reached Ma, she no longer insisted on the bra being worn. Dolores found bodies only amusing or functional; she was entirely unselfconscious about her own and openly ridiculed those of our peers, who, like me, she regarded as physically inhibited. So, she stood braless and bare chested on our street, squinting up at the boy against the sunshine, while he looked frankly back at her as if the two of them were in conversation.

Neither did I tell Rollo what she said to me afterwards, what she often said to me: 'We are all just bodies, Sunday,' she would say, laughing. 'All except you, and

I'm not sure what you are.' And it was true that Dolores was very much her body. Sugar, boys and sometimes grown men, all in various and sometimes seemingly unappealing forms, brought a depth of pleasure into her brief life that most do not know, however many years they are given.

'After the family moved away, a couple moved in, solicitors with their own practice. They positioned desks along each side of that window when they moved in. They're retired now, but you still see them sitting at their desks a lot.'

This was what I told Rollo at the dining table, while he listened and nodded along politely. The risqué element of the story was over by then, though, and he had removed his arm from the back of my chair and settled back into his own seat. But I did not say what I really believe: that all of us who have been here long enough to remember the naked boy still see him standing at the window. That we watch as he flicks his light repeatedly on and off, his pale lower body appearing and disappearing again into darkness. That his nakedness was a distress signal that we could not read then and still cannot.

The others were now back at the table, Dolly with a jug of cream and Vita with a large gilt-edged bowl containing pink-stained poached pears. Vita served the fruit and raised her eyebrows at each of us in turn for confirmation that we would like cream poured over our pudding. She looked to Rollo first and laughed as he spread out both hands to indicate that she should not hold back on his portion.

Rollo talked while we ate his smooth pears, which were so sweet and marshmallow-soft that they no longer tasted like fruit, but as an artificial confection that might be found in the jar of an exceptional sweet shop. He told us about a dance held at his boarding school, speaking with apparent reluctance. The event was attended by pupils from a local girls' day school, and he entertainingly positioned himself as an awkward and socially inept teenager amongst a crowd of sophisticated peers. He had apparently missed several romantic opportunities with various girls that night, something his friends delightedly pointed out to him – but only once they had themselves benefited from the newly lowered standards of his disappointed admirers. Rollo was good at storytelling; his obvious confidence raised the comedic value of his former ineptitude with the opposite sex. His easy self-deprecation was unexpected and attractive in a man who was otherwise so formal and composed.

Vita and Dolly watched him over their puddings, their spoons paused in concentration. They smiled in unison and laughed at him together like old friends, easily and without self-consciousness. A breaking of something hovered between them, an interruption of self that threatened to announce itself before retreating from their unity; everything amusing was further heightened by the fact that they were together. I recognised this as something of what Dolly and I shared when she put her legs across my lap, and we laughed at the girl who shook her head and said sadly that *Papa would not allow that in his house*. But, perhaps due to the recentness of their acquaintance and the addition of champagne, Vita and my daughter were almost delirious; when they laughed at Rollo's admissions, they clapped their hands and tears ran down their faces. It was unsurprising that Vita embraced excitement with such ease, but I had never known Dolly in this state of near hysteria, even when she was a child. Dolly had been born remote and reserved, I believed. Yet that night, I was already seeing a different version of my daughter. The effect Vita had on me was not this exterior and obvious change, but something more private. Dolly's uncharacteristic exhilaration, though, simply provided more evidence of Vita's charm. This is my child, and this is my friend, I thought possessively, as if in silent introduction.

Rollo's smile was as easy and engulfing as that of the King. He could have been the result of a composite sketch accurately depicting a privileged man in his forties. He had fine-boned features, smooth skin and a well-kept moustache. His face was symmetrically pleasing but bereft of individuality or character. This was not the case with Vita, whose direct stare only confirmed her loveliness, whose tiny defects, such as the delicate overbite and heavy, straight eyebrows, served to promote her features beyond obvious prettiness and into beauty. There is a Sicilian proverb that claims a girl cannot be termed beautiful until she has had smallpox. That is, the smallpox was once considered inescapable, and so a girl's appearance could not be properly judged until she had survived the illness. Only after suffering the disease could her remaining looks be qualified.

Vita, though, would be no less remarkable after suffering this illness or, indeed, any another. Her face was knowing and did not rely on youth, on innocence or on the smoothness of her skin, as Dolly's did. There was something less quantifiable about Vita, and in person, as in photographs, her image was stately and direct. She expected to be admired and did not, therefore, seek it. There was none of the wanting about her that mildly attractive people have, none of the waiting for approval that weighs heavily between you until it is addressed and acknowledged. Often, even the parents of lovely children, too, wait for an admiring comment about their offspring, and if it does not come, they will raise it as a subject themselves. It is like a tic, this incongruous referencing of the height, symmetry and loveliness of oneself or one's child. Because I have involuntary habits myself, I shrink from those I see performed; unlike Vita, who never possessed or practised such tendencies.

The pair of them were seemingly onto the disparity between their looks, because in all the silver-framed photographs of them around their dining room, Rollo looked away from the photographer, typically towards Vita when she was featured alongside him, or, when alone, simply out into the distance. Even Rollo's earliest photo caught him in this pose, a chubby little boy of two or three years old, looking uncertainly out to the side of the frame. Vita, meanwhile, looked intensely into the camera with various hairstyles and dresses, while her gaze remained direct. Sometimes her stare looked like a challenge, and in other photos it was as if she were searching for something she could not find.

Rollo passed a decanter towards me.

'Port,' he said. 'You'll break your fizzy rule for this one.'

'No,' I said, looking at the glass, stained an uneven pink by the thick liquid and sporting black-red marks in places like tiny blood clots. 'I definitely won't.'

Rollo shrugged minutely and passed it to Dolly on his left. She was speaking to Vita and did not pause in conversation, but poured some port into the smallest glass of her collection. Then she passed the decanter to

Vita, who was listening intently. Vita tapped my shoulder and, while still focused on Dolly, she indicated that I should pass the port to Rollo. He poured his drink with some satisfaction. The liquid looked old and unhappy at being disturbed; it had a quality of graininess, like water brought up from the bottom of the sea. The peculiar passing of the port was like a dance I had not rehearsed. Later at home, I looked it up in *Etiquette for Ladies. The port must be first offered to the lady on the host's right before being passed back to him, then it is passed to the guest on his left. However*, Edith warned, *the port must never reverse.*

The others continued to pass the decanter and refill their glasses.

'Would anyone object to my smoking?' asked Rollo.

We all agreed that he might, and he immediately offered a cigarette to each of us. I saw Dolly hesitate and look to me before eventually shaking her head, *no*. After Vita took one for herself, he tapped a new one to the front of the box in an easy move. He waited while she took it into her mouth and then he concentrated on lighting the cigarette for her. She stared remotely past him into the kitchen, unmoved as a queen, but I was fascinated by his deference. The lighter went out twice and he persisted, shaking it expertly in one hand. When he finally succeeded and moved back into his seat, she looked directly at me and winked, as if she knew I had been watching them. In her look, what had been between them seemed transferred, somehow, into a secret between us.

Once he had lit his own cigarette, Rollo poured more port into his glass and said to me, 'I hear you and my wife are having sleepovers already?'

'No, we aren't,' I said, factually. 'Vita left before the morning, so it wasn't a sleepover.' Rollo remained silent, and his face had the blankness peculiar to polite expectation. His was a deliberate pause, as though I had just begun to tell a story, and so I did.

I told him the folklore that I had remembered when I woke that morning on my sofa to find Vita gone. 'In historic Sicily, when a husband awoke to find his wife gone, he knew she was a witch to be dealt with. So, he would go to the *maga* and ask for a way to fix his wife, even if it meant killing her. One man was told to remove the magic salve that his wife kept under the bed and to replace it with a plain ointment. That night, when his wife jumped from the window, covered in the salve and ready to fly, she instead fell heavily down to the ground. Her husband found her lying in the street below with broken bones, and she never flew again.'

Rollo said nothing, but Vita, who I did not realise had been listening, cut in smoothly. 'Goodness, Wife,' she said. 'What *are* you talking about? I hope you aren't giving Rols ideas about getting rid of me!'

As she stopped talking, her little dog walked in. He was looking towards the French doors into the garden and seemed deliberately casual, like a teenager timing his late appearance in the hope of being offered a drink by parents relaxed after an evening of wine. He went straight to Dolly's side and sat at her feet, looking up at her expectantly. But she was in conversation with Rollo and did not look down at the little dog. Each time she gestured or moved in her chair, Beast shifted hopefully from one front paw to another and then tensed his little body, rounding his back in expectation of being picked up. At these moments of stillness, he was even more toy-like. I could not wait any longer for Dolly to notice him.

'Dolly, look!' I said, interrupting her mid-sentence. 'Isn't he funny?' My daughter and Rollo both turned, but it was me they looked at and not the little dog. I pointed at him encouragingly and said, 'He is so tiny!' The sudden silence held my observation in the air, and it echoed, so obviously true that it was meaningless. The intensity of this collective attention was too much for the dog, who began turning repeatedly around on the spot as though this was one of his manufactured functions.

'Ahh, sweet,' said Dolly in a soft voice. She and Rollo both smiled at me identically, and then she turned back to him again. 'And what did the exam panel do about it?' she asked him.

'Well, we had written just enough to pass, so we got our degrees anyway. And more importantly, we won a lot at the races. When we wrote home, we had to bump up our degrees a bit, obviously. As a boarder, you grow up away from your family; it's best to let them invent you in your absence.'

Vita leaned forward and banged the table. 'Rols! I'm too drunk to make good coffee.' She stood up and he, too, was immediately on his feet. Smiling, she said, 'Will you bring some in for us, please? Yours is much better than mine.'

Dolly also stood up and we followed Vita down the hallway. The front room didn't have a television but did have a record player, and the neatly arranged bookshelves held dozens of records along the lower shelves. Vita flicked though them impatiently and then selected one. She smiled confidingly at Dolly and me, who sat next to one another on straight-backed armchairs.

'I'll put one of Rollo's on to keep him in a good mood.'

The record featured an orchestra playing a familiar classical piece; a beautiful sound that made my skin shiver in response. Perhaps, I thought, I could have been such a wife as this, could have played the King his favourite music, could have made him into someone who wanted to bring me coffee. I had never thought of my husband in such terms, as a malleable person whose temperament or emotions I could affect. Rollo appeared in the doorway with a tray, and he paused briefly to acknowledge the music, closing his eyes momentarily with pleasure. Vita had already cleared a space on the coffee table for his carefully arranged tray, moving aside the piled magazines and art books. The bond between them was sweetly visible, and as he put the tray down, she leaned forward to kiss him briefly on the cheek. I did not expect him to acknowledge this gesture, but his features softened at her touch. In my home, I did this dance alone, every move tailored towards Dolly but received at best with adolescent coolness.

Beast had somehow made his way up on to Dolly's lap, and he was curled up on her, as frail as a kitten. His black eyes flickered momentarily as though his batteries were low, then he was gently snoring. Dolly balanced her coffee cup saucer on the sharp spine of his little back, but otherwise she seemed unaware of his presence. I resolved not to mention him or his appeal again. I refused a coffee and Rollo asked me what I would like to drink. Vita stood up and he moved to follow, but she patted him back down with an easy gesture.

'Come on, Wife!' said Vita to me. 'Let's go and see what we can find.'

In the kitchen, she took another bottle of champagne from the fridge.

'No,' I said, 'please don't open that for me. Do you have lemonade?'

'Lemonade; bleugh! Don't worry.' She smiled. 'I'll happily drink coffee with one of these on the side, and so will Rols.' She put the champagne on the counter heavily and I began to believe that perhaps she was drunk, as I had not when she announced it herself.

Turning her back to me, she put some of the pans into the sink, filling them with soapy water. 'He's lovely, isn't he, Rols? I can tell you two are going to be great friends. He doesn't take to everyone, but he understands already how I feel about you. And Dolly is *sweet*.' She turned off the tap and looked at me closely, as I did with my daughter when she was being obtuse. I never knew what it was that I was looking for, and I assumed that Vita, too, was watching me blindly. Perhaps due to the champagne, I had a brief image of her eyes, enlarged, detached and fixed entirely on me. She was still watching me as she said, 'Isn't she? Very sweet.'

We went back into the front room, with our bottle and more glasses. Dolly stood at the elaborate marble fireplace with the little dog at her feet. Rollo was seated in one of the upright chairs opposite her. She had left her coffee cup on the table and was gesticulating with both hands in explanation, while he listened to her as earnestly as a student. When he saw us, he immediately stood and Dolly dropped into her chair with a swift and invisible movement, as though in collapse.

'More champagne, Queenie?' he asked Vita. 'I thought you said you were already drunk.' But he ran an index finger over her hand when he took the bottle from her, and, as he poured a glass for each of us, he was laughing. It was 10 p.m., I noticed on the mantelpiece clock, and

I allowed for twenty-five minutes to finish my drink before announcing our departure.

We were invited for the second Friday supper before the first one had even finished, and I appreciated the lack of wanting this left.

Rollo kissed us both goodbye in the hallway and said, 'See you next Friday!' as if it were a long-standing arrangement. As if we were a close family who reserved this night each week solely for one another.

It was with pleasure that I imagined myself frowning earnestly when the King's parents insisted on Dolly spending another weekend at the farm with them. When I refused this future invitation, I would arrange my eyebrows into the straight and sorrowful expression that Vita's naturally took; would adopt, too, that downturned and triangular pout of her short little mouth. *I'm afraid Dolly must be home on Friday night. We always spend Fridays with Vita and Rollo.*

When we turned to wave from the top of the path, Vita was smiling, leaning sweetly on Rollo. She was holding one of his hands with both of hers, so she did not wave back, although he did. His wave was finite and precise; the gesture added to the almost military impression he gave, with his straight-backed posture and formal suit. Beast stared out silently from behind them, a tiny parent indulgently overseeing the extended post-party goodbyes of enormous children.

Vita smiled up at us from her husband's shoulder and said, 'Yes. Do. Come early. Come at six next time, and we can have girls' drinks until Rols gets back.'

soft-feathered and sharp-eyed

THE FOLLOWING FRIDAY, SUPPER NEXT DOOR CREATED THE blueprint for our evenings together, for a short summer of dinners that were a charming combination of predictability and drama. The former was supplied through our hosts' observance of form and the latter by their performative natures. Vita, Dolly, and I lay on our fronts across velvet-lined blankets in the back garden awaiting Rollo's arrival home. Beast curled up and slept alternately on the curved incline of Vita or Dolly's lower back in the sunshine. Each time they disturbed him with their gesturing, their storytelling and laughter, the little dog sighed resentfully.

Dolly talked on about people and personal events, most of which I had not previously heard about, and I listened as silently as a junior secretary taking dictation. Vita's accounts were glamorous and decadent, sometimes shocking. I do not often tell personal stories in conversation, cannot rework them into something amusing that begins with self-deprecation, but which ultimately recommends me. Their recounted tales, though, reminded me of many Italian sayings, and sometimes I told them translated versions of these. After all, they were using their stories as folk tales themselves, selecting one narrative to show us about something else. Mostly, I listened and did not add a postscript to the things they said. Dolly and Vita simply wanted to show themselves to one another through their own stories. I was an onlooker.

That evening, as we lay in the sun, we heard from Vita about her former neighbour and best friend who had disappointed her. She had shared a great confidence with this woman, Annabel, and intended it to stay between them. This misdemeanour had occurred at a dinner party. Vita, seated in the middle of a long refectory table, had overheard the secret repeated as evidence of her own wildness, and found she had no option other than to laugh lightly along with the other guests. Not only that, but Annabel had gone on to have a baby daughter who she could not stop talking about or leave with a babysitter, and as a result, she had become the most boring woman in London. Vita had already learned not to trust her former friend, and said that now she was also a bore, she would be glad never to speak to her again.

'A dog scorched by hot water becomes afraid of cold water, too,' I agreed gravely. It was a translation of an Italian proverb that I particularly liked.

Dolly smiled at Vita and nodded her head towards me. 'She can do this all night, you know, and never repeat the same saying.'

Vita reached across the blanket and tapped my arm lightly, which felt like a gesture of acceptance, or perhaps that was what I wanted it to be. It was precisely the type of spontaneous and pleasing touch that I was unable to make. I briefly considered saving up this gesture to copy and perform on someone else. But I knew, really, that such copied behaviours do not translate well; their success relies on instinct, which I do not have. I will hesitate and overthink the touch, which will make it uncertain, like a question, and by that point, the tap will have lost all social context. The recipient of my arm-tapping will blink and look at me expectantly, as if I have started a query that I did not finish. *Yes?* they will ask me as I retreat in silence with reddened cheeks and my hand still stiffly raised from reaching out.

'I did love her so much, you see,' Vita said into the sweet silence. 'Annabel.' She had let go of my arm and was trying, unsuccessfully, to light a cigarette. Her hands were shaking a little and I watched on, fascinated. Dolly took the gold lighter from her in the intimate and practised way of a carer while Vita, cigarette still in her mouth, leaned in to have it lit. 'People think I have dozens of friends. And I do.' She inhaled deeply and closed her eyes as if lost in contemplation of her many friends. 'But I always like to have that one close friend.' She looked at Dolly and me as she exhaled, narrowing her eyes, and then turning her head to let the smoke slowly pass her face. 'And now I have two of you. Next door!'

Eventually, out in the garden, Dolly gesticulated too much, laughed too loudly and finally disturbed the little dog from his attempts at sleep. Vita laughed at his grumpiness and called him Grandpa. 'Sorry, Grandpa,' she said when he lost patience and stalked away on his little feet, his too-long nails tapping on the path, 'are we having too much fun for you?' Beast went through the French doors and collapsed instantly on to the parquet floor, which was still lit and warm from the daytime sun.

The three of us drank champagne and ate crisps and peanuts out of a blue floral soup tureen, licking the salt off our fingers. Vita told us that the enormous tureen was a family heirloom and part of a beloved eighteen-place dinner set that was left to them by Rollo's grandparents. The rest of the set was boxed up with many other possessions, in storage, she said, as that china alone would have filled what she termed Tom's 'modestly sized' kitchen.

They would not be able to retrieve all their beautiful things from storage until they left what they called 'the little house'. Although, with the addition of Arthur's extension, Tom's house was larger than my own home, which has never seemed small to me, even when we were a family of four. My mother would have loved to own a piece like the tureen. The sheer size and ornateness spoke of enormous dining rooms peopled by unmoved guests so used to beauty they would not even notice it amongst the tableware. The fact that I saw and coveted the piece, just as my mother would have, gave us away. Ma would have placed such an item inside her locked glass cabinet and warned Dolores and particularly me never to touch it. If the tureen had been ours, it would have been the most beautiful object in our house; would have stared disdainfully out at us through the glass as we worshipped it, a little deity in our midst. My sister held on to things too loosely while I hold on too tight, but despite this, the breakages in our home were more often mine than hers.

It was almost 7 p.m. when Rollo finally appeared in the French doors of the dining room. He did not look like a man who had just driven many hours to get home, but was buoyant and immaculate in a well-fitting dark suit. He looked demonstrably pleased to see us sitting in his garden and waiting for him to bring us dinner, as if we were his beloved and expectant children, rather than his wife and new neighbours. Vita had told us that he was going to the Harrods food counter before he left town, on a special visit for our dinner. We knew, therefore, that he would have brought with him boxes filled with luxuries that evidenced his care for us.

When Vita saw him, she stretched out happily on the blanket and shouted, 'Daddy! What have you got for my dinner?'

I could not play along, for this paternal address was too close to truth. Dolly and I were more childlike there, lying on our tummies, giggling, eating crisps and eagerly awaiting a paternal arrival, than either of us had ever managed to be in our own infancy. So, I blushed instead, but I quietly enjoyed the routine, the care and the inclusion provided by this kind man. And even Dolly, with her careful and measured expressions, was visibly pleased when he arrived, with his smiles and warm greetings and promises of the special dinner he had brought home for us. Edith termed hosting prowess as an integral part of 'Gracious Living'; being Vita and Rollo's guest was a step-by-step demonstration of the etiquette her book prescribed.

'Wait until you see what I've brought with me,' Rollo announced cheerfully.

Then, smiling, he pushed his glasses back up to the bridge of his nose with an index finger, his eyes bright. And for a moment, he was not a man slick with manners, but simply a boy excited to show us something he cared about. He drained his glass and went back into the kitchen to variously warm food in the oven or arrange chilled slices on oversized white plates edged thinly in silver. We knew that, just like the previous week, he would make little towers of the food and circle it with swirls of cheerfully coloured sauce that looked more like cosmetics than something edible. We would compliment him on his cordon bleu presentation, and discreetly give each other knowing looks as parents do, silently congratulating ourselves on his pleased smile.

When Rollo finally called us inside to eat, he was keen to list the courses he was serving, and we listened attentively as he talked about each dish. He held the back of our chairs while he seated each of us, and he remained standing excitedly while we assembled our dinner choices. There was paper-thin smoked salmon on warmed blinis, and cold roast beef with various side salads, all bought at Harrods delicatessen and arranged beautifully by Rollo. Vita fidgeted as he talked us through what he had brought home; she was obviously distracted.

As soon as he paused, she spoke. Her voice was wan and intimated that she was drawing on the final reserves of her patience: 'Did you bring pudding, Rols? I was hoping there would be strawberries.'

'Yes, Vee,' he laughed. 'Lots of them, more than even you could eat. The huge ones. And profiteroles too.' She smiled widely at him in return and drained her glass, which he refilled in one practised move. He looked at Dolly and me. 'Queenie only cares about pudding. She doesn't even like restaurants.'

'I *do* like eating out, Rols. I just don't need to try every single new restaurant in town on the day it opens. They're all the same in the end. Same food, same faces, blah, blah, blah.' She tilted her head from side to side with each word of her final sentence. 'You fall for it and I don't. And I don't always want to eat *haute cuisine*.' She extended the final word – *cuisiiiiine* – and rolled her eyes when she said it. It was the expression I remembered Dolly wearing when she discussed her seventh birthday present. *But, Grandfather, I like black ponies. I don't want a white one.*

'I know, Queen Vee, and I prefer plain suppers too, when it is just the two of us.' He looked down to put some mustard on to his plate with a tiny silver spoon; when he spoke again, his gaze flickered back to us, but his head remained bowed, momentarily giving the appearance of shyness or modesty. 'My wife says I have a taste for nursery food. If she cooked at all, I would be very happy with homely dinners.' Rollo stressed the word, 'very' and the emphasis exposed his peculiar pronunciation; *vah-ee, vah-ee.*

Vita also did this with her 'r's' and I was undecided whether it was the accent of privilege or an actual speech impediment that they shared. It was a habit best expressed in the words 'very' and 'really', so it was not exhibited as often as I would have liked. Vita and Rollo were like the King's family: they shared the same moneyed confidence that ranked their personal experience at the centre of the world. The language they all spoke, therefore, was brutish with hyperbole and lacking in modifiers. Disappointing events in Vita's life were not 'really bad', but 'terrible!' or 'horrendous!' A holiday or a busy day of sales in the farm shop was not 'very good' for Bunny or Richard; instead, it was 'marvellous!' or 'heavenly!'.

'But would you really like it if I made your dinner and then complained when you were late home?' *Would you wah-ly lake it? Would you wah-ly lake it?* I silently copied her pronunciation often; this phrase, though, along with her swear words, was one of my favourites. 'Or when you didn't come home at all? That wouldn't work for you, would it, darling?' Vita said. Her voice was soft, and she smiled, but it was a measured expression, more like a showing of teeth than a kindness. She repeatedly stroked the shiny scar on the back of her hand, touching it as though it were a distressed pet. 'You would not want that sort of wife,' she continued, speaking almost to herself.

Rollo patted his hair and nodded at his wife. 'I'm sure you're right, Vee,' he said pleasantly. 'Now, who would like another drink?' He reached behind him for an unopened bottle on the sideboard and brandished it in the air. The green glass had a light sprinkling of dust as if it had been carefully powdered. The bottle looked old and as if it should not be drunk but discarded. 'Look what I've got! If you didn't love me before, you will now!' Rollo smiled broadly then, as we all did, at the implausibility of this suggestion, as if loving him could require effort or inducement.

Vita and Dolly each pushed a wine glass forward from their complicated groupings of crystal. My place setting had a water tumbler and flute, but theirs had at least four glasses and sometimes five. Dolly did not finish every drink she was given, I was relieved to notice, but instead tried a little of them all.

After filling their glasses, Rollo put a warm hand on my shoulder and poured me champagne. 'I know you'll be sticking with this, Sunday.' They would always serve strong-tasting wine that I could not drink alongside dishes that were themselves rich and dark. I did not develop a taste for wine that year, but I did find it progressively easier each week to attempt a taste of the startling food as I recognised the patterns of the evening from the previous Friday supper.

Rollo was offering the serving plates to us again in turn and when he reached me, I pointed to the dish of salmon-topped discs.

'Thank you, I do like it,' I told him, as I took some more blinis. 'I've never tried it like this before, and—'

Vita interrupted, 'But your father was a fisherman? Wasn't he?' She thought for a moment, as if she could resolve this query by herself. Then she smiled at me. 'You must have eaten fish every day as a child?'

'I was quite particular about food,' I said. As if this was a fact that no longer applied to me. 'And I saw the fish laid out all the time. Being filleted and so on.'

When my parents were still alive, the fish had laid gently across newspaper on every surface of our kitchen; each labelled for the man who had caught it under my father's direction. These were wealthy and successful city men, bankers and doctors, who did not doubt their own capabilities. They gathered in groups on our porch, and they told my father that he was the clever one; *after all, the fisherman got paid to do what these men did for leisure.* Each of the tourists said this with a feigned shyness appropriate to their first, accidental venture into philosophy. Each countered their borrowed humility with a noisy slap on my father's back or a heavy squeeze of his shoulder. Walt would make himself still during these rituals of status, absorbing their cheerful blows and balancing motionlessly on his feet as he did on the boat in bad weather. The smart men who slapped the fisherman's broad back did not want him to return their touch, did not want his weather-reddened hands on their pristine clothes and office-soft bodies. They were keen to return to their wives and their guest-house cooks, the paper-wrapped parcels of fish newly heavy in their smooth white hands.

'So you didn't like seeing them, the fish, like that?' said Vita, wrinkling her nose as if we were surrounded then by the fish bones.

'But I expect you liked going out on the boat,' said Rollo. 'My brother and I loved sailing. Loved it.'

'I loved his boat,' I said. 'It was called *Liombruno*. After the folk tale?' I retold this story often and in detail, personally fascinated but always unconcerned by the interest of my audience.

Dolly groaned, 'No, no, no. Please don't tell us now.' But she was smiling as she spoke.

'He bought it from Jerre, who has the café on the lake.' Anyone brave enough to guess at Jerre's heritage would be fiercely corrected: *Not Italian, no. I am Sicilian man! Si-cil-ia-no!* My father, fortunately, would have been characteristically incurious and unlikely to venture any assumptions about the boat-owner's homeland when he went to buy *Liombruno*. Jerre, therefore, would have remained amiable, and the two men were certainly on good enough terms for him to explain the folk tale origins of the boat's title to Walt.

'Tell us the story,' said Vita. She gently pushed Dolly, who giggled along in response although her face was now hidden in her hands. 'Hey! It isn't fair, Dolly, we haven't heard it!'

I needed little encouragement. '*Liombruno* is the story of an old fisherman who was poor because he could no longer catch any fish. One day, the Evil One rose from the water and offered to fill the nets with fish every day, in return for the fisherman's next child. The fisherman, knowing his aged wife could no longer have children, agreed that in return for the promised fish, he would hand over any such child to the Evil One. A year later, the fisherman's wife surprisingly gave birth to Liombruno, who as a teenager had to be returned to the lake where the Evil One waited for him.'

'I can't tell you how many times I have heard that story,' said Dolly, laughing.

'It's fascinating,' Rollo assured me.

Neither of my parents ever forgot the long season of 1948, when they suffered a year of such poor catches, they considered selling *Liombruno*. Finally, though, the fishing nets were again filled hourly, as if by unseen hands, and then, the following January, there was the unexpected arrival of baby Dolores to celebrate. My mother, well into her forties and thinking she was post-menopausal, had not believed pregnancy was even a possibility.

Jerre's account of the unfortunate Liombruno was a regular bedtime story at home, with Walt as the storyteller. My sister soon tired of this, but I could not hear enough of it. In an attempt to satisfy my appetite for Sicilian stories, Walt acquired a library book on Southern Italian folk tales. The book's immaculate condition and un-stamped inside cover informed me that it had not been taken out before, and my father eventually told the library that we had lost the item. I had no interest in other books and read little else, happily rereading the Italian book again and again, turning to it for comfort, as I do still.

After pudding, Dolly cleared the table, while Vita prepared a coffee tray noisily in the kitchen, carrying on her conversation with us through the open door. Rollo and I smiled at each other as she talked away. I marvelled to myself at the level of ease with which she could speak, requiring neither encouragement nor response. She was telling us about a wedding she and Rollo had attended that spring.

'It was actually her late grandmother's dress and *we* thought it quite lovely.' *Kwaite larve-lay*, I mouthed to myself as she continued. 'Didn't we, Rols?'

Rollo looked at me and silently held up both his hands in a gesture of confusion. We both laughed quietly, and he patted my arm in a little indication of complicity. I was almost consumed with my feeling for him as we sat side by side, solid and sweet as he seemed then.

'She doesn't have the bosom for a square neckline. Not like you, Sunday; you have a tremendous bosom. Doesn't she, Rols? Tremendous . . .'

Rollo put his hand to his throat and pretended to choke on his wine. Dolly was in the kitchen, and I heard her snort, with laughter or derision, I could not tell.

'Yes, Vee, Sunday has lovely boobs,' he called out to his wife, smiling at me as if this were a perfectly normal conversation. He removed his glasses with one hand and wiped them with a cloth while he looked directly at me, entirely unselfconsciously. 'You really do,' he confirmed in a lower voice. His eyes, without the glasses, looked smaller and less appealing, and I was relieved when he put them back on.

It was the first time anyone had ever commented on my body; not even the King had spoken about me, to me, in this manner. It felt like intimacy to have my physicality not only discussed but approved in such a casual way. Vita and Dolly were flat-chested in the aristocratic and athletic way that suggested they were fashioned for horse-riding and estate management, rather than for a lifetime of domesticity and nursing infants. In comparison to them, I was able to fill a modestly sized bra, but 'tremendous' was not a title anyone would have awarded my chest. That truth did not prevent me from sitting at Vita's table just then and feeling suddenly buxom.

'Of course,' Vita continued, 'that girl doesn't have the hips for bias-cut satin, but it was a sweet gesture to wear the dress . . . Apparently, she is going to have it made into a christening gown. And quite soon, I would think.' She let out a musical little laugh as we absorbed the implication of this. Then she continued in a serious tone, as if correcting an over-exuberant child, 'Although, as I say, the dress was very unforgiving, and she always did have that sort of robust, outdoorsy shape, so . . .' When Vita qualified other women's looks, which she did frequently, she would simultaneously stroke her collarbone as if checking that her own bones were still traceable. She fell briefly silent, and I imagined her out in the kitchen where I could not see her. She would be thinking about the heavy-set bride and tracing a hand concernedly along her own clavicle, feeling, with relief, the slender throat above and the visible sternum projecting below.

Rollo noted the silence and instantly began to talk. 'How is—'

But he was immediately interrupted. Vita had resumed her story, and she raised her voice as her work in the next room became louder, cups and bottles clinking together. As she began talking again, it was clear that the briefly serious tone had been replaced with a more informal one. 'The mother-in-law, though, Sunday, is simply unkind. The dress wasn't *quite* as much of a disaster as she says. That family think they can have the final say on everything. Raging snobs. People . . .' She appeared in the doorway a moment later with the coffee tray. '. . . can just be so *unnecessarily* unkind, can't they?'

I spoke as she put the tray down on the table. 'The tongue does not have bones, but the tongue can break bones.' It was an Italian proverb of which I was particularly fond.

Vita laughed easily as she poured the coffee into three

little cups. 'That's very true! I must remember that one.'

The tray contained a plate of the paper-wrapped *petits fours* that Rollo had brought home to us. These miniature cakes were to become a trademark of the dinners he provided us with. He favoured the most artificially coloured selections – the pastel blues, pinks and greens – all flamboyantly decorated with bows and patterns. I had never seen them before; I only learned that the little treats were even available in more muted colours when Vita pointed this out while comedically disapproving of Rollo's choices. He liked to eat several of the fat squares at once, a lean man playing at greed until Vita cheerfully scolded him for the vulgarity of this habit.

I typically had no idea who the people were that Vita talked about. She spoke as if we had always mixed in the same social circles, and the resultant immersive, yet distant intimacy with these exciting people was pleasurable. It had the allure of a film, the undemanding appeal of watching while not being seen.

'You know,' she would say familiarly to me, when I asked which of their many friends she was referring to, '*Sophie*. The tall, blonde one. With the lipstick? And the *awful* husband. *Sophie!*' Or, '*John-John*. Huge family. *Huge*. Charming man.' She would pause while thinking of a distinguishing feature that would identify him. Then, with a triumphant smile: 'Ran off with the nanny?'

But we both knew I was happy just to listen to her, whoever or whatever the subject. I loved the effortlessness of Vita's conversation and the earnestness of her opinions; like an uncoordinated onlooker losing themselves at the ballet. I could disappear inside Vita's inclusive stream of words, which required no encouragement, but fell as light and unprompted as rain. Sometimes the calm confidence of Vita's voice brought my words back and sometimes they did not come at all. And Vita did not seem to mind which of these responses I had, accepting my silence or my occasional interjection with the same, unsurprised continuation of chatter. She did not speak in order to entice me outside, to draw me out of my tunnel and then pin me there. She was simply expressing sound as a singer might practise offstage, a musical demonstration whose intention was not reciprocation.

Of course, now I know Vita's little bird-heart, I remember those one-sided conversations differently. I see that my frequent muteness was a convenience to someone who was soft-feathered and sharp-eyed. And who sang away to herself in my presence, happily and without interruption, for she knew I had no song with which to call back. Birds have traditionally been banned from Italian households, whether as pets, paintings or ornaments. They are believed to bring the Evil Eye, the *malocchio* curse with them. I faithfully observe every Italian custom I have ever learned: cook seven fishes on Christmas Eve and lentils on 1 January; eat rice and no flour on St Lucia's Day; take chrysanthemums to my sister's grave on the Day of the Dead, and know it is seventeen and not thirteen that is unlucky. I would not have knowingly allowed even the image of a bird into my home, however beautiful. But I lived for and loved a bird-heart that summer; I only knew it afterwards.

Dolly and I had left the first supper at ten-thirty. On this second visit, though, Dolly paused at the front door and sweetly offered to stay on and help to clear up.

'Sleep over!' said Vita immediately, stepping forward

to take Dolly's arm. 'We haven't had an overnight guest here yet. You will be our first.' They both looked at me expectantly.

'But you haven't got your things,' I said to Dolly, who was smiling and leaning almost imperceptibly towards Vita.

Vita made an easy, pushing gesture with her free hand, as if displacing something that weighed little. 'I have everything she could *possibly* need. For a month. I do keep a very well-stocked guest room, Sunday. You've seen it! I love having guests.'

'Oh, please. Please, can I?' Dolly was looking expectantly at me, her expression open and excited. 'I'd really like to stay.'

When I did not immediately agree, they frowned identically at me, holding a silence that I eventually felt obliged to fill. 'Are you sure?' Both Dolly and Vita nodded enthusiastically, sensing my softening to their request. 'All right, then. If you are sure. I'll see you tomorrow, Dolly. Call if you need anything.'

'Great!' Vita smiled and shut the door firmly between us. I could hear her talking to Dolly as they went back down the hallway: 'Now, Mummy couldn't possibly know this, Dolls, but in town, we always . . .'

It was not until later the following afternoon that Dolly finally returned. She told, with some excitement, how Vita had asked her to do some laundry and light cleaning next door on Saturdays. They had not yet engaged local domestic help. I was surprised to hear Dolly had already accepted, as she never volunteered to do such things at home, even for herself. I did not ask how much, or even if she was being paid, and I am surprised now at this omission on my part. I can only put my lack of enquiry down to an understanding of the excitement that being in Vita's presence generated. The cleaning at Vita's, however, seemed like good practice for the kind of self-discipline and independence that would serve Dolly at university a few years later. Her grandparents and I had always planned to cover all her bills while she studied for her degree in comfort. She did not need more money; she had never wanted for anything. Even on the rare occasions when I would have preferred her to wait, Richard and Bunny would immediately give her the cash for whatever she wanted – a new record player or another expensive pair of shoes. Sometimes Dolly used the money to purchase the desired item, and sometimes she spent it in ways that were undisclosed. She knew this easy and extravagant level of support would continue throughout university and even beyond.

Both my in-laws and I were eager to overfill any reported monetary gap. When she went away, I knew she would only ever have to imply that one of us was not fulfilling their financial role, or to suggest that she was missing any item, even those considered a luxury by her fellow students, and extra cheques would be hurriedly sent. We all wanted Dolly to be comfortable but, more than that, I think, we each wanted to win her. To be the one who saved her and to see that independent girl turn to us with relief, with any notice that we existed at all.

I imagined that under Vita's practised and exacting gaze, my daughter would be considerably more domesticated than me by the time she went away at eighteen. My sister and I would never have considered university for ourselves, would not have thought it possible, and I had already begun to feel the difference that my daughter's future plans would create between us. I worried about university, worried that Dolly would come home with earnest young people, who would demand brightly coloured vegetarian meals and then argue about subjects of which I knew nothing. And I worried, most of all, that she would never come back once she had left.

Dolly did not exhibit any new domestic interest at home that summer, but she did develop some peculiar tastes that must have come from next door. Her noticeable new habits included cream cheese and marmalade sandwiches, and a tightening and shortening of the dialect she had once had. Admittedly, she had always adopted a precise and clear manner of speaking when with her grandparents, who otherwise would correct her pronunciation when she sounded like one of the locals – like me. Once she met Vita, though, her vowels almost instantly hardened to become rapid and clipped, like a rebuke. She no longer called me Mum, as she had for many years, but reverted to the childhood address of Mummy or, rather, *Marm-may*. Peculiarly, it was in Vita's clear voice that she called me *Marm-may*. *Marm-may*, I will not be here for dinner tonight. *Marm-may*, I am staying next door, I am going to London. I am leaving now, *Marm-may*. More evident, even, than my new title and my daughter's elevated speech, was a new sharpness. There was a growing watchfulness about her that summer, as though she were gathering evidence to prove something I could not defend against.

Dolly, then, stayed overnight next door after each Friday supper, and this was quickly extended, first into the weekend itself and then into weekdays, too, until her absence from home was more often due to plans with Vita than with her friends or grandparents. One Friday, after finding Dolly had left behind some new pyjamas of which she was particularly fond, I returned next door to drop them off. I knocked several times before Rollo eventually answered the door. I could hear music and Dolly, or perhaps Vita, laughing, somewhere inside. I waved the pyjamas cheerfully at him and, smiling, he took them, but did not step back to allow me in.

'Sunday, you shouldn't have. We have spares of everything. But it's very thoughtful, and I should let you get back now.' He said this ruefully, as if I had a long journey and a busy night ahead, and not an empty home only a few steps away. The door was closed before I turned away.

Dolly always stayed in the guest room, which at Vita's was the rectangular room positioned at the front of the house. In our own home, Dolly's bedroom was in the same location. Within weeks, she began to keep some clothes and belongings in her second bedroom, and referred to them both as her own, as if Vita and I were divorced parents with a shared claim on her. And I was jealous of something that summer, of this easy transference, perhaps. I could have told you I was jealous even then, but I could not have said whether it was my daughter or Vita whom I envied.

this showy kiss

THE EMERGING FIXED PATTERN OF OUR FRIDAY EVENINGS WITH Vita and Rollo both excited and soothed me. At each dinner, I gratefully noted each small recurrence. It felt peaceful, and not as though I was out with new people, being presented with new foods and listening to new conversation. Just as Dolly and I spent each Friday evening next door, Vita also arrived regularly at our house throughout the week on unscheduled but welcome visits. Sometimes she came alone, uninvited, and sometimes Dolly brought her without any prior warning or discussion. We had never experienced this casualness and ease with anyone before. When the three of us were together for another spontaneous evening, I imagined, fondly, that we were experiencing what we would have had with Dolores if she had survived into adulthood.

When Vita came to us, she was dressed sometimes in nightwear, sometimes in glamorous dresses, but her style of appearance was never referenced or explained. Once she appeared barefoot, in only a large towel and with wet hair, as if she had rushed out in an emergency, but her manner was as calm and queenly as ever. She came on those nights because Rollo was away, or at the pub, or because he was simply busy, and she needed constant attention. She never appeared nervous about being alone in her house – indeed, nothing seemed to make her nervous – she simply had an unimaginable desire for company. I think this constant wanting would be highly inconvenient and like a thirst or hunger that must be met daily. She really could not be by herself at home for more than a few hours, which I found endearing, as aloneness is the thing I do best, and she was otherwise so very able. She never made it up to the spare bedroom, but regularly fell asleep on our sofa instead.

Dolly gave her our spare key, and sometimes Vita let herself in while we slept on upstairs, unaware of her presence until we came down in the morning to find her there. I bought a soft pink blanket and a matching pillow, which I put on a shelf in the front room, purely for Vita's use. She was at once childlike and sophisticated, simultaneously enjoying my care as I tucked her in on the sofa and telling me gossipy details about the latest scandal she had heard in London. It was an appealing combination, and I think one that my daughter also possesses. My sister, too, although she did not survive much past childhood, had this kind of dual charm, not ever being quite finished; neither entirely naive nor wholly adult.

I enjoyed the feeling that a third person now lived with us, at least some of the time. Of course, it was not just a third person; it was Vita. Her presence was an unexpected privilege. It was as if a rare and exotic creature had inexplicably chosen to settle in our ordinary home. Dolly and I got to look on as she lay on our sofa, singing prettily along with the radio or crying at sad films, and filled our bath with sweet-smelling oils, leaving towels on the floor, and occasionally prepared inedible food in the kitchen. We listened to Vita sing, we watched the films and cried along with her, and picked up her discarded laundry; we remade the simple meals she had attempted and served them to her. We watched one another watching her, and I believe we both enjoyed that, too. And so, our fixed little family of two unexpectedly expanded. The fourth, Rollo, was a beloved but distant paternal figure, extra attentive and kind.

One evening, Dolly arrived home at around six o'clock and opened the back door, pausing to speak before she came properly inside.

'Rollo's back in town tonight, so I've brought Vita for supper. OK, Mummy?' she said, in a gentle voice, quite unlike her own. Then she stepped into the kitchen and Vita appeared behind her with a container in her hands. They were both wearing black leggings and oversized denim jackets with the sleeves rolled up to expose thin silver bangles on their wrists. As they stood side by side, their poses and appearance were strikingly similar.

At school, I had learned that such likenesses were perceived as the sign of a profound connection, an indication of shared taste and suitability for friendship. My classmates bonded over their matching satchels, coats or shoes. It was too late, though, if I acquired these things later in the term, if they were a birthday present worn into school afterwards. When I returned to class with the popular items, the girls turned to me with faces even more eerily blank than usual, and then back towards one another with identical smiles. My heart would float up to beat fast and fluttery in my throat, while the air around me contracted and breathing required more focus than I could find. But, even then, I knew that the coat and the schoolbag that perfectly matched theirs could never be discarded and replaced. How could I explain to my parents that these much-wanted garments now marked me as a target when I did not understand it myself? Each time I boarded the bus or entered the classroom, with my new bag stiff on my shoulder and my coat earnestly buttoned to the top, the other children would have sensed me coming. Me, doing an unconvincing impression of them.

Dolly and Vita's perfume, too, was apparently the same, and the fragrance moved through the kitchen; something too musky for my daughter and too light for Vita. It somehow defined and expanded the age gap, the multiple differences between them. The distance enforced by the perfume pleased me. It felt like a space between them that I could occupy.

I was standing at the stove in my pyjamas and staring at the fish poaching in milk. It was absorbing to witness the liquid split between creamy whiteness and a watery grey swirl, not for culinary timing (my method of poaching is so gentle it could not really go wrong), but for reasons of aesthetic interest. I cook by smell and not by watching a clock, which I cannot accurately read in any case. I know when a cake is ready by the suddenly heightened vanilla scent in the air; this is what tells me when it is cooked through and not yet dry. I cannot time several different items that would traditionally be served together as a hot meal. Instead, I am used to eating only one hot element, and for this to be accompanied always by cold or room-temperature foods. I am always slightly shocked when eating food that has been prepared by someone else to find that several dishes are served together at a similar temperature. Rollo had been right, though, when he described food preparation as relaxing, the kitchen being, for me, a laboratory for heightening senses in a controllable way. I felt silent that day, as I frequently do, and unnecessary conversation seems then like an exertion that, while possible, will leave me compromised afterwards. Like running an unnecessary mile when you are terribly unfit but technically able.

Both women greeted me warmly, with Vita embracing me first. As always, she was attuned to my mood in a manner that seemed more like magic than social ease.

'Dolly told me about your quiet days. Is it a quiet day today?' she whispered into my ear: *isitaquietdaytodayisit isitisitisitisitisit* and I nodded back at her. *Yes*.

Dolly kissed my cheek several times, deliberately making an exaggerated sound that echoed around us as though we were in a vast-ceilinged cathedral and not a small kitchen. She used to perform this showy kiss when I picked her up from primary school. When she reached her final year, her classmates all believed themselves too old for such public affection, or even to be collected from school. Dolly, though, continued to stand in the playground and open her arms to me every afternoon in the stately manner of an aged grandmother. She opened the fridge and made a silent and unreadable gesture with her hands to Vita, who nodded briefly back in reply as she sat down at the table. The informal signs between Vita and my daughter were indecipherable, another social code that could not be learned. Dolly took two cans of cola from the fridge and put hers down before pouring the other into a glass for Vita.

'Do we have ice, Mummy?' she asked. *Marm-may*.

Her recent return to this more juvenile maternal address was recent and pleasing. I thought it comforted her to return to childish ways that summer, when she was otherwise becoming so independent. But before I could reply, she turned to Vita and spoke to her in a low and confidential tone. 'There won't be ice, Vee. She *never* has ice.'

There was a small porcelain tureen on the table in front of Vita, and she removed the lid with a flourish. Then she leaned back a little to admire the offering, her hands crossed modestly on the table, as if she were trying to contain or conceal her excitement. I looked inside the dish, which held raw mince with three liquid yellow egg yolks, as thick and glossy as frosting, in the centre. At that time, the local bakery was displaying a birthday cake decorated with a tennis racquet made entirely of fondant. Each string and screw was minutely fashioned and perfect. Like the cake, the tartare was neither quite the ingredients it was made up of, nor the treat that it claimed to be. I had not considered that food could be made so dishonest.

'I thought we could have this as a starter? We had it for lunch, and this was leftover. It's all seasoned and everything. It's Rols's speciality. Do you like it?' She carefully served the contents of the container on to the three plates already on the table.

'How do you cook it?' I asked, without much interest, either in the red food or in extended conversation. I had dinner planned and did not want to cook another dish, and certainly nothing so red.

Vita smiled brightly. 'You don't, silly. It's steak tartare. My favourite thing. Minced steak with an egg yolk.' I thought I must have misheard her. She continued talking. 'Rols even separates the egg for me. I don't touch eggs.' She frowned even as she considered this.

'But . . . raw beef and eggs? You eat that?' The milky steam of the fish filled the kitchen, indicating it was ready, but I was looking at Vita's food. It was so complicated, so messy and basic, that it barely resembled edible ingredients. The breadth of people's tastes in all things continues to be surprising. I want my choices narrowed so that they do not become overwhelming. I let the first, the least colourful, and the easiest, find me. It is impossible to understand the need to deviate from repetition, this ceaseless desire for the new and the colourful. Yet people's yearning for variety touches me, too, as a demonstration of hope, or perhaps it is faith. Whatever it is, I am without, and wanting. Their childlike belief that there is always something as yet untried, but superior – a different dress, or house, or menu – only to be discovered by those who keep looking, keep trying.

I looked at Dolly, who sat at the table drinking her cola without ice. 'Dolly, have you heard of this? Eating uncooked mince?'

As I turned back to the fish, Vita and Dolly both laughed, the sounds so similar that they could not be told apart.

I heard the scraping of a chair and felt a hand on my shoulder, as light as an insect landing. 'Dolly had it for lunch last week at ours, didn't you?' said Vita. She stood so close to me that I could feel her breath on my hair as she spoke. Then, in her psychic way, she answered my unspoken question. I would not have asked it out loud, but she knew it. 'You were at work, Sunday.'

Dolly nodded casually. 'Yep. It's lovely, actually. My favourite thing that Rols makes.' She smiled at Vita and shook her head, 'She'll never eat it, you know. He was right.'

I imagined Vita and Rollo sitting with Dolly in the formal dining room next door, eating this concoction while discussing my imagined adverse reaction to it. Vita's favourite classical music would be playing while the yellow and red ran together around the meat on their silver-edged plates. I put my own serving of mince and yolk back into Vita's tureen and rinsed the thin trails of blood off my plate. It seemed so primitive to eat like this. Certainly, it was impossible to reconcile such culinary habits with our neighbours, who frequently visited smart London restaurants, and who, even at home, ate like spoiled food critics. How could Vita be repelled by handling eggs and yet put this into her mouth? By the time I had cleaned the blood off my plate, Vita and Dolly were already eating their portions.

'Rols is in town for a birthday party. I told him: no, darling, I am not going, I am a country lady now, darling. Didn't I, Doll? I said, *I* am a country lady!' *A country lay-deee!* I repeated to myself, tapping along on the counter. They smiled at one another knowingly, like children pleased with their daring, and Vita repeated herself. 'Didn't I?'

'You did,' Dolly agreed, mimicking Vita's seriousness as she repeated the words herself; she did not get the emphasis right. 'I am a country lady. He couldn't believe it! He said' – she turned to me and spoke slowly as if imparting a fact of great importance – 'he said, "But it won't be a party without you, Vee."'

After they had finished their gory starter, we ate the milky fish on coloured plastic trays in front of our favourite television show, and Dolly explained to Vita about the girl with the judgemental papa. She instantly found this hilarious and was soon quoting the infamous phrase at us both, although she could not master the wistful quality of the daughter as Dolly did, with a quivering chin and impressively watery eyes. Sometimes, even as we laughed, I found myself unconsciously reaching out to comfort my daughter when she performed the role. Dolly flickered convincingly between characters like a Victorian clairvoyant, all clever and cynical show, tricks concealed below a frilled tablecloth. She would appeal to an audience of heartbroken parents, would know what they wanted to hear, and would speak earnestly, as if it were truth.

Vita was too much herself to convince as a captured girl. When Vita said cheerfully that her *papa would not allow that in his house*, she was so obviously not under anyone's rules or interested in conformity that the reference became comedic solely for reasons of dissonance.

It became the custom for the three of us to have an early supper at my house on Saturdays while Rollo hosted boys' dinners at the pub. Usually, Edward Taylor would be at Rollo's Saturday events, along with the owner of the largest local hotel, a well-connected estate agent and council members, including some of the planning committee. I learned who attended each week because although Vita and Dolly never ate at the pub, they usually went to meet Rollo and his guests for drinks after eating dinner with me. Vita assured me that Dolly only drank lemonade and that the men were not overly interested in conversation with either of them. Dolly made the evenings tolerable for her, Vita explained, as if her own comfort was the priority for all of us. And Rollo *was* pleased by their attendance, because he was always happier in Vita's presence. They did not invite me, and I did not wish to go.

The four of us were eating pudding at the Friday dinner that week when I overheard Dolly and Vita discussing a visit to Lakeview the following day.

'But don't you have work to do here tomorrow?' I asked Dolly. 'Why would you go there?'

Vita cut in smoothly before my daughter could speak. 'Dolls has got things so organised here that she gets it all done in a couple of hours now. And she has a real eye for interiors, doesn't she, Sunday?'

'No.' I said. 'She isn't interested in houses. Or interiors. Not at all, are you, Dolly?' I emphasised the name, did not want my child to become 'Dolls', another title awarded by Vita, like 'Rols' and 'Wife'.

Dolly was eating apple tart and she remained silent as she continued to eat in small, determined bites. She frowned a little, pulling down her eyebrows and conjuring tiny lines across her forehead. With her fork, she pointed to her pudding as if in apology for being unable to speak.

Vita continued. 'We do want her to help us out with Lakeside. It's challenging to start a redesign while the building is still *inhabited*. Such a lot of children and furniture everywhere.' When she said the word 'children', she drew up her short upper lip, showing her teeth. Dolly, looking on, made an identical expression, as if they had both located the same bad smell. 'It's a nightmare, really! I'm only doing it because Rols is so taken with the place.'

Rollo interrupted. 'Queenie, it is beautiful. Beautiful. It will be incredible when we finish it.'

She did not acknowledge what he said, but her face instead remained hard as she addressed me alone. 'He is paying a lot more than it's worth, you know. Because he wants them to have the money to rehome those children somewhere more suitable. Somewhere more practical. We are all so lucky, Sunday.' She gestured around the table, at the four of us, as though we were a family who shared the same home, the same lifestyle. 'It's easy to forget how fortunate we are sometimes.' Her tone, too, was tight and unfamiliar.

Rollo was at his wife's shoulder, pouring wine into her glass, his hand lightly on her back.

'But I don't understand. What can Dolly do for you?'

The three of them were looking at one another as if deciding something. They did not need words; they were communicating as silently as my classmates had when I was young. People pitch themselves, now as then, at a frequency I cannot hear. I imagined a pack of dogs gathered outside in the street, their bodies still and ears pricked as they listened in, too, nodding solemnly along with the decision conveyed.

Finally, Rollo spoke. 'Actually, Sunday, we have taken Dolly over there a couple of times. When she's been over here helping Vee in the house or . . . out shopping with her. They're always together, aren't they? So, it's natural that she would end up over there. Vee has been so pleased with her, you know, and we wanted to introduce her to the business. To see if there was something she might do.' He cleared his throat and continued. 'We wondered if she could help out there, too. Just for the summer, of course. Until she's back at school.' He raised an index finger to his moustache and stroked lightly along the length of it.

'But why didn't you tell me you had been over there together?' I asked the other two, whose faces seemed unusually serene.

'Mummy, stop it. This isn't a big deal. I had a good

time and I like the work. It's interesting. I want to learn about business, and I like Rols's people.'

'Which people?' I asked.

'The architect.' She paused and considered before continuing. 'The people who are going to be on site, the carpenters and the plumbers. In fact, I already know some of them, Mummy. You know them. Guy and Chris, who worked on the farm last summer? And William, Lucy's brother? *You know*. And Vita and I are going to London next week to look at the interiors shops and the wallpaper and fabric places. And we are going to Harrods. And Oxford Street!' Her face had become flushed, sweet and uncomplicated with excitement. She looked at Vita, who was silent and whose face was unusually blank and remote. Visibly, Dolly composed herself, and her voice, when she spoke again, was stern and censorious. 'I know it's not your thing, but I don't want to work at the farm. I certainly don't want' she gestured vaguely with both hands – 'this.' Her gesture of distaste was confusingly restricted to a small space immediately around her, as if it were Vita and Rollo's attractive dining room she was rejecting, rather than my life, her grandparents' farm, or our little town.

I had nothing to say, could not disagree with her pointing out the difference between us. The King and her grandparents would like Dolly to be involved in such a business; they would also appreciate those connections that Dolly was keen to foster. What did I know about such things, about networking and career progress? If my parents had not worked hard, leaving me the house and a modest but helpful cash inheritance, my daughter and I would probably have been homeless. My wages at the farm are below those that my mother took home as a cleaner, and I had never applied for another job. I would interview like a newly arrived foreigner, unsure of protocol and wary of the language. I had no place telling these glittering people that my daughter was not permitted to work with them. But I did. I tried to keep her, as I tell myself now.

'No. Dolly, I don't think you should be working now, or going down to London. You've only just finished your exams,' I said. 'And you will be starting A levels in September. You should be spending the summer with your schoolfriends.' I looked at Vita and Rols. 'She can't do this. It's too much.'

There was a silence at the table, punctuated only by Dolly's heavy sighs.

'That's fine, Sunday,' said Vita carefully, as though we were some distance apart, rather than next to one another. 'If you really feel that way. We thought it would be good for Dolly, and we only want what's best for her. If you would rather keep her at home, of course that's your choice.' She looked at Dolly, and her voice became a loud and stagey whisper. 'I'm so sorry, Dolly. You know we love taking you out. And we had such fun planned in London. But . . .' She held both hands up in a gesture of helplessness.

When Dolly spoke, her voice was quiet. 'Don't stop me doing this, Mummy. Really. Don't.'

'Dolly can go tomorrow, but that is all,' I said, feeling like a parent sternly addressing a trio of offspring. The three of them looked back at me; their faces were distant and unmoved, and as unlike children as they could ever have been.

Vita nodded smoothly at Dolly and then at Rollo. And I, too, nodded, aware of my daughter watching me closely with an encouraging expression fixed on her lovely face.

Vita excused herself to prepare the coffee tray. Rollo immediately got to his feet, and she made a downward sweep with her hand, which saw him sit back down as quickly as if an unseen force had been used. Dolly followed her into the kitchen, and they left a quietness behind them that was rare in that house, where hosting was an art. I noticed a pack of cards on the sideboard.

'Do you play bridge, Rollo?' I asked keenly. 'I could play all night, but I should warn you, I am excellent. My father taught me to play, and he always said I was a natural.'

'We will play tonight,' he announced grandly. 'Let's see how much of a player you really are.' He patted his tummy with satisfaction as if he had just eaten something unexpectedly good. Then he carefully poured himself the last of the wine; the darkly green-hued bottle turned the liquid within black. When the wine flowed out fast and red, the altered colour was like a trick. I knew that when Rollo looked up, he would have crafted a question designed to lead us into discussion. He deliberately controlled the conversation between himself and other people, like a ball he bounced constantly from one hand to another to distract their questions away from himself and into a winning spot. It was only that: a craft, a skill, and it could not touch or move him more than any other game.

Vita concluded the evening after coffee by announcing her tiredness. Rollo and I responded by immediately standing up as though suddenly realising we were late for something else. Dolly was staying over, and I left without either the promised game of bridge or a mention of dinner the following Friday. Were we, simply, after several Fridays in a row together, so ensconced in the weekly habit of dinner that it no longer needed to be formally referenced? Or was it, instead, a period that was never to be repeated? *Etiquette for Ladies* recommended responding to such omitted invitations with *quiet dignity. Any insult, whether intended or accidental, will fail to register if one ignores being excluded and manages to refrain from all enquiry, either directly or through a third party. The absence of an expected invitation is,* Edith assured, *an opportunity to demonstrate one's character; this is achieved by being magnanimous and restrained on the subject.*

That night, and the following day, I went over and over the evening, replaying all the conversations, but the only poorly received comment was my refusal for Dolly to work on the Lakeside renovation and to travel to London. I could not, afterwards, justify this ban, which I had imposed mainly because they had not told me about the visits, even when I must have had dinner with them, spoken with them, directly afterwards. Dolly was not my property, I reasoned; she spent time with her grandparents, her friends and her father. If she wanted to widen her circle to include Vita and Rollo, and to experience the world of work, then it was my role to support and encourage this. I felt as I had when I was a child, before I let go of my anxious hold on Dolores. Something similar had whirled and scratched inside me when I first began to hear my sister coming home in darkness.

Long before she reached Dolly's age, my sister had frequently padded up our carpeted stairs, smelling of something other than herself as she passed my bedroom in the early hours of the morning. Eventually, I no longer dared to look up at her from my bed, to see her expression or her dishevelled appearance. I did not want to wonder where she went or who she went there with. I needed to prevent the fluttering concern from entirely consuming me.

When I was woken by the sound of my sister tripping over the front doorstep and giggling nervously, I did not allow myself to think about her. I picked up my Italian book in the darkness instead and held it to my fast-beating heart as I recalled the various traditions to which the Southern Italians adhered. I whispered all the details I knew were on the pages, and the accompanying black-and-white pictures flickered across my mind, more familiar to me than memories of my own life. I lost myself in the routines and rituals that were performed in Italian villages, in those communities that held tightly to their beliefs. The people in my life were unpredictable and unsettling, but my cast of Italians were neither of these things and I loved them deeply for it. I treasured my book for containing them all and for providing me with a community, an identity where I otherwise had only a shadowy existence. While Edith counselled me critically from the pages of my etiquette book, schooling me on my regular missteps, the Italian book forced the world to retreat, along with its accompanying noises, brightness and disapproval. It asked nothing of me, but answered every question I had, and it brought me a peace I never otherwise knew.

I dreamed of growing up to become a good, if faraway, citizen of Catania, or Palermo, or any part of Sicily that would have me. I hoped all this for myself when I was a child, hearing Dolores creep through our night-time house. She and I did not speak about her late-night adventures, about the sweet and alcoholic smell that accompanied her uncertain progress through the house, but I did tell her how I felt about those Southern Italian villagers.

'You want to go to Italy?' she replied. 'I will take you to Italy myself when you finish school. It's only a year away now. And when we get back, I'll get us a flat. In town. Just you and me. We'll have a takeaway every Friday. And cider in the fridge. And I'll get you a job at my work.'

Dolores had, since we were young children, referred to a glorious future in which the two of us lived together without parents. But they had always been fantastical imaginings, of palatial houses and unlimited money to buy all the things that she wanted and would never afford. That day was the first time she had described our domestic escape in such a realistic and possible way. Although somewhere deep within, I could feel the stirrings of excitement, I was stuck some way behind, on the subject of a trip to Italy.

'No, I do not want to go to Italy. I want to live like the villagers do, to be a Southern Italian *here*. Where I will know what to do,' I said bleakly.

And in an entirely irrelevant, but well-intentioned response, Dolores scrupulously cleaned out one of her emptied hot chocolate jars and stuck a label across it on which she wrote 'Sunday's Italian trip'. She put it on a shelf in our turquoise kitchen, where it remains today, and directed all of us to put our spare change into it and then to observe as the coins transformed into an amount vast enough to buy passports, air tickets and hotel accommodation for the two of us when we travelled to Italy. Within days, however, each of them was using the collection jar for petty cash withdrawals instead, and I did not care. I was not saving for Italy. I was studying to become a proud Southern Italian villager; I think I still am.

I consciously return to my Italian book whenever the scratching creature inside my chest is reawakened, whirling around as he gathers momentum. It still pleases me to think of him trying to access my heart with the points of his too-long nails, only to find me unreachable, entirely absorbed, as I am, in my Italian book. I imagine him raging silently on in my chest, as unjustly furious as a robber meeting an impenetrable door.

'She had plans with Rols,' said my daughter in greeting as she came into the kitchen alone the following evening with her palms held upwards in theatrical surrender. 'What colourful thing do we have for dinner this evening?'

'But she didn't mention that yesterday. Chicken and potatoes.' I was at the kitchen counter, mixing salad dressing as we spoke. 'And salad. Where is she?'

'I don't know. They're doing something,' Dolly said, sitting down at the table expectantly. It was laid for the three of us, and there were bread rolls arranged on a napkin within a small basket, just as Vita always had at her dinners.

'But I was expecting her here. We will see her on Tuesday, won't we?' I felt then as if I had inadvertently banned that which I wanted from my home, and, for the first time ever, Dolly no longer felt like all there was or even like enough. She shrugged in response to my question, and I resolved to try and concentrate on her instead, a practice that had once been effortless.

'How was the home today? What are the children like?'

She drummed her fingers lightly on the table. 'It was fine. They are sweet kids.'

I smiled; many of the home's residents were teenagers, and some would have been the same age as my daughter.

'But really, the building is falling to pieces, so I think they are excited about the move.'

'When are they moving out?' I asked.

'Some of them have gone already, out to a big place in Lancaster. And the children who are going to foster homes are leaving on Monday. So, it will be all ours after that.' She rubbed her hands together as if trying to generate warmth. 'I told the kids what we are going to do to the place, and they were really interested.' I raised an eyebrow at the casually employed 'we' as she thickly buttered a small roll and then put it into her mouth whole, as she used to when she was little. How odd, I thought, that my child talked about these strangers as if they were family or long-standing friends. But I had already planned what I would say about this, and so I continued.

'Yes, well, I have decided it's fine if you go over there again after today. To the home. And to London with them, if you want to. Sometimes. But you must let me know exactly when you are going and where you are. It all sounds fine, anyway. I was just surprised that you hadn't told me about it before. And that Vita didn't.' I sounded, to my own ears, like a sulky child.

Dolly, though, was surprisingly gracious. She had matured so much already that summer that I felt ridiculous for daring to tell her where she could go and who she could see. 'Mummy, it's fine. You always get strange about new people. I told Vita and Rols, and they totally understand.' She smiled winningly. 'And I told them you'd change your mind, too. Don't worry about it.'

I prepared two supper trays so we could eat together in front of the television, and as I did this, I wondered if

I *was* strange about new people. We had never had enough of those in our lives for me to have developed a pattern for it. My daughter's gentle face and tone did not match her words, which felt sharp and disloyal. Her father can predict people's behaviour like this; he, too, would have guessed I'd relent about Dolly working with Vita and Rollo. He shared intimate knowledge about others easily, as though secrets were just another disposable possession to be given away.

Dolly cut into my thoughts. 'They will be able to house the children much better now. Because of Rols. It's so expensive to run Lakeview, Vita says. It costs six times more to keep each child there.' She looked at her hands here, and carefully held up six fingers to demonstrate. It was not the gesture itself, but the way she counted up to six, her earnest concentration, which made her look far too young, suddenly, to be working, even on the pretext of being a companion to Vita. 'Six times more to live there, in a big old house, than in a foster home. Rols says the council don't find them good enough foster families, though. He says they need purpose-built children's homes, smaller than Lakeside. It's criminal, he says, for the children to live with bad foster parents or in huge institutions with leaky windows and ancient plumbing.' She pronounced the word 'criminal' with a dramatic and seemingly random inflection, like an incompetent actress in a radio play, and fluttered her hands as if in agitation. I heard her roll and soften the 'r' in the way that Rollo and Vita did. Perhaps it is an affectation, then, and not an impediment, I thought. The word 'institution' too, would have come straight from Rollo. He could have persuasively constructed Lakeview as a Dickensian 'institution' and then positioned himself as the rescuer. 'He wants the council to commission him to find sites and manage new residential builds. Once we finish Lakeside.'

She was watching me for my response. Dolly and her father were the only people who have ever been able to read my face; it remains blank to most people, including me. They are gifted translators of people, of course, and I am without a social language. I have a photograph of myself holding Dolly the day after she was born. I know I was high, at the time, on a post-labour cocktail of drugs and hormones, but my flattened expression tells nothing of this, or of anything inside. Even my eyes, fixed on the photographer, who I think was Richard, look dull and disinterested.

But I remember the intensity of feeling I harboured after birth, the wanting to inhale and consume the little body I had recently produced. I even briefly understood those peculiar stories of tiny, sweet-faced creatures eating their young and leaving no trace in their immaculate plastic cages, those notorious little rampages in suburbia that made their owners shudder even as they shared the news at the school gates the following day. Possession is a form of love, after all. The warm weight of my daughter in my arms was all I had ever wanted, before I even knew I was wanting. Before Dolly, I had thought myself to be missing the basic components that would make me human. Her little body made me real and not only paper, like my own family; just as I had made her, she fleshed me out. Yet, when I look at the one picture of myself as an unsmiling new mother, I wonder, where was I? Inside, I was euphoric, transported suddenly into the world of others. But none of that is visible in my flat stare. What was it like for Dolly to be mothered by that hard and unmoved face? Perhaps even my own mother's disapproval was better than that.

'What does Rollo know about parenting? Or foster care?' I asked Dolly.

'Mummy!' *Marm-may!* She spoke in a warning tone, as if shocked by my irreverence. 'He went to *boarding school.*' This was whispered in hushed tones, as if she had delivered a secret and devastating revelation. In fact, Rollo often referred to his time at a well-known public school, where he had studied alongside the sons of rich and aristocratic families, many of whom were even wealthier and better connected than his own. His time there, punctuated as it was by exotic holidays and regular visits home to the family estate, did not sound particularly brutal. School was where he first learned to make money, he had told us proudly; he had taken bets on national sporting events and, for a huge profit, had supplied his peers with various contraband, from cigarettes to spirits. He had apparently even arranged, on occasion and for a large sourcing fee, for a friendly local woman to visit boys in their dormitories, an admission which Vita immediately laughed off as one of his poor-taste jokes.

I smiled. 'Not really the same thing, is it, Dolly? I expect there are benefits to being raised in a foster home, though, whatever Rollo says. It's easier to care for children in a family environment, isn't it? And in a more comfortable place. You would rather have been brought up here than in an enormous building by various strangers, however kind they were.'

'But he knows what it is like to live in an entirely unsuitable old building. With cold showers and freezing cold rooms.' Dolly pouted unhappily. 'He says new buildings are the way forward. Not paid foster parents or huge old houses.' She blinked at me uncertainly.

Invoking her own domestic situation with me had apparently not helped my argument for the desirability of foster homes. And how could Dolly really appreciate the benefit of a devoted parent at these children's sides when she had never known anything else? I expected that the freedom created by a procession of lively children and a rotating group of untrained staff would thrill any visiting teenage girl. But these were children, and vulnerable ones at that.

'Well, I certainly would not want to live in a children's home. Even a new one,' she said unexpectedly, and I thought that I had perhaps underestimated her attachment to me, and to our home, after all. 'The kids don't even have their own stuff; they wear clothes from a shared pool. I asked one girl where she bought her jeans from, and she said they weren't hers. They showed me where the house clothes are kept, sorted by size, and shared by all the kids. It's like a really shit sort of shop.' She shuddered with distaste, as remote and private as a cat.

Our supper was ready; we each took a tray into the front room, but Dolly left the room long before our programme finished. When I turned the television off, I could hear her on the telephone in the hallway. From the pitch of her high and excited voice, I knew that it was Vita she was speaking to.

I avoid the telephone whenever I can, using it only for short and necessary calls, or for Dolly. My mother had found this aversion particularly troubling and, for a few painful weeks when I was a teenager, she had ordered me to answer the telephone whenever it rang. Dolores, who loved the telephone, and my father, who used it only for work, were both ordered not to answer it, for this task was mine alone. Typically, the phone went unanswered during mealtimes, but my mother even changed her position on this, and, when the shrill tone began, she would point a raised fork first at me and then out into the hallway, where the telephone was.

I fidgeted and spoke over the floating voices that had no faces to follow. I sweated and became nauseated and could not hear. I misheard and took messages that made no sense. I began to run out of the house at the sound of the first ring, regardless of bare feet and inappropriate clothing, or hiding upstairs. I became nervous simply passing the handset in the hallway. It was fortunate that Ma soon tired of the outcome of my brief period as her home receptionist. Casual callers quickly hung up on my stuttering and confused replies, and I translated the queries of the more persistent ones into inscrutable messages; at last, she forbade me from touching the telephone at all, as if it were an item I longed to use.

'Vee! Vee!' repeated Dolly from the hallway in mock outrage. And then: 'No, don't bother. She's changed her mind. It's fine. Leave it for this week. No, she wouldn't anyway. She doesn't like the telephone.' She made a snorting sound that could equally have indicated disapproval or mirth. 'I know! I *know*.'

And I, in the sitting room of my late parents, remained immobile and silent on what they would have called a settee and what both Bunny and *Etiquette for Ladies* insisted was a sofa. I felt that mounting panic in which you are so scared of doing another wrong thing that you are frozen into stillness. It is like a social coma. Some people see it and move hurriedly along, either embarrassed or uninterested. Others are drawn to it; they will step closer. These are the ones who first check you are still breathing; they will stick pins in the soles of your feet and scratch them lightly along your wrists. This is where it begins.

Dolly remained uninterested in discussing the etiquette of Friday Night Dinner for the rest of the week. She knew Vita and Rollo had plans on the Friday to which we were not invited. She was focused on locating a favourite blouse and packing her bag, as she was going to stay with her grandparents for the weekend. She made a studiedly casual remark that the King might make a short visit to the farm at some point, to collect a machine for the smaller family acreage in Lancaster, where he lived. She reassured me that she would be back to help Vita on Saturday as usual, and then go back to her grandparents afterwards.

The Friday evening passed slowly, and I did some work in the garden, hoping Vita or Rollo might come outside. At nine o'clock, I was at home alone and in pyjamas, but still expecting Vita to knock at my door. She would be in one of her long and flowy dresses, with gold threads of jewellery around her throat and wrists. She would be barefoot, with her hair worn loose and shiny, in that way my mother termed 'undone'. She would be breathless and expectant: *Wife! Why are you still here? Aren't you coming over? Get dressed!* But she did not arrive, and when I finally went to bed, it was in an empty and quiet house.

the sleep of cats

NEAR THE END OF HER LIFE, MY MOTHER FINALLY SPOKE IN A rare moment of full consciousness. She had turned to look closely at me as I sat next to her hospital bed, reading my book. I could feel her watching me, but I kept my eyes fixedly on the page. *Sundays are special occasions in many Italian families and among* paesani *from various regions of Italy . . .*

'You're not wired right, you,' she said.

She had deteriorated rapidly during the last week, and her original south London accent returned more strongly each day, seeping like water through the rounded vowels she had cultivated during her time in our lakeside town. She no longer sounded like herself, or at least not like the version of herself that I knew. I waited expectantly for her to say more, but she lay back in bed, breathless with pneumonia, and stared up at the ceiling. During this final illness, her pallor, once the temporary sign of a recent lake swim, had become permanently tinged with the blueness of chilled milk left on the doorstep, a paler shade of her hair. Her bony chest rose with each shallow breath and then fell too deeply, as though repeatedly collapsing.

Eventually, she continued. 'My mother knew. She called you "That Child". "That Child," she would say, "that Child watches us as if she is behind glass." And she would never look after you. Not even when I begged her.' As she said 'begged', she grimaced, showing both rows of her small teeth in a terrible smile. 'And I did. All the time. But you, you *scared* her.'

A young nurse was circling the ward, topping up the plastic tumblers of each patient, and my mother fell silent again as she watched her progress. The clock above the ward double doors became unbearably loud, filling the large room, and I stroked the smooth cover of my book for comfort.

'I know,' I told Ma as she lay in the bed, rigid with resentment. I wanted to find the thing that would soften her and make her finally understand that I was trying. The lack of visible social effort on my part was what she always criticised me for most harshly. I believed, even then, that if I could only convince her of my constant attempts at normalcy, she would forgive my resultant failure. She thought my difference was a deliberate pose; thought my remoteness was something I was consciously doing to her. As if, deep down, I had always known all the secrets of communication, just as my sister had, but I had wilfully turned away from that knowledge. 'I try. I have always tried.'

Ma made a short sound deep in her throat; it could have been a laugh or a cough. I persuaded myself it was the latter. She turned her gaze back to me and cleared her throat. 'Tell me, then. If you are really *trying*.' She pronounced the last word in a slow and doubtful way, as if she were unfamiliar with it. 'If you are trying, then tell me about Dolores, about what happened. What you did.'

'We went swimming and she got caught, she went under. But she got out quickly. She seemed fine. I went into her room the next day and she was asleep. I heard her breathing heavily, then. I thought she was sleeping.' The Sicilians consider light sleep to be *the sleep of cat*s. My sister, however, did not sleep the sleep of cats; she slept hard and could not easily be disturbed. She worked in the local hotel, and her shift patterns meant she often slept in as I left the house for school in the morning. But I had tried to explain all of this before.

'Is that still all you can say? She was breathing heavily? So why did . . . you . . .' my mother croaked at me, visibly running out of breath and gasping for more. We already knew every one of the whys: why hadn't I told them my sister went underwater, why had I gone to school, why had I just left her? And the biggest why of all, the one so obvious it did not even need to be voiced: why, why, why, was it her who was taken and not me?

When Ma first asked me about my sister's death, I had not understood what details she wanted; it seemed impossible, then, to know what would help her and what would hurt her. In fact, I learned, all the questions could be satisfied only by my regular admissions of guilt. And of course, I knew Dolores' death was my fault, had always known it, but it pained me to say out loud what I carried with a silent reverence.

I inhaled deeply and spoke on the exhalation, letting the words all run together so I would not feel their truth so sharply: 'It-was-my-fault-I-should-not-have-left.' I looked towards Ma and saw that we had not yet finished; one of her eyebrows was still raised in expect-ation. 'It-was-my-fault-she-died.' My hands had fluttered, palms upwards, as I spoke, and I placed them gently back together, fingers entwined as if recapturing something precious.

As Ma settled back into her pillow, she was almost smiling. The nurse finally reached us and leaned close to refill the glass. Ma extended a bony finger to tap the woman's arm. It took a visible effort for her to perform this minute gesture.

'Tell her to leave. *Please*,' my mother stage-whispered to the woman, nodding at me. Her voice was loud enough for the patients on either side to hear what she had said. She pronounced the word 'please' breathlessly, as though it was costing her valuable air to continue speaking.

The nurse slowly straightened up. She looked at me and not at Ma. The woman's cheeks were flushed pink, and she said to me, in a genuine and confidential whisper, 'They don't know what they're saying sometimes, when they're like this.'

As I turned to go, my shrinking mother spoke from her bed. Perhaps the nurse's gentleness with me, her apology on Ma's behalf, had been audible from the bed.

No longer whispering, my mother said conversationally to the entire room, 'I never did like that girl.' Her reclaimed accent made the word 'girl' sound like 'Gail,' and I momentarily persuaded myself to believe that she was referring to someone else, a forgotten and fictional woman named Gail, who we had both once known and disliked. Ma continued, unflinchingly direct. She raised her hand to point at me, and all of us, the nurse, the patients and myself, knew exactly who she was naming. 'Her. No, I did not like her. *Never did.*'

And it was not the condemnation of me that was painful, for I already knew this pronouncement of her feelings to be sincere; it was the public announcement and the flippancy in her voice that finished me. Ever since her death, I have consoled myself with the thought that wanting your mother to find something worthwhile in you was probably the most normal condition I would ever find myself in. I am certain Ma would have spent my early days searching for something appealing in me, for she saw herself as a good mother.

She and Dolores liked to cook together, to read and draw, and, looking on from the doorway, I had often imagined myself in the place of my sister. When Ma spotted me watching, as she occasionally did, she retained her smile with an effort so evident it was painful to witness. When her gaze landed on me, it became something fixed and uncertain, until she looked back at Dolores. Ma learned that a closed door did not deter my observations; I could listen to them as fervently as I watched. I tiptoed nightly up to my sister's door to marvel at the barely disguised impatience with which she tolerated our mother reverently brushing out her braids each night. And in this way, at this distance, I learned about Ma's other voice, which was soft and sweet. I heard my mother sing love songs with a little catch on the lyrics she felt, and I knew what it might be to have her softly stroke your hair and laugh at the silly things you said. I had been a witness, at least, to her maternal love.

I deserved the pinching flatness of my mother's resentment as she lay dying in the hospital bed. The slow, gasping and bed-bound manner of her demise must have compelled her to think of nothing in her final days but my sister, stilled in her bed by death and not sleep. Dolores' lungs, too, had finally been overcome on dry land, and by the same lake-water that was slowly reclaiming our mother, calling her back. As I left the ward, Ma stared pointedly up at the ceiling, remembering, no doubt that I had also walked away from the bedside of my dying sister.

My sister and I had been in the water together each evening of the holidays that year. Then, in August, she took six days of holiday from her chambermaid position, and we had swum together two or three times each day, challenging one another to keep going and only allowing ourselves to emerge when we were too exhausted to last any longer. By September, the edge of coldness was already beginning to threaten, but we always wanted to extend the swimming season for as long as we could. Dolores and I had an unspoken agreement not to mention the transition until the cold visibly manifested in our bodies, until the post-swim shiver and blued skin began to outlast both our lakeside dressing and brisk walk home.

The night before, the water had become unexpectedly vicious as my sister floated sleepily across the waves on her back and I dried myself on the shore. She was a strong lake swimmer, her body trained to the sudden currents in a way that pool users were not. The function of my swimming was exploratory. I was convinced that one day I would discover, deep in the water, the thing that drew my mother there, and that it would become a shared and bonding secret between us. Dolores did not search the water when she swam, did not care to know what Ma saw and loved there. My sister's lack of curiosity regarding our mother was characteristic of her in all things. She had an ease about her, an acceptance that enabled her to find joy without examination; it was a gift I coveted. As she swam lazily out that evening, though, allowing herself to follow the gentle pull of the light currents, the water changed. The waves were insistent, pulling Dolores inside and then expelling her violently out on to the stones where I waited, motionless with fear. Her skin was seal-grey, and I looked up at the sky, expecting a sudden darkening. But the bright yellow-pink of the late sun persisted, colouring all below it, except Dolores. She lay gasping at the edge of the water, an offering considered and rejected by the lake.

I did not know, then, that neither of us would ever swim in the lake again; that the lake had only just begun, and was coming for all of us. It is not always possible to recognise an experience as the final of its kind – such things are often known only in retrospect – but I am grateful for what I did not know as I stood and shivered on the shore that evening. The secret was that an ending was approaching my family.

We walked home afterwards in a silence that I did not question. I could not see, as we walked together in the darkness, that my sister was still submerged; was, in fact, a dead girl walking. I did not know, then, that she would struggle all night with an invisible and watery enemy; that she was being kept somewhere below the surface and unable to summon help. I still believed, then, that my way of not seeing only made me strange and unpopular; I did not know that it blinded me to all the fires that were not in the fields.

The morning I left my sister at home and in bed, I sat alone on the bus, missing her company now that she was fortunate enough to have finished with school. The bus followed the popular tourist road, which offered views of the lake, and I remember the water was placid as I passed it, an entirely different creature from the one it had been the previous evening. I did not know as I went to my lessons. I did not know until I had been home from school for several hours. Until my mother, growing impatient, finally stopped calling and went upstairs to tell Dolores to come down to dinner. Instead, she found her beloved child cold and still, oblivious to the heavy duvet that still blanketed her blue skin.

Walt and I heard the screams and went upstairs to find my mother pointing at Dolores in shock: 'My child! My child!' She moved towards the body with her arms out, as though prepared for an embrace that would be returned.

As I stood in the open doorway, I copied her exclamation: 'My child! My child!' The flattening and the emphasis were unusual. I spoke under my breath, but I expect it was still audible; I was less discreet back then. And, of course, I was very distressed, although I do not think this was necessarily evident. Then I found myself saying Ma's phrase repeatedly and loudly. My voice had never sounded, to my ears, so clear or so definite. 'My. Child! My. Child! My. Child! My. Child! My. Child!' I am sure my index finger, too, would have been raised at this point, stabbing the air to locate the exact note my mother had struck.

She came at me so fast, it seemed she was flying. Walt had to position himself between us, and he shut me in my bedroom while the ambulance was called. Hours later, when I heard them carrying out the body of my sister, I went on to the landing and followed them out of the house. I became one of the *prefiche*, and felt them, too, marching sympathetically alongside me, those black-veiled Italian women in funeral processions of the past, who loudly demonstrated their grief to onlookers. It was with reverence that I sang the only Italian song I knew as I escorted them to the ambulance. The song, from my precious book, was dedicated to the *Borda*, who visits children in their beds if they do not sleep. My mother lay on the sofa in our front room while Walt and another man hovered uncertainly in the doorway, as if awaiting instruction. I sang even louder as I passed them in the hope that Walt would join the procession for Dolores. Even in death, we could not distract him from our mother. My singing did not rouse her; she was fast asleep and fully dressed. Entirely still, with her shoes on, her coat buttoned, and her handbag placed on her midsection below her clasped hands, she seemed like a displayed corpse herself, so great was her determination to be back with Dolores. Later, I learned she had been heavily tranquillised, and she remained in this chemical suspension of time for many weeks.

On the day of the funeral, I found Ma in my sister's bedroom. She was sitting on the bed with her face hidden in a piece of Dolores' clothing. The door was open, and she had heard my step out there on the landing, so I went in and placed my hand lightly on her shoulder. It was a gesture I had seen passing like a baton between my parents since my sister died.

'You were a good mother,' I told her, attempting the soft tone in which they often spoke to one another. 'You really were.' Her shoulder stiffened and turned to rock beneath my hand.

She inhaled deeply and spoke on her exhalation. 'Get the fuck out,' she said. Her voice was so low it was barely audible. This calmness was more disturbing, even, than the shouting.

My parents' insistent questioning – *What happened? Why didn't you tell us? Why didn't you check on her?* – lasted until their own deaths. They believed my answers could raise Dolores from the lake, and I, too, sometimes felt my words might bring my sister back. But I was haunted by the prospect of her emerging once more from the water, now eerily dry and accusing. I embarked on two months of silence so that I could not inadvertently summon the grey and gasping sister that I remembered. The coroner brutally termed the death 'dry drowning'. This is something like burning to death after escaping the fire.

My parents each succumbed to premature death within a year of their daughter's passing. Each died from what were typically non-fatal conditions. First, my mother developed pneumonia, and then my father's heart faded and eventually failed, for it had no purpose without Ma. These deaths were not resisted or fought against, but were instead welcomed as transport. In the twenty years since the dry drowning, I have tried to live above the surface. But my condition did not remain in my childhood; it will not be confined to my little house by the lake or be discarded along with all those perfect little fish bones. This difference accompanies me, uninvited, and I exist uncomfortably in the shallows. I can pass as one of you for a time until I am submerged again. When it comes to claim me, it is sometimes the relief of summer broken by cool water, and sometimes an undertow that drags me beneath.

the fondness of possession

AFTER A LONG WEEKEND THAT SHOULD HAVE CONTAINED VITA and Dolly but had neither, working on Monday was a challenge. The plants seemed to have rapidly deteriorated and become fragile, despite my increased attentiveness. Their thin bodies were needy and disagreeable beneath my hands, which, in turn, felt like clumsy and oversized tools. The plants responded to the distress of their caretaker as young children do, by signalling their own need more insistently, their own panic fluttering at the edge of their demands. My fingertips typically work in conversation with the plants; this is a language I understand. I feel their wanting and meet it coaxingly, with water, light, shade or replacement soil. That day, though, work was more like a social interaction, communication interrupted by interference like a lost voice on the radio, coming through uncertainly and then fading back into undecipherable crackles. *This soil is too dry, no, it's oily, and this leggy plant needs pruning, but not that hard.*

David worked diligently opposite me, the neat plants behind him making a pleasing and orderly row. He had let his hair grow longer that summer, and he occasionally touched it with one hand, a suspicious, light stroking, as though the feel of it were still unfamiliar, while he periodically signed to me with the other.

Several times during the morning, he knocked on the counter to get my attention, then signed: *You OK?*

I am fine. Yes, yes. Thank you, I signed, my actions becoming more precise each time he asked the question. Eventually, I acquiesced to his obvious concern. *Dolly was here all weekend, and I missed her.*

Was she? he signed back easily with one hand; his mouth was downturned in doubt. *Here?* He shook the soil off his working hand and used them both to shape the last word, holding the position for longer than usual, his index fingers still pointing downwards while he considered this.

Yes, here. Why? I signed.

I went in to see Richard early this morning; he had just got back. He and Bunny were away all weekend. At a wedding, David signed. He smiled and continued. *Someone very important, Bunny said. Very important!* When he paraphrased Bunny, he widened his eyes and moved his fingers in a frantic and busy way, the opposite to his usual easy communication.

I could imagine David standing impatiently in Richard's kitchen, waiting to learn something about the harvest or about crop rotation plans, and instead having to endure Bunny showing off about the social circles in which they moved. Richard was discreetly conscientious about facing David and pronouncing words evenly in order to make lip-reading easier. Bunny, though, was a little showy about it, and I never liked her less than when she tugged on David's arm or patted at him repeatedly, as if he were an untrained pet of hers. She raised her naturally carrying voice even further when she spoke to him; I had told him this once, expecting that we would laugh together about it. He replied that he knew this already; could tell from her reddening face. He knew people's accents from lip-reading. He knew, for example, that Mr Lloyd had an attractive accent, and he had once asked me specifically what it sounded like. I had tapped out the intonation of various phrases in the Welsh lilt out on his arm and he had nodded; without any signs, I understood that nod had meant: *Oh, I see.*

In the greenhouse, David looked serious again and signed in slow and definite movements: *Dolly didn't go with them.*

OK, I signed. He looked at me. *I don't know!* I signed, as if in response to a question, before I went back to the plants. He, too, resumed work, and I waved exaggeratedly until he looked up, eyebrows raised. *Are you sure, David?* An explanation came to me. *Maybe she was looking after the house while they were away?*

David looked steadily at me. *They had Katie staying,* he signed. *She was just leaving when I got there.*

Who?

The vet's daughter. In case the little dog started labour. Bunny's dachshund had been taken to a well-bred male of the same breed some months before. Customers at the shop, even those who had never seen Bunny's dog, received regular and unrequested updates on her subsequent confinement.

All that morning, the air in the greenhouse felt dense and unyielding, as though the plants were greedily storing all the oxygen for themselves. Eventually, David tapped on one of the glass walls until I looked up from the work counter.

Lunch, he signed, and smiled briefly. *Aren't you hungry yet?*

He looked a little older with his grown-out hair, but remained boyish. I followed him over to the table, where we often eat together. He typically eats with one hand because he likes to keep a hand free to sign. I enjoy watching his animated talk more than I enjoy hearing conversation. I have always cared for this good and gentle boy, who is easier to care for, who is warmer and more responsive than my own shining daughter became in adolescence. David is a good man.

Before I first introduced my daughter to David, I had reminded her how to sign the simple greeting we had used so easily when she was a small child and we had enjoyed silence together. But she kept her hands by her sides when David signed *hello* and only smiled back in a brief and perfunctory way, before instantly frowning at me.

'I want to go home now,' she said to me directly as I stood next to David. 'I've been at school all day.'

'Stay for a bit,' I said, to allow her time to make up for her unfriendliness. 'We need to finish up here first, don't we?' And I did not sign as I spoke, to remind her that David could lip-read.

'We can't speak,' she said. She moved closer to me, pulling her school jumper over her hands impatiently. 'He doesn't understand me,' she continued in a loud whisper that spoke more of anger than caution.

David turned to me and signed in his usual, easy way. *I'll close up. You go home.* He smiled broadly at me and gestured towards Dolly: *I don't understand her. She is a very complicated woman.*

Dolly, recognising that she had featured in our

conversation, immediately turned to leave. She pulled the glass doors shut with obvious force, but the fragility of their aged hinges meant they responded weakly, taking some time to come to a final close as David and I looked on and she stared in at us. Whenever she came to the greenhouse after that, she waited for me outside rather than speak to David. After their first meeting, I tried to reassure her that David would be keen to talk to her and that he was used to slightly laboured conversations with non-signers. Dolly was on the sofa, wearing pyjamas printed with tiny rabbits and reading a library copy of *Lady Susan*. At that time, she was very taken with Jane Austen and was rereading all the novels chronologically.

She shrugged and replied without looking up: 'Great. He's happy to talk to me. But I don't want to talk to *him*.' She turned a page with a showy flick of her hand, signalling that our conversation was finished.

Dolly's friends did not cut their mothers' conversations off in this way, I knew, from observing them together. In fact, other mothers spoke to their children with the seniority that Dolly reserved to address me. Although this assuredness was typical of my dealings with my daughter, it sat oddly with her smooth and girlish face. And David, too, did not want to discuss Dolly. When I spoke about her, his face closed into uncharacteristic stillness.

Usually, when David and I have lunch together in the greenhouse, I take the shaded side and he, with his tanned skin, seats himself opposite, underneath a large square of glaring sunshine. That day, I did not want to talk to him about where Dolly had been. Instead, to make him laugh, I told him about the steak tartare incident, emphasising my disgust at the dish.

Your face! he signed, pointing towards me and comically assuming a look of revulsion to mirror my own. *Although*, he signed, *fair enough. I would not eat that shit either*.

I waved an admonitory finger at him for the swear word and he grinned back, entirely pleased with himself. We both know I don't really mind his language, but this pretence of gentle rebuke is something we do occasionally, and it seems to satisfy us both. It fulfils my instinct to mother him and perhaps meets a maternal need in him, too, whose own mother is so aloof and immaculate. Since infanthood, Dolly had been violently outraged at the mildest disapproval of her behaviour. So, instead, in the greenhouse, David and I act out a parent-and-child relationship where I can caution him because he knows that this is qualified by care.

Dolly says it's really tasty, though. She loves it, I signed back, feeling protective of the admittedly bizarre taste my daughter shared with Vita.

David nodded; his expression was serious, almost severe. *Yes*, he signed. *Yes, I can imagine she does*.

After work, I went to Vita's house and knocked at her door, and there was no reply for some minutes. But as I turned, finally, towards my house, she appeared, dressed in a short kimono and with her face shiny and clean. Her late afternoon daily bath, I remembered.

'Oh. You,' she said. I could not recall ever seeing her face so unanimated. She appeared hardly to blink or even breathe.

I had my invitation prepared and so I did not respond to her words but repeated my own lines. 'Hello, Vita. We haven't seen you for a while and wondered if you would like to join us for supper tomorrow? We are having chicken with a cream sauce.' I hesitated and then spoke into the growing silence. 'Because Dolly told me Rollo is away this week, and I know you don't like being at home on your own.'

The final line was unscripted and voiced as a response to her stillness; an effort to claim some knowledge of her on my part, some reason for my being before her, talking. However, as soon as I had spoken, it seemed vaguely daring to have referenced her husband and their domestic arrangements; our friendship had cooled so dramatically. I felt I was an interruption; it was like catching someone in a private moment, an uninvited intimacy clumsily taken. But Vita did not rush to reassure me with an embarrassed apology, as people do when inadvertently discovered in an embrace or berating their children. Instead, she slowly took a lighter and a package from the console table next to her and lit a cigarette. Her eyes remained fixed on me throughout, as if I were an unpredictable stranger from whom she could not afford to look away.

'Dolly said,' she paused to inhale, and then exhaled deeply, an exaggerated smoky sigh – 'she said she is allowed to come to Lakeside now. Is that right, Sunday?' Not 'Wife' any more, then.

'Yes, that's right,' I said.

'And she can come to London with me. Yes?'

'Yes. She can.' I did not ask if they had already taken her to London, if they had all been there for the weekend past. It was already too late.

'Because you know, her grandparents are very happy for her to be down there with us. They can see what an opportunity it is for Dolly.' Vita was watching me closely as she spoke.

'I didn't know that you had spoken to them . . .' I said. 'When did you see them?'

'We've been in for drinks a few times,' Vita said. She inhaled slowly again, and as she blew out the smoke, her face began to soften behind the little cloud. She raised an eyebrow and lightly shook her head as if in denial. 'They invite us in whenever we pick up Dolly from the farm. We have to accept *sometimes*, or they'll be *offended*. So,' she said, 'I will come to your supper tomorrow. And we'll see you here for Friday dinner this week, won't we.' And this assertion was not a question, but a statement of fact.

I felt myself blushing with pleasure, and I smiled. 'Yes, that would be lovely. Thank you, Vita.'

She patted my arm and moved to close the door between us. As I reached my house, I heard her door opening again. 'See you tomorrow, Wife,' she shouted cheerily. *Wife*. And I waited for the comfort to descend, knowing I should have felt that I was winning once again by being back in her favour. But it did not seem as if I had won. Rather, I knew I had given away something valuable, without even realising I had once held it in my own hand.

The following evening, Vita and Dolly arrived together for supper. Dolly did not use her key, but rang the doorbell, and I let them in, feeling as I did so that I was hosting a young couple. They were giggling together, and Vita was too absorbed in their conversation to observe her usual warm and tactile greeting.

Instead, she patted me distractedly and pointed at Dolly in explanation. 'So funny!' she said. But she had stopped laughing as she moved towards my kitchen, leading us purposefully as if she were now the host. 'I must eat soon. I'm starving!' she warned as she sat down expectantly at the kitchen table.

She was wearing a red cotton sundress in a similar shade to Dolly's oversized and tightly belted T-shirt, which stopped mid-thigh. Both of them wore bright red lipstick that had a matt finish and was so expertly applied that it was incongruous with their outfits, which, for Vita especially, suggested sunbathing rather than a supper engagement. I felt awkward and matronly in my best blouse, which had a rounded collar and small pearl buttons.

'The chicken isn't ready,' I said. 'Can you wait for a bit, Vita? Dolly, can you put the bread on the table, please?' I turned the oven up and put some frozen vegetables in the saucepan.

When I returned to the table, I was surprised to find them both teary-eyed with silent hysteria. Dolly had obviously attempted to wipe her face, and her lipstick was smeared on to her cheeks and her fingers. Vita passed her a paper napkin and gestured to her own face, unable to speak for her suppressed giggles.

'What is it?' I asked. 'What is so funny?'

I took the napkin from Dolly's hand; she was helpless with laughter and released it without resistance, hardly holding it at all. When I leaned in to wipe the lipstick from her face, Vita snatched it from me. She was utterly serious, without a trace of the humour that had consumed her moments before.

'I will do that,' she said brusquely. 'Thank you.' And, standing, she bent over Dolly, gently dabbing at her face with the napkin, just as I had done so many times when she was small. I do not think, though, that I had ever looked so possessively at Dolly as Vita did just then, with an intensity that spoke of a claim.

When I finally placed the plates of chicken casserole on the table, the two of them were serious. Dolly's face had been wiped clean of lipstick, and, in fact, they had both cleaned all traces away from their mouths, too. Each looked down at her supper with little interest, despite Vita's recent claim to overwhelming hunger.

'A seven point five,' announced Dolly.

'No, more of a nine, I'd say.' Vita spoke cheerfully, but she picked up her fork between her thumb and finger, curling the others away in a gesture of distaste as she stabbed at the chicken.

'Are you rating the food?' I asked, trying to smile. 'You haven't even tried it.'

'We are rating it for colour, Mummy. Zero is for brightly coloured and a ten would be utterly white.' Dolly took a mouthful from her plate and smiled brightly at me. 'Yummy.'

Vita helped herself to some sweetcorn from the dish on the table. 'This looks fine, Sunday,' she said in her silvery voice. 'It's simply not how we eat in London, is it, Dolls?'

'What were you laughing at?' I asked. 'Before.'

This set them both off again immediately, and I quickly lost patience in pursuing it. We spent a fairly short evening together. They were planning to watch a film that was playing on television at 9 p.m. I did not ask them to stay and watch it at our house. I cannot say, even now, if I did not want them to or if I simply did not want to hear them make excuses for declining. Vita left first, sternly reminding Dolly of her time restrictions as she left. Dolly stayed behind only for a short time to pack some things that she needed. When I kissed her goodbye, I asked her what they had been laughing at.

Dolly giggled lightly, even at the memory of Vita's amusement.

'Margarine,' she said. 'I put it on the table, for the bread. And it always just makes her laugh. *Marg.*' She pronounced it slowly, deliberately accentuating her northern vowel extension. She must have said this to Vita at the table, in that same mocking way. To Vita, who spoke only of *butter*, her vowels so clipped you would hardly know they existed in the word. I looked away from Dolly as she spoke, feeling I had caught her in something that should have remained private between them. I could not tell if it was an intimacy or an unkindness of theirs; I knew, though, that I did not want to observe it, and that they would not invite me in.

On Friday, Rollo was home early enough to greet us as we arrived, and he held me for an extra moment when he greeted us at the front door, silently acknowledging our period without contact in his gentlemanly way. When he released me, his round glasses were slightly askew, and he adjusted them awkwardly, with both hands, as though unfamiliar with this occurrence. Before we sat down at the table, he proposed a toast to me; it was a vague and wandering address, as though avoiding something unsavoury. It was as if our routine had been interrupted by my taking an unsanctioned trip that could not be referenced. Vita asked Dolly to help her bring dinner from the kitchen, and for a moment Rollo and I remained silent, listening to them chatting animatedly and clinking plates in the next room.

'Rollo,' I said, before he could say something smooth and distracting, 'are the plans at Lakeview going well? Have the children been moved out now?'

'Yes, it's empty now, which makes things easier. But we have some concerns about overdeveloping such a large single unit in this area. Property prices have a different ceiling here, which I hadn't planned for.' His gaze flickered towards the closed kitchen door and he sighed lightly. He took a long sip of red wine and when he spoke again, I saw that his teeth were stained pink. Rollo's small teeth gave him a childish look when he smiled, a schoolboy playing at being one of the grown-ups. His glasses were large and performed like a borrowed prop of maturity. I liked the incongruity of Rollo's face against his sophisticated suits; the little teeth and oversized glasses only added to his charm. 'But I mustn't bore you with the day job – shall I top up your fizz?' He reached towards the bottle, his pose and restraint that of a formal sommelier rather than a private host.

'No. Thank you. But I do want to know about it. It's Dolly's job at the moment, and she doesn't tell me much at all.'

Rollo patted his already immaculate hair and then stroked his smooth jawline, as if feeling for regrowth. 'Well . . .' he began, stretching out the vowels, *weeeeell*. 'Hmm, well, it's complicated, darling.' Rollo did not often call me this; although Vita used the word frequently and indiscriminately, even as a reprimand, her husband did not.

Vita appeared in the doorway, holding a large platter of antipasto with both hands. 'Look what I have made!' she said cheerfully.

Dolly followed behind her with a glass bowl of brightly coloured salad.

'What *you* have made?' teased Rollo. 'That's funny, I seem to remember buying that in Harrods deli only this morning.'

Vita put the platter on to the table and placed Dolly's salad bowl alongside it. 'Nonsense, darling,' she said, entirely seriously. 'Now go and get the salad dressing so we can eat.' She patted his bottom as he walked past her to the kitchen. He made an exaggerated jump away from her as if startled, then stepped neatly backwards into her still-raised hand, and they both laughed. They smiled broadly and solely at one another when he returned to the dining room, holding several glass bottles of dressing.

Dolly watched them thoughtfully and I wondered if she was remembering the short time that her father and I had lived as a couple. And that he and I had never behaved in this intimate manner, with practised little routines and responses reserved only for the other. Vita and Rollo's playfulness suggested that the time they spent alone would never be enough to express their attachment, that it necessarily spilled out into their public life because it was too large to contain privately. I remembered Dolly as a child in Jerre's café, eating ice cream from a tiny spoon and sternly instructing me about the love the King had for his new wife. 'Because they love each other so much. All the time. You don't see what I see, Mummy. You do not see it.' Beside her in my thoughts, Ma smiled grimly. *You're not wired right, you.* And my sister Dolores flicked her pale hair back, dripping water and laughing as she said, not unkindly, *I don't know what you are, Sunday.*

'Sunday,' Rollo said, 'let me talk you through this antipasto. It is a little different from the one we had before. This one . . .' The three of us had already begun to choose items from the platter, and, as he talked on, he fussed over our plates as if we were infants being carefully weaned. He was at his most ebullient and distracting, putting pieces on our plates and raffishly removing those that he said we would not enjoy, before dropping them on to his own plate. I already knew that I would only be eating the doughy white roll from my side plate. I knew, too, that none of them would mention this when they cleared the plates and saw my starter untouched. And I looked at Vita and Dolly, protesting but laughing along excitedly with him, and I did not ask any more questions.

After dinner, Dolly brought the coffee tray in from the kitchen, and she put it down carefully next to Rollo. She looked out on to the terrace.

'It's still warm, isn't it?' she said. 'Let's take it out there.' She paused before moving the tray, and looked at me. 'Is that OK with you?'

My daughter's association with our neighbours seemed to be encouraging a gentleness that I had never seen before in her. I nodded happily and followed her outside. She frowned with concentration as she set out three tiny cups, a jug of cream and a French press on the narrow garden table. Rollo and Vita followed us politely outside, as if this were our house and they were the guests. He nodded for Dolly to pour his coffee, and, with some enthusiasm, they discussed the coffee press, which he had brought home recently after a trip to a casino at Deauville. At home, Dolly always used the same saucepan my father had for making coffee. Her grandparents were more concerned with tea, and Rollo's press seemed to be a symbol of sophistication for her. Dolly had already informed all of us that making coffee in a saucepan was basic and old-fashioned by comparison.

'We'll get you one in John Lewis when we are in town, Dolls. You can choose it yourself,' said Vita airily.

'No, don't, Vee,' said Rollo. 'I will get a proper one for her next time I go to France. Just like this one.'

And Vita did not respond crossly to his command, as I had thought she would. Instead, she beamed at Rollo as if he had unexpectedly yielded to an overly optimistic request. Dolly, too, smiled at him, her face unusually open, and she put down the press to give him a brief embrace.

'Thank you, Rols! I will use it every day!'

He leaned back in his chair with a deep inhalation, and his chest visibly expanded, the garden lights bringing his handsome face out of the darkness. The coffee tray also held Rollo's garishly coloured petits fours and an iced soda water for me, served in a heavy crystal glass. I coveted their crystal for the reassuring weight of it in my hand. The surprising heaviness of small crystal glasses somehow makes them both alive and trusting; they double in weight like a sleeping child in your hold. *Here I am*, whispers crystal, *made heavy by my trust in you*. Rollo and Vita always kept a stock of soda water in for my visits. Their attention to my preferences touched me. I had not been known in this way before and found acceptable. There I was seen, and approved of, even indulged.

I have heard families speaking of one another's eccentricities as Rollo and Vita spoke of mine. I had begun to notice that, just like my new friends, other people laugh about their loved ones' observance of peculiar habits, but with the same fondness of possession. *She wears a coat even in summer. He won't talk to anyone before breakfast.* I realise, now, that my mother could still have loved me, if she had chosen to. It is possible to know the oddities of people and to love them regardless. I want this to comfort me, but it does not. I had always thought that I was an unloved child purely because of my peculiarities. Since Vita and Rollo and their cheerful celebration of my strangeness, I wonder if there was something else Ma witnessed in me, something that she found not simply different, but abhorrent.

On the terrace, Vita and Rollo decided to show us the complicated first dance that they had learned for their wedding. This event had taken place over twenty years ago, he reminded us, as he made an uncertain face. Vita was wearing a sleeveless yellow dress without jewellery, and her skin was even more deeply tanned than when we had first met. Rollo, lean and handsome in his dark suit, was an excellent dancer, and he began by taking their routine very seriously, but she kept forgetting what came next. They gave up on their recreation of the original and finished the dance by circling the terrace instead, with her standing barefoot on Rollo's big, shiny shoes. She kept a comedically pained expression on her face and held her exposed limbs all stiff like a little doll, while the rest of us laughed so much, we were actually crying instead. But Rollo was so gentle and patient with her that I was grateful for the laughter to cover my tears. I had not, have not, ever been looked at or held in such a way. And I hoped that Vita knew her good fortune and did not take it for granted. But, like Dolly and Rollo, she did not have to sacrifice very much of herself to be lovable, and this perhaps spoiled them for others. Should great love be attained without effort? I do not believe that anything so easily won can be prized at all.

When we began to feel a chill on the terrace, we moved indoors to the front room and watched as Dolly leafed familiarly through Tom's vast record collection.

Occasionally, she held one up and Rollo said, 'No!' Eventually, he shouted, 'No! What is wrong with that fucking man?' *That facking man.* 'He listens to a load of shit! Shit!'

Unlike Vita, Rollo swore very rarely, but when he did, it had the same effect on Vita as someone leaving or returning to the table had on him. She would leap to her feet as though summoned. That evening, she rose from the sofa instantly, gesturing silently for Dolly to move away from the records before crouching in front of them herself. While Vita flicked efficiently through the records, Dolly sat down without a word; her gaze was fixed on Vita, as though studying her process. Vita quickly found the record she wanted and, when she put it on, Rollo settled back into his chair and closed his eyes.

'He's tired,' she said to me. 'All this driving . . . He doesn't need to be going back to town so often, but he is so conscientious. To a *fault*, I think.' She and Dolly exchanged a glance, which Vita broke first, looking away with a slight blush as Dolly continued to watch her, thoughtful and unmoved.

'Rollo told me that Lakeview is becoming more complicated,' I said to Vita as she sat down next to Dolly on the sofa, uncharacteristically fidgeting with her hair and smoothing down her dress.

'Yes, it has.' She stopped picking at her clothes and sat back against the cushions. 'He told you we have to break up the estate?'

'Yes, he did,' I replied with more certainty than was required.

'So, we are splitting the estate. The grounds will be sold off in plots once we get the permissions in place. And the house will be divided up into several units. You know, apartments. Very nice ones. Possibly a retirement block. Rols is just looking at the numbers before Dolly and I start to design.'

'Yes, he showed me his plans earlier,' said Dolly. 'I still think some of our initial ideas could work by just shrinking down some of the layouts, Vee.'

Rollo snored lightly as the two of them talked on about the apartments, about bathroom suites, kitchen plans and colour schemes. They discussed what their own perfect house would look like; it would, apparently, have been aesthetically very similar and situated in London. The two of them sounded as much like a couple as Vita and Rollo did, their communication easy and effortless, interrupting each other smoothly without the need to apologise. The music played on as the two women spoke.

At work the following week, David commented on my restored cheerfulness. I told him about the evening before, and he nodded encouragingly.

Excellent. The mysterious neighbours, he signed. And then, impatiently, exaggerating the movements as though raising his voice: *Go on. Tell me.*

And I told him about the champagne, the petits fours, the stories and the laughter. When I talked about Vita dancing on Rollo's feet, I did an impression of her, stiff-legged and confused, and he shook his head.

You would have laughed. It was funny, I signed. *And they have given Dolly a summer job. She is going to work in their building business.*

Why? he signed.

Because they are kind. Good friends. I added the last word randomly, because I could not explain why they wanted to take her to Lakeside or to London, or why she would want to go. I imagined she would be roped in to perform menial chores, telephone calls and orders, of which there must be plenty. Dolly would probably lose interest in going to Lakeside after some work there, once she saw how thin the veneer of glamour is on such places.

How old are they? he signed.

My age. No, a little bit older than me, I replied. *He is perhaps forty-five.* I considered Vita's age, then remembered our conversation about how they had met at university. *So, she is in her fifties.*

He nodded and went back to pruning; the small secateurs looked like a pencil in his large hands. After a few moments, he tapped on the table, so I would look at him.

Is he handsome? His signing became rapid, and I concentrated to keep up. If he had been speaking at that speed, I would have been floundering. *This man? And is she? Are they rich?*

Yes and yes, I signed back, deliberately abrupt in my repetition. I considered the final question and signed, *They have nice things. Yes, rich.*

Children?

I shook my head instead of signing with my fist: *No.*

And Dolly? he signed. He reverted to using the sign for a children's dolly, cradling it in his arms, but I ignored this. He repeated the sign: *Dolly likes them?*

I nodded, tightly. David nodded to himself, as though considering, and carried on with his work. While I was still watching him, he put down his secateurs and signed, his eyes still on the plant in front of him. *You are a good mum. Really good*, he signed enthusiastically with the thumbs of both hands before he returned to the rose.

When I tried to engage him in conversation again, his responses were brief. His face was closed down as though in repose, and I thought he must have been tired; perhaps he was still adjusting to living away from home and alone for the first time. At lunchtime, knowing he would be working out on the hot fields all afternoon, I got a bottle of lemonade and a packet of biscuits from the farm shop and put them both in his rucksack before zipping it closed.

something markedly different

THE FOLLOWING FRIDAY, DOLLY SUGGESTED WE WEAR SIMILAR black dresses and identical velvet Alice bands to dinner. We had not matched outfits since she was very young, and I found it touching, although I disliked the fit and fabric of the dresses she insisted on. When we arrived, Vita met us at the door in one of her brightly patterned kaftan-style dresses, and I was glad she had chosen something markedly different from what we both wore.

She greeted and kissed us both, then she stood back, clapping her hands and making a little shriek as if just seeing our outfits for the first time. 'Ahh! You two look so sweet! Dolly and I did that the other day, didn't we, Dolls? To go shopping? It was so lovely.' She leaned in towards me and lowered her voice, as if to impart something Dolly should not hear. Her perfume surrounded me; it had notes of almond and marzipan, the sweet and artificial smell of celebratory feasts. 'The cashier told me she could tell instantly we were mother and daughter . . . imagine!' She looked away modestly, sweeping past us to close the front door, and then gestured expansively towards the kitchen. As we walked ahead, Vita followed us and kept on talking. Her much-raised tone demonstrated that Dolly and I were both included in the conversation now; that perhaps even Rollo, if he was already somewhere in the house, was also intended to hear. 'I think it was just the matching outfits, though. It's deceiving, isn't it? Even if you aren't anything alike. It makes you *seem* similar. Even if you aren't, really.'

Dolly turned to smile back at me as we entered the kitchen. I noticed that her hairband had moved backwards a little, allowing random strands of hair to escape, and I reached up to fix my own in the same, looser style.

Over dinner, Rollo talked about his plans for Lakeview, gesturing as expansively as a television magician. I watched his hands as he weaved them through the air, and had to remind myself to listen to what he was actually saying.

'The alterations are going well. The council have been extremely . . .' He paused, as if considering how to phrase something sensitive, and then continued. 'Receptive. They are very good chaps, you know. Accommodating. They realise they need new life in the area, new ways of thinking. Lakeside is going to make some beautiful apartments.' He exhaled with exaggerated satisfaction, in the same way he did after trying a new wine of which he approved.

'Have you got the builders on site now?' I asked him.

'We have, yes. For the moment, at least.' He looked at Vita and, as she looked back at him, her face was unusually blank. It looked, then, as faces generally do, and it unnerved me, as if she had somehow disappeared behind her features. One of the reasons I loved Vita's face was that it was so mobile and expressive that I felt like one of you in her presence. Like a mind reader. Rollo continued: 'But we have just received a very good offer. From a company in Lancaster who would like to buy the plots once the planning comes through. They want to take over the conversion of the main building from us, too.'

'Oh, no!' I said. 'Are you going to take it? Dolly will be disappointed.' I turned to look at her face and see if she had heard. She and Vita were both watching Rollo, and both wore the same uncharacteristically serene expressions.

'Well,' said Rollo, 'it is an excellent offer.' He reached for his wine glass to take a long drink. As he swallowed, he put down his glass and spread out the fingers of both hands, his palms facing upwards. The pose could have been that of an evangelical speaker, or of someone trying to catch stray pieces of something falling from above. He took another drink. 'Selling would free us up. We could return to town whenever it suited us, rather than staying here until the build is complete. I think Vita has taken to country life rather better than me.' He righted his spectacles, pushing them back up in that gesture I had always found endearing. Then he continued the upward gesture, fixing his hair in place with the same hand. He looked directly at me. For once, his expression bore no suggestion of his easy smile. 'I'm getting rather itchy feet, I'm afraid, Sunday. I'm ready to go back to town soon.' For a moment, I believed he meant he would be going back alone, that Vita would remain with me. But he looked towards Vita. 'We are both ready, aren't we, Queenie?'

I began to flick through the Rolodex in my mind, that limited reference for human behaviour. This conversation had begun to feel like the announcement of an ending. I recalled the King talking about 'positive change', about 'company expansion' and 'personal growth', all key words that alluded primarily to his leaving Dolly and me. I thought, too, of Dolores' grim silence just before she died, and of my parents' last conversations. These had typically been focused on practicalities: the garden, the milkman's account and which of the neighbours needed to return borrowed household items. None of them had looked at me steadily, as Rollo did, and announced that they were ready to leave. Perhaps this straightforward and flattened announcement was not, after all, the way in which people actually ended things. It seemed, at once, too simple and too abstract to openly refer to one's exit plan before executing it.

'But you are staying here for the year, aren't you? Vita said . . . or you said . . .' I was still flicking through possible interpretations of Rollo's announcement, and could not remember which of them it had been, or when, but I believed it had been said. Or implied, at least. 'One of you said that you might buy a house up here. And not go back to town, to London. At all.'

Vita patted my hand and finally spoke. 'We haven't even accepted the offer, darling. We don't know that we will take it. Nothing has been signed.' She looked at Rollo and stroked her forehead with one finger in a repeated and horizontal motion. It looked, to me, like a sign as deliberate and exact as any that David made in conversation. 'And, anyway, we've still got this house for a few months, Sunday. Nothing's really changed.'

'Thank goodness!' I said. 'I am really looking forward to seeing what you and Dolly do with the apartments.'

'It's fine either way,' said Vita, her voice unusually low, as if she was speaking from a distance. 'We have other projects that Dolly can help me with.'

'Are you buying more houses here?' I said, excited at the thought of them making more commitments in the area. 'Where are you thinking?'

Everyone had put down their knives and forks by now. The meal that night had been a complicated sweet and savoury affair: chicken with sticky dates, yellow rice dotted with raisins. I had retired from the main course early to eat bread rolls instead. My dinner plate was still full, and this, I knew, would not be mentioned, a fact that made me happier than I could ever have explained to my hosts. Vita stood, beginning to clear the main course from the table. Dolly stood at the same time, and she carried Vita's little pile of plates into the kitchen. Vita smiled down at me.

'We don't have any firm interests here, Sunday. But we have a lot in town. And you are OK with Dolly visiting us down there now, aren't you?' She put an arm around my shoulder and rubbed it vigorously with her flattened palm, as if I were cold. 'We are so lucky to have you two.' There were four of us at dinner. And I did not know which 'we' were the lucky possessors and which the owned pair. I took some comfort, though, in the fact that we were somehow paired up, at least, and that I was not alone in this equation of fortune. Vita should not have studied history of art; she could have been a professor of semantics.

Rollo told me about the new car he was planning to buy that weekend when he returned to town. The quality of the leather seats was apparently a feature peculiar to this model alone, and one that he was keen to detail. He knew facts about the car that rivalled my depth of knowledge of Sicilian tradition.

'You know a lot about Lakeview, don't you, Rollo?' I asked him. 'And this town, too. Did you do a lot of research before you bought the home?'

He gave a wide and involuntary smile, so different from the expression he assumed when he was charming the recipient of his attention. Rollo liked to talk about his work process; while he was guarded about the figures and deals themselves, he invented himself through his business practices. 'Yes. Of course. That is where I would start with a purchase. I know London well, but this place is . . .'

'But have you ever been to the lake, Rollo? Have you seen the lake?'

'Yes! I've seen the lake dozens of times. I drive past it whenever I leave this house!'

'So you have passed the lake. But have you ever been there, Rollo? Have you ever stood and watched it?'

He looked at me. He had reverted to his careful and winning face, chin slightly dipped, eyebrows raised and a small, thin line of a smile, which suggested we shared a secret we were not speaking of. 'Tell me,' he said, gesturing generously with one hand as if directing an unseen person through a doorway ahead of himself. 'Tell me about the lake, then.'

But my version of the lake is not what people want to hear. I told a different story instead: one about my father at the lake.

Walter was a tall and well-built man. Long after his death, local people continued to refer to him with something between fear and admiration. I watched him once as he kicked off his shoes and dived gracefully into the lake to rescue one of the tourists, who had fallen from the fishing boat while taking photographs. Other men were already in the water, trying to save the drowning man, but, mad with fear, he pushed away the float and pulled them underwater when they came near. Walter decisively knocked the flailing man unconscious with one punch and brought him to land, where he laid him on the stones with enough tenderness to draw sighs from a group of local women who had stopped to watch. My father's navy shirt clung sleekly to his body as he stood at the lakeside and pushed his hair back from his forehead. He called out sternly to one of the onlookers, a neighbour of ours and a former nurse, to come and check on the man. Meanwhile, the man lay gasping on the ground in his soaked suit, marooned in the heavy wool fabric.

Rollo did not respond to the story, but instead asked a series of polite and distant questions about my father. *Had he always lived in our town? Oh, he had not? And had he missed the city?* He only fell silent as Dolly came into the room with a glass bowl of trifle, as he always did when pudding was brought to the table, to allow the two women their moment of performed domesticity. He sat very straight in his chair, though, and in an even more formal pose than usual, his chest stretching the neat confines of his navy suit. The evidence of his obvious pride in this new purchase was childlike and moving. I had not imagined Rollo would feel so serious about anything outside himself, except perhaps Vita. I had only ever been close to Dolly, who talked a lot, but told me little about what she cared for. Of course, I realised, Rollo and Vita would have their own lake, their own Sicily, and I could only know it when I was in a longer-standing relationship with them.

Dolly was followed by Vita, who was carrying Beast. The little dog leaned against his owner as he sat up, watching her face as if fascinated. He did not hold himself tightly, as dogs often do when held, but surrendered completely like an infant would, his limbs floppy and trusting.

'Vee!' Rollo said earnestly. 'This looks wonderful. And tell me, did you make it yourself?'

This was a script they had begun to run at dinner, the idea that Vita had made the pudding herself. The pretence sometimes extended to other courses, but always applied to the final course. Vita always served the pudding, and did so in an uncharacteristically modest way, which added to the impression that the confections were of her own making. We all played along, complimenting her sincerely each week. And, each week, she blushed prettily and fussed with the pudding, debating its qualities and the ways in which it might be improved. I could not, of course, eat any of the enormous trifle. It always strikes me as something an unsupervised child might put together: the layers of basically all textures mixed together, then randomly doused in sweet sherry and covered in hard sugar sprinkles, as if there were not already enough competing tastes present. It is so overblown and loud, the polar opposite of white food. As an adult, I have taught myself to turn away from noise like that of the trifle.

Vita asked if I would like some, and I declined bluntly.

'It's just not right. There is too much to it. It's so . . . busy,' I explained. Vita was holding the silver serving spoon still poised in the air, as if demonstrating it as a possible instrument of discipline. For a moment, I thought I should have just mumbled about how I was too full, but it looks delicious, really it does, and I just couldn't eat another thing. As I would have said at anyone else's table. *Never just say what you are thinking*, Ma had reminded me, often. *Nobody wants to hear that.* 'Or, er . . . it reminds me of school cafeterias.' That seemed better and certainly less personal.

And then Vita laughed loudly, and the other two looked up from their conversation, startled by the sudden noise. She stood up and launched the long spoon into the trifle, where it landed noisily across the pudding, exposing and mixing the different layers, some of which rose up on to the tablecloth. Then, leaning over the table towards us, she placed an unlit cigarette in her bottom lip and let it dangle crookedly to one side.

With one hand on her hip and the other poised over the spoon, she said, 'Quiet, you lot! Who wants some of this lovely cake?' *lover-ly kaaaayke!* Her new accent was actually very believable, and certainly better than her attempt at the girl from our programme with the strict papa. It was the precisely enunciated cockney that a classically trained Nancy in costume would conjure to sing 'As Long as He Needs Me', her corseted cleavage enhanced by the arm held up to her cosmetically applied black eye. *But all the same, I'll play this game . . .*

Rollo and Dolly must have had no idea why Vita had suddenly become an angry dinner lady, but they laughed along good-naturedly and held out their bowls as if her performance were perfectly normal.

As Vita served some trifle into a silver-edged bowl for Dolly, she addressed Rollo. 'Rols, do go and get a plate of cheese and biscuits for Sunday. Of course she wouldn't eat *trifle*. Trifle! Why would you buy a pudding like that?'

We all smiled at her admission that the pudding was Rollo's choice and not a home-made dish. And her voice was her own again, crisp and commanding and lovely.

My mother would have said something like this, would have apparently accepted my refusal as something predictable and reasonable. And she would have commanded my father or Dolores to go and get me a plainer alternative to the original dish; then, when they began to follow this instruction, she would have shouted at them to sit back down again. It would have been a trick. But at least Ma quickly learned not to make me eat the offending item. We both knew it would make me gag and this, thankfully, made her uncomfortable. At Vita's house, too, there were tricks. But they were not exposed over tantrums thrown at the table; they were played as a long game and could only be recognised some time afterwards.

Rollo rose smoothly and went into the kitchen. Vita did not ask Dolly if she wanted pudding, as she had me, but simply served the trifle into three bowls.

Once she had finished, she spoke again. 'Sunday, Rols is going back to town tomorrow. Dolly and I thought it was a good time for us to visit, too.' She smiled brightly and picked up her spoon. 'OK, darling?'

'You mean London?'

'Yes, town, London . . .' Still holding the spoon, she spread out her hands, palms up in a gesture of openness or, perhaps, impatience.

Rollo returned to the table with a plate of roughly cut cheese and some crackers. He had foregone the elegant presentation that he always seemed to enjoy, and I watched him as he sat down, looking to find a reason for this change. Dolly passed his pudding across to him.

'Thanks, darling.' As he took it from her, their hands touched, and he held on to hers absent-mindedly for a moment. She looked as sharply at me as if I had just called out her name.

Vita stood up and I was surprised by the firmness with which she guided Rollo smoothly back into the kitchen, whispering softly to him and closing the door behind them.

Dolly and I remained at the table in our usual silence for some moments. It was not for us to guess at what they were discussing in the kitchen, just as it was never for Ma or the King to comment when I spoke of Sicily, or speech patterns, or etiquette.

'So you are going to London tomorrow then, Dolly?' I said.

She nodded, unsmiling, and began to eat her pudding, taking small and perfunctory bites. She did not share a preference for sweet things with the first Dolores.

'You are ridiculous, Mummy.' She spoke in a soft and gentle way that suggested infinite patience. 'Trifle should not frighten you.' She stabbed the air with her spoon and made a ghostly noise. 'Wooooo!'

After pudding, we listened to Rollo's classical music while he apparently dozed in his chair and occasionally woke briefly to critique whatever track was playing. None of us commented on the music or his responses to it, but politely fell silent, as if we had been waiting for his review and were just filling in the time between his remarks.

'Why is Rollo so keen to go back to town?' I asked. 'I thought you were both enjoying it here.'

Vita shrugged and picked up her glass, clearly disinterested in the conversation.

'Well, I am excited to be going . . .' Dolly began.

'But have you changed your mind about staying on?' I addressed this to Vita only and as if Dolly had not spoken.

'We have interests in London, you see, darling, and it's important for us to keep up with our contacts. Otherwise, Rols won't hear about new opportunities. We mostly convert buildings that were offices or commercial places, and they sell quickly. They are becoming rarer. That's why he hopes Lakeview will be taken over, so he can work on other projects. And do more nationally. And perhaps start sourcing or renovating buildings for councils.'

'Yes, I told her about that,' interjected Dolly. Vita looked at her in silence. 'That was all I said. Just about trying for the council contracts.'

This was not an answer as to why he had lost interest in our town, so I waited for her to continue.

After a short pause, she said, 'He is, you know, staying connected, and so on. And of course, you wouldn't understand this, but property really is quite a little world of its own.' She looked at me without expression.

'But does he need to actually *go* there? For work?'

'Work! Work is terribly vulgar, darling.' Her voice was suddenly different, borrowed. She smiled and the smile was not her own, but something tight and restrained. 'That's what Tom would tell you.' As she spoke, she gestured around the elegant room, as if Tom was still somehow inside this, his second home, and not in London with his frail and pregnant wife and their children. We looked towards Rollo as he slept on, still immaculate in his suit and his shiny leather shoes.

'Tom works,' I pointed out. 'Like Rollo does.'

And then Vita spoke again, in her own voice, which was still confident, but sweet and soft, as her version of Tom had not been. 'People like Tom don't really work. Not in the way we know it, Sunday. Rollo and I are extremely comfortable; we have nice things, but we aren't like Tom. He is the oldest, so he will have a lot of the family money.' *Famil-ay mon-ay.* 'Rols has an older brother, so he won't get anything.'

'Don't his parents like him?' It was difficult to imagine anyone disliking Rollo. And surely if such a charming man was your own, your love would be enormous and augmented further with pride at the admiration he received. It would be like being the parent of a much-loved celebrity and a little of the public's awe would naturally fall on you. It would not be the experience Ma had with me, but perhaps like being the mother of Dolly. Or Dolores.

Vita laughed, but it was not in her usual and involuntary way. The sound was contained and finite, the teeth-showing snort of a displeased exotic pet. 'Like him? Rols? Of course they like him. Everyone loves Rols.' *Ah-vary-won laaaves Rols*. She made this statement with the reverence of Bunny making another confident pronouncement on the Forresters. Then she looked at Dolly, who was nodding encouragingly, as if they had already confirmed this point about Rollo's appeal many times between themselves. 'But the estate must remain entire, you see. Rols's father only got it himself because his brother died before inheriting.'

Dolly leaned forward. 'Was that Freddie?' She glanced first at Vita and then at me. She leaned towards me to put a hand over my arm, as if breaking bad news. There was no pressure in the touch. Her hand was entirely weightless and without warmth; if I closed my eyes, I could not have known it was there. 'He shot himself, Mummy. Didn't he, Vee? Before you even met Rols. How sad.'

Vita nodded gravely. 'Yes, Dolly. How sad.'

And I found I did not care for them so much that night, as they sat prettily side by side on the sofa, trying out morose expressions for an Uncle Freddie neither of them had ever known.

The following Tuesday, I came home from work to find Dolly and Vita sitting together at the kitchen table. They were quiet and hunched over their coffees as if very cold. They both had their Levi's on; they wore these jeans in a distressed and baggy fit. Above this seemingly relaxed style, though, their belts would be strapped as relentlessly as that of corseted actresses in a period drama. Dolly was wearing a navy silk jacket that I had not seen before. It was appliquéd with butterflies and flowers, and had lots of tiny badges sewn all over; it was fussy and unlike her usual style. Vita wore a similar jacket in red silk. Both looked up with similar little smiles when I came into the room, but did not perform their usual greetings, the kisses and girlish exclamations.

'Hello, you two,' I said. 'How are you? Did you have a good time?'

They looked at each other as if silently deciding which of them would respond. Dolly took a slow sip of her coffee and Vita spoke.

'We're fine. We had a lovely time, and Dolly met lots of our friends.' She looked at me thoughtfully. 'We got some ideas for our new house, too.'

'What ideas?' I asked. 'What did you do?'

Vita stood up and made a fluttery and impatient gesture with both hands. 'You know, fabric shops, wallpaper, that stuff.' She leaned down over Dolly to kiss her head possessively and then patted me on the shoulder as she passed on her way out. 'I'm off for a nap. See you on Friday, Sunday.'

I sat down opposite Dolly in Vita's chair, but did not speak until I heard the front door close behind her.

'Where did you stay? Who with?' I asked Dolly.

'They've got a new place, and Rols went there. Vee and I stayed in a hotel. We could have stayed with Rols, but Vee wanted to make it special. Their house is a terrace, and it hasn't even got a functioning bathroom at the moment, but it's awfully grand. It will be, anyway, when we have finished it.' I no longer queried her use of the collective 'we'.

Dolly was sniffing her coffee intensely, as if there were something specific in the steam that she needed to absorb before properly waking. I went to the cupboard and found a packet of chocolate biscuits, which I pushed across the table towards her. They were continental-style thins wrapped in gold foil, a present from one of Rollo's trips that glittered against the otherwise ordinary contents of our pantry. 'You need some sugar, Dolly. It will wake you up. Tell me about the hotel.'

My daughter stroked the shiny wrapper without interest. 'Rols told me something. He worries about Vee being back in London. He likes me to be there with her. She was a bit troubled, he said, before they came here.' She continued in a low voice, as if the two of them might be hiding somewhere in our house, listening to her. 'Her best friend had a baby and Vee couldn't cope with it.'

'Why couldn't she cope with it?' I asked.

'She took the baby out on a walk.'

'That's OK, isn't it?'

'But, Mummy, she actually went into the garden and took her in the pram. She didn't ask Annabel, the mother, didn't even tell her, and she was gone for over an hour.' For a moment, the adolescent thrill of recounting an adult drama was more to Dolly than her constant celebration of Vita. She widened her eyes as she spoke. 'When she got back, the police were already there. It was quite a scandal,

Rols said. It was the reason he sold the house.' She remembered, just then, where her loyalties lay, and she adjusted her expression, continuing in the phrasing Vita might have used herself. 'Poor Vee. People are so unforgiving, really.'

'Do you think it was OK for her to take the baby?' I asked.

She paused. 'The baby was fine,' she said eventually.

'But the baby's mother didn't know where she was. If you had been taken away as a baby, Dolly, even for a moment, I . . .' And I trailed away, initially unwilling to explore how such a loss, even temporarily, would have felt. 'It must have been terrifying for that family. Terrifying.'

Dolly shrugged, obviously unhappy with the tone of my response. I patted her hand in a slow and reassuring action.

'But we weren't there, were we? So, we can't know what happened.' Her face was remote, and I knew the subject would be closed.

'What did you do this weekend? Tell me about the hotel.'

She remained silent, though, and eventually I raised an eyebrow at her. She looked sideways, as if recalling her weekend and deciding how best to describe the place in which they had stayed. Apparently, though, she decided she would not after all, for she continued, 'It was . . . an expensive London hotel. You know. Like in a film, Mummy.' She spoke kindly, and as if to a devoted and much younger sibling. 'Do you mind if I just go up to bed for a bit?'

I got a tray and put a glass of milk and the biscuits on it. She watched me as I rinsed out her coffee cup and arranged her tray, then she picked it up with a nod. She started towards the door, then stopped. 'I'm supposed to go over to the farm for supper. Could you phone Grandma and tell her I'm . . .' She paused, deciding what to say. '. . . I'm not well?'

I nodded immediately, shamelessly pleased to help Dolly cancel on her grandparents and happy to be at the centre of the deceit for once. It often felt as if she, Bunny and Richard were in on a secret without me.

I listened to her progress upstairs. When she reached the top of the stairs, I raised my voice to be heard. 'And are you not well, Dolls, or are you tired?'

She must have been on the landing then, and as she replied, her voice was fading along with her step, and I could only just make out what she said.

'Tired,' she said, her voice disappearing, as she was herself.

Alone, I thought of the baby who had been taken as she slept in her pram. The scene played before me, involuntarily and in unsettlingly vivid detail. Annabel, lovely in a floral dress, went out into the sunny garden to retrieve her baby for the feed that she would normally have already woken and cried out for. On finding her navy Silver Cross missing, Annabel would not, at first, have allowed herself to believe her baby had been taken, but would instead desperately search her mind for an alternative explanation: she had put her down in her cot upstairs, or in the wicker carrycot, which was usually kept in the kitchen . . . But, no, she remembered, she had left that with her in-laws, at their request. She had . . . And all the time Annabel was trying to solve this puzzle in a rational way, one that meant her baby was still with her, a rising voice inside would be scornful at her own wilful refusal. *You'll have to face this now it's happening it's already happened the baby has gone-gone-gone.* And then, in the pretty garden, after the silence, the screams.

It was easy to imagine Vita casually pushing the pram along the street to Annabel's house later that day, her smile only growing brighter when confronted by the frantic parents and the solemn-faced policemen.

'Annie,' she would say – she would, of course, have a nickname for Annabel, as she did for all of us – 'Annie, you did say I should take her for a walk. Do you remember, darling?' And to Annabel's husband, to the policemen: 'She's *so* tired, poor thing. A new baby, it's exhausting, of course.'

But perhaps the shocked fury of the parents, and the policemen's questions, too, would unsettle even Vita. Unused to rebukes of any kind, she would mumble unsatisfactory defences of herself as she backed minutely away from them with a little stumble. Their move to Tom's, Dolly's reference to a scandal, suggested that even Rollo had apparently been unable to persuade their friends to excuse his wife for what she had done. Although he would have tried, in his most charming way, to do so; would, on that day, have gently reminded the couple of what Vita had been to them, and would too, I expect, have been shocked to discover this was not enough to pardon her.

Later that day, when the policemen had finally driven away, Annabel would be acclimatising to her new world, one in which her baby could be taken from her, even if she was then returned, unharmed. Annabel would never experience again the undimmed sunniness of that day before her baby was taken. Her life would necessarily be tainted by the shock she had experienced, by the ongoing and profound loss of trust. I thought of Annabel in the nursery, holding her sleeping infant close while staring, wide-eyed and fearful, into the new darkness.

The only aspect of the day that I could not conjure was the conversation between Vita and Rollo in the privacy of their home afterwards. Would she have attempted to explain her actions? Would he even have asked her to do so? I did not believe he would have. In my mind, when he returned, defeated, from Annabel's house, they shrugged silently at one another in feigned tolerance of parental unreasonableness and simply debated where to go for dinner. Vita had already bathed and was elegant in a new dress, and he was still so immaculate in his daytime suit that she pleaded with him not to change.

'It's been such a long day, Rols, darling. A simply awful day. You can't imagine,' she would have said. Adjusting her frown into something more persuasive, she would look up at him prettily as she took his arm. 'Could we please go to dinner now?'

The following day, David and I took some of the potted plants into the farm shop. I felt that some of the younger plants appeared more fragile underneath the shop lights, but David disagreed. I put my hand into one of the pots and felt the crumbs of earth that moved in stagnant waves, breaking dolefully over my skin, and I knew they were not yet ready to go. I took one of David's hands and put it into the soil to demonstrate this.

'Am I interrupting something?' It was Vita. She wore a fitted dress in pastel colours and one of the shop's wicker baskets hung uncertainly from one wrist. She looked as if she had been styled as a woman shopper but had yet to find a convincing pose. She was smiling as she extended a hand towards David in that regal way she had. '*I am Vita. How do you do?*'

David had been watching her carefully as she spoke. He nodded slowly before showing his muddied palms to her in silence. His usually open face was entirely impassive. She blinked back at him, unmoving and with the same smile frozen in place.

Turning to me, he signed, *OK*, and he began to place the youngest plants carefully back in the tray.

'Let me introduce you,' I spoke and signed. 'Vita, this is David, who works in the greenhouses with me. David, this is Vita, my neighbour.' Edith Ogilvy reminded me that *informal introductions benefit from a reference to an interest or acquaintance shared by the two parties.* I looked at Vita, her hand still expectantly inclined, and then towards David, who was selecting plants with exaggerated concentration, and I said nothing.

'And do you like working here?' Vita asked him in the kindly way of a visiting patron. *And do you lake working har?* Her question cut through the silence and inexplicably expanded it.

David nodded; his eyes were watching her, but his hands moved consideringly over the leaves of the plants in his tray.

'It's fun, yes?' she continued. And he did not nod again, but a muscle twitched at the corner of his mouth and then stopped abruptly. He had the loaded tray in both hands and, looking at me, he nodded towards the greenhouses before leaving the shop.

'He is a lovely boy, Vita,' I said. 'We've worked together for—'

'Yes, and it's *so* sweet of you,' she said in a tone of

finality, as if I had reached the end of an unnecessarily pro-
tracted explanation. '*Exactly* what I would expect of you,
Sunday.' She reached out and took my arm, speaking in a
theatrical whisper. 'Darling, Richard is hovering. Will you
come and do the till before he sees me waiting? I simply
haven't the *energy* for one of his long chats today.'

Sometimes that summer, I came downstairs in the
morning to find Vita sitting quietly in my kitchen, wearing
her dressing gown, and smoking a cigarette. Vita was a
different person early in the day. She moved slowly and
talked little, like a patient emerging from a long confinement. She also liked to smoke while sitting on our
front step or her own identical one. She did this in Rollo's
pyjamas or in her own pretty nightwear, or occasionally
(and my favourite), still dressed in a glamorous and
becomingly dishevelled way from the night before. It
pleased me to see her on the front steps of either of our
houses, her colourful clothing fanning out around her
on the austere stone floor like something spilled or
thrown. Our Victorian builder must have imagined that
it would be severe-looking parents and lines of neat
children stepping over his threshold, all shining boots
and serious faces. He could not have conjured an image
like Vita perched on his front step, as I could not have,
before she came. Straight out of bed and draped in
silky fabric or clad in a brightly coloured minidress paired
with my slippers, her hair falling out of whatever style
she had constructed the evening before, Vita was always
a vision. After she had smoked two cigarettes, which
she needed to do in complete silence each morning, she
gradually returned to form. She was at her most cutting
at this time of day, when she first recovered her voice,

and Dolly and I laughed along with her little cruelties.

Vita did impressions of the local people; my surreal postmaster, who did not address her, as he does me, about the weather, but instead gave her shy and mumbled compliments. She also copied Phyllis, with a loud, carrying voice, and an imaginary chicken tucked under one arm. Our favourite, though, was her impression of Bunny, whose background is certainly more privileged than my own, but who is not from asset-rich farming stock like her husband; nor is she a wealthy and well-connected urbanite, like Vita and Rollo. My former mother-in-law married up, both socially and economically, something that Vita saw the first time they met. Marrying so well is not accidental; it takes focus, said Vita, and she ridiculed Bunny for the efforts she believed it must have taken for her to become a Forrester. She never mocked me, although I, however briefly, was also a Forrester wife who came from a lowlier position. When Vita was Bunny, she lowered her voice and wore a pained expression.

She said, 'We use our indoor voices, don't we? We talk quietly, don't we? We make statements into questions? Because we have.' At this point, she shook her shiny hair and looked around anxiously, before whispering – '*money*. Everything is a bit *embarrassing*.' Part of this comedy was the ridiculousness of Vita performing self-consciousness; she was so supremely certain of herself. Vita was a marvellous mimic, but she was always Vita, an essence too powerful to be eradicated, even momentarily, by an impersonation, however cruel or skilful. Bunny-Vita spoke of her Forrester privilege in hushed and shy tones: '*Pretty baby, new car, gifted child*'. She announced with a sad smile that her charity work was 'for the *poor* children. I'm very *sensitive*. I care *too much*.' This, with a slow and helpless shake of her head. '*Too* much.'

Dolores would have appreciated this, I thought when Vita performed, and Dolly and I laughed again. I can still imagine my sister and me as teenagers, spotting the exotically dressed Vita chain-smoking unapologetically on the next-door porch as we walked off to school in the mornings, and being thrilled with our discovery.

My mother would have been disparaging of Vita. She would have relegated our glorious neighbour to the group of 'lazy mares', those local women who did not conform to Ma's exacting ideas of decency, and whose eccentric dress or manners she correlated with low morals and promiscuity. Idleness was one of the two behaviours she found the most unforgivable; the other was peculiarity, and both were criticisms often aimed at me. She frequently held Dolores up as a beacon of decorum and normalcy. While Ma lectured me on this, my sister would stand behind her and perform outrageously. She would flip her skirt up to expose her knickers, or hold her hands together as if in prayer. In either pose, her face would be serene, and when Ma turned, Dolores would frown and nod along with her as if in concerned agreement.

Leaving Vita, sleepy, friendly and half-dressed, at home while Dolly slept on upstairs had felt a little like being a husband going out to work. For a brief time that summer, I was a man who was indulgent where his family were concerned, a responsible provider and protector, a man good enough even for the exacting criteria in *Etiquette for Ladies*, where the women were lovely, and the husbands were courteous.

Vita, too, must have felt something of this. She

regularly waved me goodbye from my own step, kissing my cheek, then sitting back down and closing one eye as she exhaled smoke from the side of her mouth. 'Have a good day at the office, darling!'

And I walked around her in my utilitarian workwear. It was ugly and plain, although I had never thought of it in such terms before Vita came, with her silky, bright clothes and her delicately soled sandals and shoes in every colour. I had never seen an adult wear red footwear before. Or green, or gold, or silver. But I did not need lovely shoes. Indeed, I did not need to be lovely, because Vita did that, excessively. She did so even without recourse to *Etiquette for Ladies*, and Edith's extended advice on cosmetic preparations and feminine appeal. And I went off to work in my sturdy boots, my mud-coloured trousers and loose shirt. All those items that David or any of the male farm workers would comfortably wear themselves.

Vita and Dolly gradually increased their time in London, though the visits and the sleepovers became less and less frequent, until eventually I could not quite believe they had ever happened. I had even begun to go to Friday dinners alone, meeting Dolly next door as if she were one of the hosts and not part of my household. I was pleased, then, when she finally came home one Friday, even though she went straight upstairs to shower and change for dinner. When it was time to leave, I knocked on her door, and when there was no reply, I went inside.

'Dolly?' She was lying on top of her duvet, looking up at the ceiling thoughtfully, as if considering it. 'Are you ready to come next door?' I asked, but I could already see she was newly smart in a violet taffeta minidress that I had not seen before, paired with electric-blue sheer tights.

She and Vita often wore brightly coloured tights and accessories, in shades that did not feature anywhere in the rest of their outfit, as if deliberately chosen for their incongruity. There was also a lot of heavy gold jewellery, of a weight and width that looked highly uncomfortable. So much of Dolly's wardrobe that summer was new, bought on their London visits by Vita, who often had similar, if not identical, pieces herself. I had begun to feel sentimental on the rare occasions when I saw Dolly in any outfit that was not chosen and purchased by Vita. The taffeta dress was very her: sleeveless and full-skirted, it spilled out prettily on to the white cotton sheets.

'Mmm, yep,' she agreed, without moving.

I sat down on her bed, putting her feet across my legs, so we were sitting as we used to on our Tuesday nights on the sofa, and I leaned back against the wall. 'Dolly,' I said, 'do you like working for Vita?'

'Well, I work for Vita *and* Rols, actually,' she pointed out, her gaze still fixed on the ceiling.

'And do you enjoy that?' I asked.

'It's money, isn't it? A lot of money, in fact,' she said, her voice flat. She looked down at me without her usual indifference, as if suddenly interested in what I would do. She watched me closely as she continued: 'It's more money than I have had before. Loads more than you and Grandma give me. And I don't even spend it on clothes, because Vee is always buying me more.' She gestured apathetically towards her wardrobe, which we both knew was full of new things, so many that some were still unpacked, wrapped in tissue paper, and left in their bags and boxes. She brought her arm back to her lap and laced her fingers together over her midsection. She was serene and untroubled as she lay there, motionless. 'I'm just saving it all. It's a lot.' She was looking at me expectantly, but I was unsure how to respond.

'Lucky you! Perhaps you could save it for university.'

She snorted humourlessly and her mouth remained in a firm and unmoving straight line. Then she turned her gaze back to the ceiling above. 'I am saving. Lots.' She put a hand on my arm. Then, distracted, she straightened her fingers out to examine the flaking nail polish, the lack of repair a rare and welcome reminder of her girlishness. 'Ask Rols about me tonight . . .' She paused, still considering her nails. 'He says I am doing a *marvellous* job.' She emphasised 'marvellous' by stretching out the syllables slowly. This was a habit that Vita, too, had with hyperbole. They each stilled their tone at the point of exaggeration; it had the effect of self-parody. Like a girl at a staid dinner announcing what *enormous* fun she is having, the emphasis gave a peculiar air of cynicism. Dolly began to speak again, but then stopped, and I remained silent, waiting. Eventually, into the silence, she said, 'Do you miss me at home? Vee thinks you like being on your own better. That you hardly notice the difference.'

I thought of nothing but my daughter for hours after I waved them off each Saturday. I did not know, then, that we were about to attend what would be our last Friday night dinner. That they would start going to London for long weekends, which increasingly ran into the week, too. Dolly came home less, and Vita often came with her when she did, as if they were a couple whom I might reasonably expect to see only in each other's company. I watched the three of them leave every Saturday morning as they sped down our quiet street in Rollo's new car, which was the same vivid red as the first stupid one, with loud disco music playing from the open windows. Vita would only drive on short journeys: 'I don't have the concentration, darling. I fall asleep after twenty minutes in the car!' It surprised me, though, that Dolly travelled in the front seat next to Rollo, while Vita sat in the back. In my own household, even the celebrated Dolores would not have been offered the front seat, because it was strictly reserved for the wife of the driver. Dolly told me that Rollo listened to Radio 1 on the journey to London and to classical music as he drove home. To get him in to the right frame of mind for each place, she confided once, earnestly, as if I were an outsider compiling facts on each of their preferences, as if this were something I cared to know.

Now, when I remember those early mornings on which I watched my daughter leaving, I do not, as I did then, allow myself to stand and silently watch Dolly go. I do not stand motionless at the window as she climbs serenely into the red car and Rollo closes her door with a flick of his hand. In my dreams, I run to my daughter, pull her from her seat (she does not object to this as she would have in real life, but instead surrenders to my embrace) and take her inside with me. But I am unable, ever, to prevent the rows of Lakeside children from being removed from their too-expensive home to be scattered amongst strangers as randomly as salt.

'Of course I miss you, Dolly. I would rather you were here. But you were so keen to go with them,' I said.

'I think they really need me. You know?' She smiled, indulgent as a fond mother herself. 'Rols says Vee is only really happy when I am with her. Even when we are just at home together. He says he doesn't know what she would do without me. What he would do, either.'

'What do you do? Is it mostly telephone calls? Arranging deliveries? Things like that?' I asked, genuinely interested to know how she spent her days with them.

Dolly started as if slapped. 'No! No, it is not. I help Vee here. And when we are in town, we see people . . .' She pointed vaguely in the direction of her wardrobe again. '. . . we go shopping. For interior pieces, too. Whatever needs doing. You know.' She looked at me appraisingly. 'Or perhaps you don't really know. You've only ever worked at Daddy's farm, haven't you? So, I suppose it's hard for you to imagine what work is really like. It's complicated. You just have to adapt, to do whatever needs doing.'

I sighed. 'You don't have to work so much this summer. And you can't be responsible for Vita – she is an adult. It's too much. You are away too much. When did you last see Grandma and Granddad? Or Daddy? I'm proud of you for working hard, but you don't have to tire yourself out. Shall I tell Rollo for you? He'll understand. And Vita will, too. Shall I—'

Dolly abruptly sat upright. 'No! What *are* you talking about? Don't.' Her tone was sharp, and she shook her head, either at me or in the process of correcting herself. 'You are mad, Mummy,' she continued, but she spoke gently now, as though admonishing a toddler whose waywardness only slightly exceeded the entertainment they provided. 'Absolutely mad. Come on, let's go.'

The dinner next door was a little plainer than usual, but still strange. Rollo brought us a soup that he called *vichyssoise*. When he pronounced this word, it was with an impeccable French accent and a peculiar stretch of his fingers, as though he were a conductor. The soup was not simply cool but iced like a cocktail. A salty vegetable cocktail. I tried one spoonful.

'Rollo.' I took a big gulp of my tonic water. 'This is terrible. It is not soup.' And he put down his own spoon immediately, laughing as he passed me the bread basket instead. They always had soft white rolls with dinner, although Vita and Rollo rarely touched them.

'Don't rich people eat bread?' I had wondered out loud at an early Friday dinner. Our hosts, for once without an answer, had looked at one another in silent mutual query and then shrugged.

There were always uneaten rolls left over at our dinners, and Rollo used to wrap them up in an unused napkin for me to take home. The use of the square white linen rather than a plastic bag was a very Rollo gesture, and I kept the napkins because I knew he would never ask for their return. I have them now, folded and immaculate in a cupboard.

Later, Vita told me that people who entertain formally often serve food that is rich and heavy. In consequence, the guests tend to eat less of the starchy dishes. 'But a good host insists on lots of fresh rolls at the table, because parties work best on a theory of comfort and over-abundance. So, the trick is to provide too much of everything.' Vita said this as seriously as if she were talking about a long-observed religious practice. 'Because it alludes to that feeling of overstocked comfort.'

Dolly, by her side, nodded along with equal earnestness. 'My room is so comfortable. I love the way you—'

'Your room, Dolly?' I said, challenging this claim for the first time.

She shrugged unapologetically. 'Yes, my room here.'

Vita put her hand on Dolly's back and gave her an indulgent smile. 'Of course it's your room, darling!'

The main course, that last Friday evening, was coronation chicken with various salads and small savoury pastries, which had been carefully folded in on themselves. Rollo passed around the serving bowls and got up to make sure that everyone had exactly what they wanted. His own plate, though, contained little. He was the only one of us drinking red wine, and he quickly had to replace the first bottle with another. During dinner, Vita and Dolly spoke mostly between themselves and in little bursts of energy, like over-excited children. For the first time at a Friday dinner, there was no pudding for Vita to present to the table. Instead, Rollo brought a tray of cheese and biscuits in from the kitchen. He passed me a small plate and I took some slices of cheddar. He pointed to a soft, white-crusted cheese, and with his other hand he made a circle of silent approval, as if the recommendation were a secret between us, so I took a piece of that, too. He did not take any for himself, but passed it down to the others.

'It's great how those two get on, isn't it?' he said, as I, too, watched them in conversation. 'Vita always used to say she couldn't stand teenagers.' He said the word 'teenagers' carefully, grimacing downwards on the first syllable and drawing out the word into separate parts, as if unsure of it. *T-eeen-a-geeers*. 'But she really loves Dolly. No doubt about that. It has been very good for her being up here. Dolly has made her so much better.'

'Was she unwell?' I asked.

'No, not unwell as such. Just had a little wobble back in London. Her closest friend had a baby and, I don't know, it . . .' I saw him, for the first time, struggle to find the right words. He was not speaking, as he typically did, as from a known script, but was actually telling me something. 'It disturbed her. But look at her now.' We looked again at Vee and Dolly, so much a pair and so oblivious to our gaze on them. He finished his wine and showily checked everyone else's glasses, before he refilled his own, emptying the bottle. He spilled a little, and the red stain spread rapidly across the tablecloth, as if trying to reach me. 'What about you, Sunday? Did you always want to be a mother?'

'No, I did not.' And I turned the conversation back to him. This was a trick I had learned from both of them. He and Vita handled discussion like expert craftspeople, manipulating language into something new and deliberate in their hands. 'Of course, Dolly isn't quite a child any more. But she is still so young, really. What were you like at her age?'

He raised an eyebrow. 'Haven't you heard enough about my errant schooldays?' And it was true that many of his stories came from his time away at boarding school, where he had apparently escaped expulsion narrowly and on a regular basis.

'OK, at eighteen, then. I suppose you were at university . . . had you already met Vita? Did you know she was the one straight away?'

'No. Well, yes. Not really. We got together when I was in my second year, so . . .' He spread out his hands, then lightly clapped them together, in a gesture of closure. I remained quiet, though, and he continued: 'We were on and off for a time, as young people are, I suppose. There was certainly a period of adjustment. Of course.' He smiled winningly, 'it was my behaviour and not Queenie's. I am not an easy man to live with. As my wife has no doubt informed you.' He glanced momentarily at Vita,

225

who was listening intently to Dolly. 'Anyway, on to happier things! We are so looking forward to Dolly's party.'

'Dolly's party?' I said.

'At the farm, the garden party,' he clarified.

He was referring to Bunny and Richard's annual garden party, which this year was going to celebrate Dolly's GCSE results.

'Oh! I didn't know you would be there,' I said. I was made to feel extremely fortunate to receive an invitation each year. Bunny made a special trip to the greenhouses in midsummer to present me with the engraved white card, so stiff that, even felt through the envelope, it seemed outraged and aloof. She handed the invitation to me with a light giggle of excitement. It was always addressed to me in my maiden name, prefaced with 'Ms' and not a 'Mrs'. Dolly was never included in the invitation, because, as she liked to patiently explain, she was family, so technically she was actually the inviter, the host.

'Dolly is keen that we go, so . . . And she tells me her father is coming down for the party, too? We haven't met him yet, so we are looking forward to it. She hasn't stopped talking about the new baby. She is very excited,' Rollo said.

I was confused. Why would they care about meeting the King? I only saw him annually, at the garden party, and Vita and Rollo were neighbours, not family members.

Rollo was standing up. 'Excuse me, Sunday.' He left the table briefly and returned with the port. When he sat down again, he moved automatically to pour the port into my still-full champagne glass, and I quickly put my hand over the top.

'No, Rollo. Thank you.'

He laughed. 'Sorry, Sunday. Wrong glass. And, of course, you don't like it. Here.' He put the port down and looked at the others. Then he stood up, slightly unsteadily, to offer Dolly and Vita the port. Both of them shook their heads, *no*, and waved him away without looking up or pausing their conversation, as though rebuking an intrusive waiter. Rollo took his seat again and refilled his port glass. 'I am really tired. All this driving . . .' He said this to no one in particular, and pushed his hair back off his forehead, as though hot. He had the heavy, straight hair that I associate with privilege, with people like him, people like Vita and Dolly, too. Perhaps it is a result of genetics, of the good breeding that the Forresters and others like them claim; the years of careful nurturing by a team of admirers; the nannies, teachers and parents all invested in a successful outcome. Like the prizewinning animals that populate the King's farm, such people are glossy-coated and selectively bred.

'Rollo,' I said, as I remembered, 'you said something about the new baby? Who is having a baby?'

'Exactly! What baby? God, I am drunk. Sunday, please ignore me. Vita will be furious if she hears all the nonsense I've been talking tonight. Terrible hosting,' he continued, shaking his head and wagging his index finger as though berating someone else. He stood up and stuck his elbow at me crookedly; I saw how unsteady he was on his feet. 'Come on, Sunday. It's our secret. Help a drunken old man into the sitting room and you can choose the music.'

I quite liked this version of Rollo, who was less smooth and polished and wanted my help. And it was with real fondness that I took his arm to help him. He leaned on me a little as we left the table, with Vita and Dolly eventually following us. Like a couple, their heads were close together and their conversation was pitched low so only they could hear one another. Even as I watched them, it felt something like a memory. Dolores and I must have looked like that, I realised. And I am glad to have had that once myself, for I do not think I will ever have it again.

a kind of confession

DOLLY STAYED AT HOME THE NIGHT BEFORE HER GCSE RESULTS were due, an increasingly rare arrangement and one for which I was grateful. In the morning she was downstairs before me, sitting at the kitchen table in a white nightdress that had been a favourite of hers when she was much younger. I had not seen her wear it for some time; had assumed it discarded along with other outgrown clothes. The nightgown was sleeveless, trimmed with broderie anglaise, and although it had been bought primarily because it was ankle-length in a satisfyingly Wendy from Peter Pan way, it had quickly come to reach her knees. It was startlingly at odds with the sophisticated wardrobe she had acquired since working for Vita. She had made coffee in the press bought for her by Rollo, but apparently had not yet eaten. When she spoke to me, she kept her eyes fixed on the table.

'I should tell you something, Mummy. My results might not be what you are expecting. I didn't work as hard as I should have.' Her eyes were hard and glittering, though, as if she were waiting for something promised to her.

'But, Dolly, you worked really hard. All that time you spent revising,' I pointed out. I moved from the fridge to place a hand on her exposed shoulder, my other hand holding on to the cold milk.

'I was out. I wasn't revising. You are so literal. So . . . simple. If I tell you something, you just accept it because you can't come up with an alternative scenario. That's not even trust. It's stupidity.'

'I know you are feeling nervous, Dolly. Everyone worries on results day; it's perfectly normal.' I was determined to soothe her, to keep her calm until she had collected her grades.

'Do they? And how would you know that? Oh, yes, from all your vast academic experience,' she said, stirring sugar into her coffee. She looked up through her eyelashes, and even at that moment, I felt a jolt of admiration for her loveliness. 'Am I right?'

On the rare mornings that Dolly was home, the French press bought for her by Rollo in Deauville was always on the table. I had come to dislike this object, with its silver lines and smug perfection. Dolly treated it with reverence, rebuking me if she found me cleaning the press, or putting it away, as apparently only she was allowed to handle it. I flinched at her words but did not reply to her question.

'You will want to take that to Grandma's with you, won't you? When you stay over for the party?' I said conversationally, indicating the coffee press.

I cooked her favourite poached eggs and served them on a thick slice of ham. She finished several cups of coffee but little of her breakfast before going upstairs to dress. The mother of a friend was driving them both to school. Dolly had not invited me to go along, and I had not asked.

*

David was covering for me at work so I could be home when Dolly returned with her results later that morning. I was sitting in the kitchen and heard the slam of the car door outside. She appeared in front of me and dropped a large envelope on to the table. I reached for it, but she waved me away with some irritation.

'Oh, don't worry, I've done it,' she said to me, warily, as if in defence against a challenge. She looked very tired. Or perhaps it was relief on her face, I couldn't be sure. 'I've got eight As. And one B.'

I could not allow myself to be proud, as it suggested I shared some responsibility for my child's achievements. But I was filled with something like awe. I automatically reached for her.

'Dolly,' I said, speaking into her neck, as she released herself from my embrace, 'that is incredible. Well done!' And she smiled, but she was silent, and when she sat back down at the table, she exhaled through her nose. It was the soft little sigh that Ma had begun to make as she aged, whenever she took a seat or stood up from a chair.

'I didn't even study. I didn't do anything for this,' she said. Her voice was flat.

'Dolly! You worked very hard. All those evenings revising . . .' I said.

'I hardly ever revised. On those nights. Or at all, in fact.'

I thought she was making a kind of confession and my reply was intended to comfort her. 'Dolly, you have done really well. You should be proud of your results,' I said. She remained silent. I could not tell what was happening. 'Dolly?' I said, too sharply, and she looked up, surprised I was even there.

She was not confessing anything to me; she was really talking to herself, and I happened to be in the room. Interrupted in her thoughts, she kept her gaze fixed on me. Her face had a burning concentration that I had not seen on anyone before. When she spoke, her voice was low and controlled, the same unchanging and unmoved tone as a doctor relaying bad news.

'It's all so easy, Mummy. So fucking easy. It all just . . .' She snapped her fingers together and they made a satisfying, noisy *click*, like a shot going off. She leaned back in her chair and looked past me, up at the ceiling. 'Why do you struggle? What is it that you find *so* difficult?' Her voice broke a little on the final word. 'If I listened to you . . . if I lived like you do . . . I would be too scared to do anything.'

'We're different,' I told her. My voice, even to my own ears, sounded flatter than usual.

'You are even worse than I thought. Because this' She gestured around her and then to the window – 'it's so easy! So simple! And you can't even do it.'

'I like my life, Dolly,' I told her.

'This isn't living. It's . . .' She paused, then spat out the last word like something filthy: '*Small*.' I had never seen her so furious. I had never seen her angry, I realised. Surely, I thought, surely, she has been angry before. Had I missed her anger, or had she deliberately kept it from me; another secret my child could not trust me with?

I found, though, that I was telling the truth. I did like my life, and I did not want to live like her, or like Vita, however easy they found it. Everything came effortlessly to them, and was therefore replaceable and without value. Dolly does not know if she has it in her to struggle, I thought. Or even to try hard at something, or with someone. She does not know what it is to be misunderstood, or disliked, or simply not adored. When I put my hands on my plants, or immerse myself in Sicilian culture, I am gifted with something more than I really am. The awkwardness of being no longer exists when I am part of these other worlds and aligned with something bigger. I would rather be a tiny person who wonders and trembles at their surroundings than rule over everything, manipulate it to my preference, and in doing so, come to despise it.

Dolly left the house and went next door, with her results paper in her hand, without saying goodbye. And although I heard her come home later that night, when I was in bed, she never really returned to me.

Vita put a note through my door explaining that Fridays were not good for dinner any more, that she would be in touch when things were less chaotic. That was the word she used: 'chaotic'. And I returned to my previous routine, to the life I had once lived without them.

After her results, Dolly was at home much less. When I asked about where she had been, she would answer that she had spent a few days in town, even though this was not always true. If I challenged her or Vita about the presence of Rollo's car, or about a brief local sighting of them when they had claimed to be in London, they were both flippant in response. They had always just been briefly home before leaving again, they would assure me in turn. Even if their stories varied, their unflustered demeanour was identical. Typically, Dolly came home in clothes that I did not recognise. She had always been fastidious about her possessions, but that summer she seemed to develop a perverse pleasure in leaving new items on the floor of her room, sometimes only wearing them once or not at all, before abandoning them to the discarded pile under her bed. Eventually, I collected them all up and washed everything that was not made of an exotic material. I took everything else to be dry-cleaned. By the time she returned home to pack for the garden party weekend, the Cellophane-wrapped items all hung pristinely in her wardrobe; the hand-washed items were folded in her drawers. She did not mention any of this, and I found that I did not, after all, want to discuss my domestic efforts or her new clothes, either.

On a Saturday morning late that summer, Dolly was at home preparing for another weekend in London. We stood in the kitchen while I made her breakfast. She wore a short shift dress that I had not seen her wear before, and I thought it too short to wear for anything except perhaps the beach. Did people wear dresses on the beach? Vita's clothes, too, had come to seem like something non-functional; the style that I had once admired now looked to me to be primarily impractical. Since working with Vita, Dolly had stopped wearing the oversized fluffy jumpers and the tight-fitting jeans that she had once spent hours shrinking in the bath. She had begun to dress fashionably and uncomfortably, and as if she were pleasing someone other than herself. She was dressing to another person's requirements, something I have never been able to do. I wonder how it would feel to satisfy someone's aesthetic wants so effortlessly, to know intuitively what was expected and what would appeal. The King, certainly, would have liked me to know such things; and then, presumably, to care for them, too. His second wife dresses like his mother; both women are as clean and tidy as good nurses.

Dolly's silver-blond hair was pinned up neatly. She had painted thick black stripes along her upper eyelids, which extended their natural line and gave her a watchful look. When Dolly was still a child, a fox moved temporarily into our garden. He lived, for one winter, in a hole under the shed that had been there and empty for years. We had assumed that he was injured because he first appeared looking awkward and thin. He only appeared in darkness, slinking in and out of our garden occasionally, with his shoulders held high and his head down low, like a criminal, ready to bolt when necessary. But at our last sighting of him, some months later, he was glossy, and his bones were no longer visible. Looking at my sharp-eyed teenage daughter, I thought that perhaps the fox was not injured after all, but was instead very young and growing into himself under our gaze. I was glad, just then, for each plate of milk and dog food that I had carried down to the end of our garden every night that winter.

'Do you want to go to London, Dolly?' I asked her, only half-turning as I stood at the counter buttering her toast. 'You look tired. You could stay in with me instead,' I pointed out, as if she did not already know this. I handed the toast to her.

She gave it back. 'Crumpet toast, Mummy, please.' This was what she called toast buttered twice; once hot, so the butter disappeared from the surface, and once when cooler, so it remained visible in raised yellow stripes.

As I finished buttering the toast, I felt her resting her chin lightly on my shoulder, and she stood there silently for a moment. She put one hand on my head, stroked the hair that was a thinner version of her own, and I wondered if she was thinking of this similarity between us, unalike as we were in every other way.

'If I stayed here this weekend, Mummy, what would we do?' she asked eventually, in the encouraging and slightly dreamy tone she had used when she asked me for stories as a child.

'What do you want to do? We'll do whatever you like,' I told her.

She put down the plate of toast, opened the fridge and took out a Tupperware box of leftovers. 'Mashed potatoes? Is this tonight's dinner?' she asked.

'Yes. And it is mainly potatoes, but essentially that is vegetable soup,' I corrected her.

'With white bread?'

'Yes,' I said. 'And vanilla custard afterwards . . . I could do cheese and crackers.'

And she laughed quietly to herself. I felt her tense and draw back from me; she straightened up and shook herself as if getting rid of something.

'I miss you here,' I said.

She looked at me closely and smiled. 'I'll be back on Tuesday – let's watch our programme together,' she said. 'Just us.' She said the last phrase sternly and pointed at me, as if I regularly populated our evenings with various people and needed to be warned against this habit.

'OK, Dolly. That would be lovely,' I told her.

'Off to work, then.' She left the kitchen, and I heard the front door close quietly behind her. As always, once I heard the door close, I went to the bay window in my front room. From there, I could discreetly watch the three of them getting into Rollo's second car.

Rollo opened the passenger door in a sweeping and deferential motion, as if making up to a spouse for a recent oversight. My daughter received all attentions without acknowledgement; they were, after all, what life had accustomed her to, and Rollo's courtesy was no different. She took her seat in the queenly and elegant way she did with her grandmother, with me, with everyone who offered her something. And, because she was both lovely and beloved, everybody did.

evie-loves-the-water

EVERY AUGUST, DOLLY'S GRANDPARENTS HELD A GARDEN PARTY at their rambling farmhouse. The themes varied and often expanded to include an event or achievement within the family. The year the King remarried, for example, the marquee at the garden party was decorated with white flowers and photographs of the couple on their big day. When Dolly was born, the subsequent party had a pink theme and a baby announcement card on each table. That summer, the party was celebrating Dolly's GCSE results, and there were many pink balloons and shiny silver banners announcing: 'Congratulations!'

The day of the party was unnaturally bright, and I knew that Richard and Bunny would insist all the guests stayed outside in their large and beautifully kept garden. I grimly prepared for what would be a day of discomfort, choosing a long-sleeved white shirt, loose blue skirt, dark glasses and a wide-brimmed hat. This, although I antici-pated that the other women would wear large pieces of jewellery and tight-waisted sundresses, some with bare shoulders, building on their already established tans.

A hat is correct etiquette for all formal occasions, of course and, on behalf of Edith Ogilvy, I would privately count the number of women who did not wear one. I knew some of them would be noting my oddities in conversation and behaviour; perhaps later they would bring them to Bunny in cupped hands with their heads bowed, little offerings to the mother of the King.

Dolly wore a boxy hat with a white ribbon, a navy dress, and a single strand of pearls. All of these were chosen and bought by her grandmother; they were too solemn for a young woman and resembled the formal wear Bunny herself favoured. But my daughter was still radiant, without make-up and wearing her hair loose under her hat. The incongruously mature style of the dress and necklace only emphasised her young face. We circled each other in our little hall awkwardly before we left home, unused to attending formal events together. That is, I was awkward, she was entirely relaxed and unfazed. A party at which Dolly would be the star turn was only another pleasing diversion for her; she would navigate the smiling faces without effort or concern. She was naturally gracious – was so even before Vita and Rollo – but her social ease had flourished even further since she had been working with them both. She would accept the afternoon's kisses and congratulations with the same sweetly bemused air Vita would have done. If the party had been for anyone but my daughter, I would have preferred not to attend at all. I did not want to see the King talking to his pretty wife, or Richard and Bunny greeting impatient friends, all of whom work to the same rapid and unfathomable script.

But I could not miss a party for Dolly. I could already imagine her wedding. The guest list would be the same as today, because Richard and Bunny would arrange it all and their people must be kept happy. I would pace my hall as I was then, and my mother-of-the-bride outfit would also mirror today's effort, being technically appropriate but not quite right.

I had hoped Rollo would be able to take us to the party, but he and Vita were going to the farm straight from London. Vita had apparently been reluctant to go without Dolly, but Bunny insisted that Dolly spent the day before the party at the farm to help with preparations. So, without Vita next door, Bunny had to drive over to the house to collect us. 'My friends don't want to see you two getting off the bus,' she had insisted with a high-pitched laugh and an unsmiling face. And she held the passenger door open to Dolly, as deferential as a chauffeur. I sat behind them and listened to them talking, interested as always in what it was that they discussed together. My daughter never spoke about her grandmother, but Bunny talked to me about Dolly whenever we met, her eyes sharp and her voice hopeful with the possibility that she knew something that I did not. Those were conversations in which I was grateful for the blankness of my expression. Even Bunny, with her watchful eye, could not know from my inscrutable face what I was hearing about my child for the first time. The Land Rover's engine rumbled collusively above the sound of their voices as I listened. All I could discern was that Bunny was asking questions and Dolly was answering them briefly, looking out of the window, which muffled her voice further. When we arrived at the farmhouse, Bunny turned off the engine and sat motionless for a moment, allowing Dolly to admire the large porch, which had a pink and white flower arrangement built in the shape of an archway.

Dolly leaned across the seat to kiss her grandmother on the cheek.

'Well,' she exhaled. 'The house looks very pretty.' Her voice was restrained, correct, and entirely empty; both the tone and phrasing were recognisably my own.

Bunny and Dolly went through the open side gate hand in hand, the older woman now an infant led by my daughter. I followed them through into the garden, where the rest of the King's family were waiting. They were a handsome group, a living demonstration of what a comfortable life, good genes and focus can accomplish. My daughter was moving purposefully towards her grandfather and the King, no longer allowing Bunny to guide the reveal of each party detail. However, even without Dolly at her side, Bunny continued to gesture around her like a wilting game show hostess, as though to point out the open-sided canvas tent, with the buffet and the bar laid out underneath, and the uniformed staff fussing around both areas. Dolly embraced Richard and her father before moving to her stepmother. As the woman raised her arms to return Dolly's greeting, I noticed her distended stomach pulling against her dress and I flinched, stumbling slightly backwards on the even grass. The group turned to look at me in collective acknowledgement, and I held up my palm, a sign that could be interpreted as either *hello!* or *stop!* Then I found I was walking into the house and through the kitchen, while Bunny shouted helpfully after me that *you needn't go indoors; guests are using the gardeners' lavatory over there. Over there, Sunday!*

The downstairs loo is at the side of the farmhouse, and from there I could hear cars pulling up on the gravel and the voices of guests as they moved into the garden, strangely hushed as they presumably scanned for people they knew. Vita's voice carried through the loudest, clear and authoritative, and she sounded as if she were hurrying a less enthusiastic Rollo along, although they were not late. I took off my shirt and sat on the floor. My mind and my body were on fire and there was not enough water in the whole lake to put them out.

An insistent rapping on the door was followed by a voice saying, 'Are you ever coming outside?'

I thought it was Vita, but when I finally stood up and opened the door, Dolly was standing there. I was ashamed by my disappointment; I had spent little time with Dolly that summer. I imagined future birthdays and Christmases, long summer holidays, where Dolly had other commitments, with people she did not yet know. And now I would also be sharing her with another new little person. One who was half the King and would naturally have his charm.

'Mummy, why are you . . . ?' She gestured at my half-dressed body. Then she shook her head, dismissing the query. 'Vita's here. And Rollo. Are you coming out to see them?'

'Yes. Dolly, you didn't tell me . . . she . . . is pregnant?'

'No. What do you think?' She was watching my face intently and her words were flat, as though scripted and read aloud for the first time. She sounded again like her own impression of me. 'Vita thinks the baby should have a name with my initials, and Daddy agreed.'

'I am very happy for you.' This was the proper tone of a party conversation at the King's family home, measured and polite. Although the fact that I was dressed in only a bra and a skirt probably negated the propriety of our talk. I tried to add the words, *A little brother or sister for you!* but I found that I could not, after all, say this. Dolly returned to the garden alone without either of us mentioning that I was crying.

Soon afterwards, there was another knock on the door.

'Are you coming out? Dolly says you aren't in the party mood.' Only Vita would use a phrase like 'party mood'. She *was* the party. 'I met Alex,' she continued cheerfully. 'Quite pretty, darling, but God, how dull!' Her tone was conversational, as if we were face to face; she spoke in a loud voice, which any of the visiting strangers or the King's family might have overheard.

I opened the door. Vita was in a bright red dress. Her delicate matching hat featured a red-netted veil that obscured and exposed her face in a contradiction of modesty. I had missed her face intensely, I realised, as I found myself examining the netting between my fingers. Her lips, too, were painted bright red, which I liked very much on her. She did not move, but instead stood patiently while I traced my fingers along the trim of her hat, feeling the peculiarly soft and inflexible veil. No one else, even Dolores, would ever have let me do this; no one has ever stood in a comfortable silence while I patted their hat, their hair, their clothes. Concentrating on the feel of the veil beneath my fingers made the heat and the noise less fierce.

When I finally dropped my hands, she moved past me into the little room. 'Your face!' She giggled cheerfully. 'Here, let me sort you out. And, by the way, that is the ugliest bra I have ever seen. Where would you even buy something like that?' She lifted her dress, showing her entire body, but pointing at her bra, as if the rest of her were somehow irrelevant. 'Look, Sunday, this is a bra.' Her underwear was lace and satin, small and navy blue. Her breasts rose above her bra in the same unhappy way that her hips and legs appeared to be escaping their own encasement, as if in discomfort from a rapidly decreasing space.

I sat down on the loo and shuddered, considering her underwear as I had never considered the appearance of my own, which I selected solely on the grounds of the soft material and the pale colour.

'I think your bra, and your knickers are terrible. I would never wear those.' 'Terrible' was another word I had acquired from Vita. As a result, our conversation often sounded like that of excited children; we threw around the most dramatic and pleasing words we could conjure without regard for accuracy.

Vita laughed cheerfully and stuck out one hip in an overblown pose, her body still exposed. I remembered her in my kitchen, weeks ago, the pleasing lack of concern over her milk-covered lip. I knew, of course, that the King's wife would also wear this sort of underwear, of the type designed for the pleasure of the spectator, rather than the comfort of the wearer. Perhaps that was why I disliked it, not just for the imagined discomfort it conjured. I had resisted wearing anything the King suggested. The few such items he had bought me seemed intended for someone else, for a smaller and more obliging kind of wife, perhaps, while I was the kind who was more sensitive to the pinching and painfulness of the little pieces than to his aesthetic requirements. Suddenly, I was very tired and thinking only about the cool familiarity of my home. I had left all the curtains drawn, as I often do at times that are both demanding and bright, and it means the day never quite gets through.

Vita filled the sink and floated several tissues in the cold water. She produced a large make-up purse from her handbag; she selected several items, which she lined up on the sink, as efficient as a doctor preparing for surgery. She placed the cold tissues lightly over my eyes and cheeks, leaving me in a cool darkness. Then she waited for some minutes, while I felt the coolness soothing my skin. She chatted easily and without pause about the guests outside. No response was sought or required, so I let her words float past like music, as I did when I listened to Mr Lloyd in the farm shop. I received only pieces of information. There was a woman wearing a silk floral dress that Vita coveted; another wearing sharp-heeled shoes, which kept getting stuck in Bunny's prized lawn. Rollo had already apparently rescued the inappropriately shod woman twice while she floundered ridiculously on the spot. It was with some pleasure that Vita described how the woman's arms flailed about while her feet were restrained as if in cement.

'I mean; is she a *child*? Who would wear those shoes to a *garden* party?' Vita sounded genuinely perplexed by the error.

Of course, Vita would have dressed correctly for any event. And she would have done so without recourse to an etiquette guide like mine. Edith's book had schooled me on dress, but what I knew was learned and not innate. *Flat shoes on a yacht and knee-length fitted boots for hunting; the leather of the latter would be clean but gently worn. If the boots are too pristine, it would suggest that they were bought for the event, and flaunting the newness of belongings is always vulgar. Ostentation, in dress as in manner, must be avoided above all else.* And if Vita did not wear the right thing, she would have known it, and she would have found it funny, as she did when she sat on the doorstep on our street, clad in a silk robe and my work boots, with a cigarette in her hand. And that, then, became something quite different, for it was a wrongness that was enchanting and not at all common or gauche.

I thought of the woman outside, who was in the wrong shoes, but did not know of her error until she began to sink slowly into the lawn. Perhaps she caught her husband's gaze as she began to drop downwards; at the same moment, they might have realised: *Oh, no!* The other guests would know, as Vita did, that the woman had made a mistake, that she had dressed inappropriately. And the woman would give herself away when she did not laugh unselfconsciously, as Vita would have done. Instead, after several miniature descents, the woman would blush, apologise and limp awkwardly to a nearby chair; she would refuse to leave her seat until the party finished and she could walk, barefoot and shame-faced, to her husband's car.

Vita talked and talked and did not pause for replies. Her voice in the darkness and beneath the cool was again like pleasant background music. My throat and chest began to expand back to their proper capacity, so that I could breathe again; it was as if Vita's words had brought in the air I needed. It was like being back with Dolores.

Eventually, Vita stopped talking and put her hand on my shoulder. 'I am going to take the tissue off now, darling,' she warned, as gentle as a mother. Not my mother, but a mother. Light flooded in like a blind being snapped open, and I was back in the loo at the terrible party. She began to apply her make-up to my skin, her cool fingers moving lightly across my face. Her hands

246

were always cold, which was a gift she had. However, the light could not be properly dimmed, even by Vita. It made me as uncomfortable again as one of my failing plants; hot and overexposed. Always, there is too much light.

'You do know, Sunday, don't you? Rols spoke to you, didn't he?'

'About what?' I asked, adjusting to the too-brightness, which must be endured.

'That he and I . . . that we care about you. Greatly.' She shook her head minutely. 'Forget it. Move on!' She pointed to the door. 'I'm going!'

'He and I care about you. Greatly. Forget it. Move on. I'm going. We care about you. Greatly. Forget it. Move on. I'm going,' I mouthed the words back to her, only just audibly, and she drew back at first. She gasped and her hands went up to her mouth. Then she put her arms around me for a moment in a tight hold that was unlike her usual, easy embraces.

Outside in the garden, the King and his pregnant wife waited.

We went through the double French doors together and Vita took me to the marquee, where a breeze moved through the rolled-up canvas sides. She ordered us both champagne and ordered me to drink mine as fast as she downed her own. Then she asked for two more glasses and advised me to sip this one; she was already on first-name terms with the barman, and I imagined she would be the first to be served if a queue appeared later on.

Dolly appeared at Vita's side.

'You haven't spoken to Daddy yet, have you?' She smiled at me and then at Vita. 'Vee, tell her she needs to say hello.'

'Of course, darling. We'll go over now, won't we, Wife?' said Vita as she took first my arm and then Dolly's too.

As the three of us made our way towards the King and his wife, Rollo joined us, falling into step on my other side. He greeted me uncharacteristically quietly, as if we were in an organised and covert operation that demanded we did not draw attention to ourselves. He was tanned and handsome in a pale linen suit with an open-necked white shirt. I had never seen him without a tie before. I felt I had caught a high-ranking officer out of uniform, mid-change and exposed. The King, of course, intuited that we were making our way over to him, and he turned smoothly, as though performing a rehearsed camera close-up, to acknowledge our approach. I admired his face again; my knowledge of him has not diminished his beauty.

'Sunday!' The King leaned in towards me. I was apparently further from him than he realised, and so he was forced to step further forward after his first kiss, and even on his second attempt, he did not quite make contact with my cheek. 'Vita. Rollo. So how are you all enjoying being neighbours?'

'We feel very lucky.' Vita's speech was clipped and direct with him, more like my own than her usual excitable chatter. 'Sunday is fantastic. We don't *ever* want to move.'

'But Dolly tells me you are all off again soon?' The King was gleeful, as if the move were his own idea and he were in charge of Vita's housing arrangements himself.

'Well, we will go back to town, yes. But now we have Sunday, so we will be coming back to visit.' She had not mentioned Dolly as a reason for returning, and I glanced over to make sure this had not been noticed. Dolly was smiling and must have been unconcerned. Vita put an arm on my shoulder then and leaned in to me; her small-ness making me the mother of that pose. 'And we have the house until October, so there's really no rush,' she continued. Vita remained brusque, still an elegant version of me, and Rollo took over with his easy charm, chatting to the couple about the housing market in London.

'And I hear you'll be busy yourselves soon, too?' Rollo said. He was careful to reference the fact he had been told; he could not insinuate that the pregnancy was visible, had still not named it directly. He was a joy to propriety and convention; Edith Ogilvy would have loved him as I did.

The presence of the King overshadowed not only Rollo's pleasant looks but those of all the men there. It felt disloyal to note that Rollo looked more feminine next to Dolly's father; he was smaller in feature and build than the King. And Rollo's eyes were enlarged by his thick glasses; the King has long eyes that seem to narrow in displeasure only with me.

'You have to eat whatever you crave,' I told the King's wife, who was listening to the two men in silence. She didn't respond, so I repeated loudly: 'Hey? You need to respond to your cravings. Whatever they are.' She and the King both looked at me, but still she did not speak, so I continued, my words expanding to fill the silence. 'Sicilians say that a pregnant woman must feed all her cravings. If the woman ignores her desire for something, her baby will be disfigured by the lack of that food. For example, a woman who does not ask her neighbour to share the fish she can smell cooking will have a baby covered in scales. You must always ask for whatever you want.' But you can only ask for things and not for people, I found myself thinking. You did not ask for my husband. And I would not have shared him if you had.

The King's wife took what she wanted, but not in the Sicilian way. And I wanted to believe it was solely her quiet theft that had damaged me, and not the King's desertion, not his continuing disdain. As I fell silent, I began to feel that pregnancy was perhaps an inappropriate subject for polite conversation. I remembered, too, how the King's face always hardened when I spoke about Italy, and I could feel myself reddening. I found I was unable to look at him, did not want to see his mouth tighten and his eyes turn dark and flinty.

'Yes, I've heard that, too,' said Vita, patting my back gently. 'Excellent advice, Sunday. And did you follow that when you were pregnant with our lovely Dolly, too?'

It pleased me that she referred to Dolly as *ours* in the King's presence, as if he had no claim or involvement but was merely an onlooker. When I was pregnant with Dolly, my behaviours and decisions were no longer entirely my own. I believed sometimes that I was a vehicle being driven around by the tiny person working inside me. It made pregnancy tolerable, enjoyable even. It felt like turning off the switch to a machine that requires enormous and exhausting amounts of energy to power. People who perform on instinct do not keep vast libraries of information in their heads. They do not concentrate in company as if taking an important exam. They do not need to shut down frequently and turn off all the lights to find relief. And even then, find that peace does not often come.

The King's wife was watching Vita uncertainly, with her white-gloved hands crossed over her rounded stomach as if in protection. Of course, the King's second wife would be correctly dressed; her gloves were immaculate, and her hat was becomingly trimmed with real flowers. The rest of the group, though, looked at Vita with smiling faces. She was a good friend; being married had not, ever, been like that. The King never helped me along with conversation as she did. He laughed at whatever I said for the first year we were together, and after that he would flinch and hold his mouth in a pinched line when I spoke, as if he believed a demonstration of his own silence would silence me, too.

'Yes,' I replied earnestly. Although what I had truthfully wanted most for myself when pregnant was the King. And he was not for me; not then, or ever. The King's wife was looking up at him and had taken hold of his hand, but his gaze was fixed on Vita, who was especially pretty when wearing the hard, glinting smile that she reserved for new people. I did not want to be on the King's arm, as his wife was, ever again. I had already been round-bellied and dull and had lived only for a brief glimpse of his affections. They all remained quiet, perhaps waiting for me to continue, but I found I could not speak further just then.

'Well, of *course* you did, Sunday.' Rollo's voice was raised and lightly bewildered. He seemed somehow affronted, as if defending me against an accusation. 'You're a *wonderful* mother. Wonderful.' He smiled reassuringly at me before turning to the King and his wife. 'And you must both be very excited about the baby,' he said. 'Congratulations!'

'Congratulations', that word that covers so many situations and that I cannot use in conversation, because it requires both substantial consideration and in-depth prior knowledge. People seem thrilled to hear it in the proper context, but this term demands an understanding of their very private desires. How can you always know that they even want the outcome for which you are congratulating them? What if they are embarrassed by the specific change and you draw uncomfortable attention to them by celebrating it? It is impossible to know another person's unspoken wants, and, conversely, to guess at their secret horrors, too.

Rollo raised his glass and we all looked at the King's wife, who held up her glass limply in response. She was lovely in a clean and uncomplicated way, with her shiny skin and her square, white teeth. I imagined she smelled permanently of soap and laundry. She would give birth naturally and without complaint, returning to her normal self within moments of the baby being born; or at least, that is what the King would expect. That was what he had presumed of me, too. His second wife would not need to be restrained by a team of sharp-fingered nurses under fluorescent lights, as I had once been. *To prevent you from injuring yourself*, they said afterwards, when they saw me examining the bruises they had left behind.

I imagined the new wife instead, lying in a calm and gently lit ward, being presented with a baby blanketed tightly into a bee-shaped thing. I found myself hoping that she would instantly know the little face, as I had known Dolly's. That she would immediately realise, *Of course it's you! Where have you been? I have been waiting, always, for you.* I hoped the King would hold the baby, often, as he had not with Dolly; that the warm and trusting weight of his second child would furnish him with a tenderness so substantial it would include his girl-wife, too. I wished her the version of the King I had once faithfully believed in, but had never actually known.

Rollo and the King were deep in conversation about obscure farming techniques. Rollo said things like: 'Well, of course horses should never be allowed near agricultural ground.' To which the King would quote a statement made by his uncle, which negated this theory. Then, as the King recommended another farming approach, Rollo would politely detail how European farmers would disapprove of it. They sounded like schoolboys competing for the superiority of their beloved fathers. Or perhaps this is how wealthy people argue, I thought. They come at it from behind another person and are not required, then, to acknowledge their own differences with one another.

Vita was talking to the King's wife, recounting a friend's experience as a new mother, '. . . for years, yes. She's called Annabel,' she was saying. I stiffened uncertainly at the name. 'A lovely girl, a great friend, but, oh . . .' She shook her head gravely and paused to inhale deeply through her nose. After breathing out a long sigh, she spoke again, in a quieter tone. '. . . Really changed by the whole thing.' She tilted her head and widened her eyes, as she did when granting an intimate confidence. '*Really* changed,' she mouthed.

Wah-lay charng-ed, I repeated to myself, silent and self-soothing.

The King's wife had leaned closer to listen intently, as to a warning. But Vita was already smiling again, and she continued in her own louder and cheerful voice: 'Of course, she couldn't walk for weeks afterwards! Still wets herself when she laughs . . . which she doesn't do much, admittedly, now, because she is so tired. Baby has colic, you see. Screams all the time. Gosh, well, motherhood! But you' She paused here, to inflict her most winning smile on the woman – 'you will be an absolute *natural*, darling. It's *such* a blessing.' She paused again, grim-faced now. 'Isn't it?' Her question met with silence for a moment. Then, as the woman began to speak, Vita patted her arm. 'I know, I know,' she said in a very soft voice, quite unlike her own. Then she smiled brightly at me in the manner of a nurse transitioning from a broken patient to one who was both fully recovered and appreciative. 'Come on, let's go and get drunk.' She looked at the King's wife. 'Oh. Sorry. I would ask you to join us, but . . .' She pulled an exaggeratedly sad face and gestured broadly around the woman's midsection, the circles covering a vast area many times larger than her actual stomach. As we walked away, Vita carried on over her shoulder. '. . . Congrats to you, though! Best of luck!'

The King's wife was smiling uncertainly as she shrank into the distance behind us, blinking hard as though dazed by the sun. She appeared misshapen from afar as she had not close up. She became a rounded circle of a person, a planet with thin and weightless limbs. The King took one of her white-gloved arms firmly in his own, as if anchoring her, and I imagined her circular figure, filled with air and not with a sibling for my daughter, floating balloon-like as he attempted to hold her down, alarm distorting his lovely face.

Vita took my hand as we walked towards the bar and linked her fingers through mine. 'What a drip! God! What was he *thinking*, darling?'

While Vita got us drinks at the bar, I sat down at one of the tables, which all featured stiffly posed flower arrangements. I stroked the roses, which were real but might as well have been plastic. All were entirely without smell and their precise uniformity in colour and size marred any natural aesthetic. I had offered to pot up some plants for the tables, which could have been given as party gifts later to the departing guests, or planted up in the garden after the party, creating a new flowerbed to mark the celebration. Bunny declined: allowing me to dress the tables would have caused great offence to the local florist, who would also be attending the party.

When I looked up from the unscented flowers, I recognised the woman seated opposite me. Carole was another guest who my daughter probably would not know; I expected she had received an invitation purely on the strength of her regular and generous patronage of the farm shop.

'Beautiful flowers, aren't they? And Dolly looks lovely,' Carole said brightly to me, her eyes fixed on my daughter, who was some distance away and posing for a photograph with her grandparents, one on either side of her.

'Yes,' I said.

'Like my Evie. Evie-loves-the-water,' she told me in a confidential tone, as if the other party guests were waiting for precisely such information but she had chosen to gift it to me. Carole had two adolescent daughters whose existence dominated all her conversation. When she spoke about them, she acquired the look of an aged widow recounting something lost. She described her daughters in sentimental and disjointed fragments, as if trying to make sense of confused memories. Sometimes, when she came into the shop and talked about the girls in her intense and searching way, I found myself uncomfortably convinced that one of them must have recently died or

255

met with some other tragedy. Their lives, though, seemed to remain entirely free of excitement or even interest.

'Evie loves the water?' I repeated, as if for clarification, but actually in order to create some time to craft an appropriate response. Did this woman want me to tell her about one of Dolly's activities in return? Other mothers typically required a show of returned interest in their own offspring, rather than facts about my child. Normally the stories were more carefully crafted, however, in both structure and subject. A child who liked water was so routine that I was unsure how to proceed with this conversation.

'Yes, she does! She is *such* a swimmer. I expect Dolly has told you all about it, though.' Her eyes returned from the distance to focus on me. It created an uncomfortable feeling. The assumption that Dolly, unprompted, would tell me about a girl I did not know and who could swim was a peculiar one. I could not recall Dolly ever telling me about any of the hobbies of her peers. Or even her own. She swam. I no longer swam. We did not need to talk about it. What was there, even, to discuss, in those facts? Carole was still watching me, and she repeated herself: 'I said, I expect Dolly swims at the lake with my girls? She'd have told you about my Evie.' Eventually, I shook my head firmly, No. *I am already full. I am full of information, of facts and words that occupy me, that overwhelm me. I do not want pieces of your life to carry around with me too*. This is what I wanted to say, but I remained silent. Carole raised her eyebrows, causing several half-circle lines to form above them and emphasising the depths of her effort with me. 'About Evie's swimming? And her competitions?' She was prompting me because she wanted an answer.

'No. No, Dolly has never talked to me about your girls,' I said, honestly, and glad to finally be dealing in facts.

'Well, of course,' said Carole, 'we can't all have that kind of relationship with our daughters. Can we?' She was smiling, but her eyes remained unaffected by the expression. So, I remained silent while I considered reparation, and I smiled deliberately widely at her as I thought. My mother always told me my facial expressions were too small, too subtle. *Smile more, try harder! Always, try harder! Why don't you try?* Only Dolores ever thought I did enough, tried hard enough. And, for a time, Vita did, too. I decided to provide Carole with some information on my reluctance to let Dolly swim in the lake with her friends. Mothers shared seemingly random facts about their lives. It was just knowing what exactly they wanted to hear back from you that was difficult.

'My sister drowned in the lake,' I told her. 'And my parents, too. Well, not exactly *in* the lake, but they all died because of the lake, anyway.' And as I spoke, the information landed, and it pained me. I realised that my voice had become very quiet, and I was muttering this to myself, so I repeated what I had said, loudly this time, and still Carole did not say anything at all. I thought I was more socially appropriate and polite than Carole, who was not even trying to respond to what I had told her, at some personal cost to myself. Under her squashy hat, I noticed her hair, which was the dull brown of a child's fat crayon. It was evenly curled, and the ends were first pinned under, and then into, the nape of her neck. It looked terribly uncomfortable, but the texture of it was fascinating. I would have liked to feel that restrained, net-like structure in my hand. 'I like your hair, Carole,' I told her. I took off my gloves and touched the loose bun under my own hat in an attempt to create the sensation of touching her coiled hair. 'I really do like your hair.'

'You two look serious,' said Vita, announcing her presence by placing a hand on my shoulder, as I had often seen Rollo do to her. She sat down and placed two drinks on the table. 'What am I missing over here?' She looked at Carole and reached out a hand to her. 'How do you do? I am Vita.' The way in which she always phrased this introduction, never contracting the 'I am', was rather grand.

Carole shook the proffered hand. 'Carole,' she said. 'Pleased to meet you.' In fact, she ought to have returned Vita's 'How do you do?' and I was pleased she did not. Neither was she wearing or holding white gloves. I cheerfully imagined Edith Ogilvy, bejewelled and ball-gowned, shuddering in distaste at Carole's omissions.

'Vita. Pleased to meet you,' returned Vita. Her expression was unusually flat, and I knew she was sharing a joke with me by copying Carole's address, acknowledging that we both understood Carole had got it wrong. 'And how do you know Sunday and Dolly?'

I was glad Vita had referred to Dolly and me as a couple. She and Dolly so often spoke of their shared plans and preferences that I, too, had found myself beginning to think of them as a pair, separate from me.

'We . . . my husband and I, we are good friends of the family. Of the Forresters.' Carole had apparently learned to pronounce the name in the way Bunny did, emphasising the first syllable, then the short pause, before quickly proceeding with the rest of the name. 'And how about you, Vita?'

'My husband' – Vita paused to locate Rollo and gestured in his direction – 'and I are great friends of Dolly *and* Sunday.' Her emphasis on the connective somehow spoke of pride in this intimacy and also expanded my small family into something far more substantial and impressive than the Forresters. 'We just think the *world* of them both.' And we grinned at each other, and I felt like a bride, as I never had.

'Sunday and I were just talking about,' Carole paused here for effect. 'My. Daughter. Evie. Evie-loves-the-water,' she continued formally and very clearly, as if announcing her child's full name to a waiting official. 'The only thing Evie loves more than her swimming is art. Since she was very small, she has always drawn foxes' heads as a circle with two triangles. It is very stylised. Very artistic. Everyone always says so.' She was looking into the distance, in that peculiar way of hers, as if recounting distant and painful memories.

I had still produced no response to this unsolicited information about a child whom I do not know personally. Swimming and drawing were routine among my daughter's friends, and it would not have occurred to me to share Dolly's participation in these activities with minor acquaintances. Would 'That's interesting?' be appropriate? People typically responded well to this.

I looked to Vita, who was nodding patiently at Carole, as if waiting for further explanation as to why she was being told about Evie-loves-the-water. But, for once, I was ahead of Vita; I knew this was the full statement.

'That is very interesting, Carole,' I said.

'Isn't it?' agreed Vita instantly. 'Fucking fascinating. Fox-heads. Imagine.' She looked at me, nodding and exaggeratedly narrowing her eyes, as if in serious con-templation. She magnified her expressions deliberately for me, I thought, so that we could communicate wordlessly, as other people did. Carole, who had been visibly startled by Vita's enthusiastic swearing, nodded slowly in response to this apparent acknowledgement of artistic talent. She was obviously glad to have been joined by someone who recognised the gravity of the discussion.

Vita took my arm showily. 'Sorry . . . er . . . Catherine? We have just seen a neighbour who we must speak to. Excuse us.' And she led me over to Phyllis, who was sitting alone and staring into her glass.

Phyllis looked up and smiled enthusiastically as she recognised us. She was wearing a bright pink hat with a collection of brownish feathers tucked into the ribbon trim. As we reached her, I realised they were chicken feathers, presumably from her own flock. Vita kissed her loudly on both cheeks, and I patted her arm awkwardly.

'Hello,' I said. 'I like your hat, Phyllis.'

She reddened but smiled, and her hands went up to her hat, patting it as if checking that the feathers were still in place. 'Do you, dear? It's always been a favourite of mine. It needed a little updating, but I'm always happy to give it an outing.'

Vita said, 'You look lovely, Phyllis. It is a very pretty hat. How *clever* of you to fix it up.' She pronounced the word 'clever' slowly, as though it were a word that might be difficult to comprehend. She leaned forward to pet something in Phyllis's lap, and they both cooed at the little creature. At first, I thought it was one of her chickens, but it proved to be one of the family of farm cats who all looked identically brown and thin. It was impossible to tell which were friendly and which wild, and so I avoided them all.

'I love cats,' said Vita. 'But Beast is so anti-social.' She smiled at Phyllis. 'He's my little dog. When his time is up, we are definitely getting a kitten.'

'I haven't seen your little dog. Where do you walk him?'

'I don't,' said Vita. 'He's too little for walks.' Phyllis was looking intensely at Vita, who had already straightened up and was shading her eyes from the sun and looking over the garden, perhaps for Rollo or Dolly.

'Has Sunday told you about her cat, Vita?' asked Phyllis, smiling up at me.

'I don't have a cat, Phyllis,' I said.

'Exactly,' said Phyllis triumphantly. 'You *don't* have a cat. You never have.'

And this was one of the reasons I loved Vita, still. The King would have walked off to speak with a more glamorous guest, leaving me frowning at Phyllis in confusion. But Vita, I knew, would solve the puzzle, gently and with a social grace so abundant that it settled on me, too.

Vita had already taken the chair next to Phyllis and was looking at her encouragingly. 'You've been here a long time, Phyllis, haven't you? I bet you know all about Sunday.' I had never told Vita about the period of guardianship that Phyllis had once held. My scrupulous silence on the matter was, in fact, evidence of my regard, but I knew it might be taken as an absence of such. This awareness, though, did not alter my need to keep it to myself. One of the qualities I loved most about Vita was her easy lack of scrutiny, so unlike the demands of other people and the offence taken when they discovered something you had not disclosed but apparently should have done, according to their rules. Vita bounced lightly in her seat like an excited child. 'Tell me about the cat. The whole story. Oooh, I love *stories*!' On the last word, she spread out both arms widely, demonstrating the breadth of entertainment that Phyllis would be providing.

Phyllis turned to Vita happily as they both stroked the cat on her lap.

'Well,' she began, turning both her hands palm-up as though opening a book, 'when Sunday was about six, she was obsessed with a story about a family who lived in a caravan. She carried the book with her everywhere and read it to anyone who would listen. She even took it to bed. She was always asking her mum, "Where is our caravan?" And we all told her that she lived in a house, instead, which she accepted. There were two children in this book, a girl and a boy. Sunday asked where her brother was, and we said that families are different, which was fine. The family in the book also had a cat, however, and this is what caused the problem.'

She paused dramatically at this point, like a newsreader looking down the lens at the scene of a tragedy, lights flashing behind him as he began to speak: *What caused the problem was . . .*

Vita touched her arm. 'Go on, Phyllis.'

'She used to ask, "Where is the cat?" Long after she gave up on the caravan and the brother. "Where is the cat?" she would ask everyone on the street. Running around as if she had just lost it.'

'How sweet!' Vita said cheerfully. 'And did she finally get a cat?'

'Oh dear, no. You didn't know Sunday's mother. Very strict, she was.' Phyllis glanced quickly at me. 'But of course, it was different then. Children weren't spoiled like they are now. You should see those Fraser girls with their dad . . . Oh, they—'

'She threw the book away,' I told Vita. 'She watched me looking for the book and finally she told me not to bother. That she had got rid of it because she could not listen to another question about it.'

Vita put both hands up. 'I know what to do! I have an idea!' As if we had found ourselves in a sudden emergency, which she was going to solve. She stood up and gestured impatiently for me to sit in her chair next to Phyllis. Then she promptly sat down sideways on my lap, her small frame warm against me. 'We should get you a cat, Sunday. Shouldn't we, Phyllis? Do you know anyone who has kittens? I know someone in town who breeds Siamese. Beautiful creatures, but you wouldn't want one in your house . . .' And already, Vita was regaling Phyllis and me with a story about a Siamese cat who ruled her friends' house, who sat at the head of the dining table during smart dinners and spat at anyone who tried to move it. This cat walked unchallenged along the long table during parties, amongst the decadent food and the crystal glasses. And Phyllis and I listened and laughed, and we both forgot instantly about my book, about my mother and all the sadness. And this was another gift of Vita's. I was no longer preoccupied by fact, by whether the Siamese actually existed. By whether he was really walking, disdainful and thin-hipped, through formal dinner settings in a smart house somewhere. Phyllis and I smiled at one another as we listened to Vita. The stories were evidence of Vita's care for us. And that had become much more important than the truth.

Waiters began to circulate among the guests with trays of champagne, and I watched as one of them handed the King's wife a narrow flute of orange juice. She took the glass from the young man without eye contact or acknowledgement, as though collecting her drink from a conveniently placed table. Her face was impassive, but

I know something that is more telling than a fleeting expression. I have learned to see inside to the repeated pattern on their hearts. It is that phrase that first woke them roughly from childhood sleep, that sudden recognition of self while in a crowded place one day that instantly set them apart from everyone else, the separation of self that both terrifies and exhilarates. The King's little bird-heart bears only his own lovely image, while his wife has a heart that reads, *I can, I can, I can*. I do not allow myself, though, to imagine Vita's bird-heart; I am not ready to look beneath the mechanical tick-tock and identify whether it is a clock or a bomb inside her.

'Speeches, I think,' said Rollo into my ear, indicating the circling waiters, straight-backed and precise as dancers. He sat down next to me, and winked at Vita, who looked back at us, unmoved. The afternoon sun cast precise shadows on her face through the hat netting. Each enlarged square framed a tiny piece of loveliness: an eye, a cheekbone, one nostril.

'Sort of,' I said. 'Really, it's just Bunny making family announcements. And bits about the farm. It will all be about Dolly and her GCSEs this year.'

Bunny was shushing people in an authoritative way; she has been chairperson of the local WI for as long as I have known her, and it is easy to imagine her in this role. She would have been one of those children who told off her classmates when they wore dirty shoes, who scolded them when they playfully swapped names to confuse visiting supply teachers. Her shyness is reserved solely for talk of her fortune, altered through marriage alone. Eventually, the spreading quiet among her guests was to her satisfaction, and she took her place next to her husband in a peculiarly showy act of deference. The King stood on the other side of Richard. He is taller than his father, with impressively square shoulders. His generically handsome face and broad smile believably cast him as an actor paid to attend, a brand representative for the Forresters. Typically, Richard thanked the attendees and then introduced Bunny, who would give a speech outlining all the family's achievements since the last party.

'Thank you all for coming today to celebrate with us,' Richard began. Then, instead of turning to Bunny, he continued to speak. 'And we have a lot to celebrate this year. Firstly, we are so very proud of our lovely grand-daughter. As many of you know, Dolly recently got her GCSE results. She was awarded eight As – eight!' He did not mention the ninth, the B grade, which surprised me. 'And, of course, the school are very keen for her to stay on for sixth form. But Dolly also found the time to get a job in property development this summer!' He did not speak in his usual jaunty way, which was structured around rhetorical questions. He spoke instead as Bunny did, in short, boastful epigraphs; it was uncomfortable to hear his wife's voice come through him. I thought she must have prepared his talk. Each of his lines was followed by a silence into which the references to family accomplishments were allowed to settle. Only when the audience begin to fidget and mumble amongst themselves did he talk once more. 'She has decided not to return to school, but to explore this new career.'

It was a summer job, I thought irritably, a couple of months that seemed to mainly involve shopping and lunches with Vita, and it was never a career. She would, in fact, be starting her A levels within a few weeks and still spoke, hopefully, of going to Cambridge eventually. Was Richard simply making up news to show off this year? Bunny should have made the speech after all; she had never lied in all the years she had done it. Surely Dolly's exam results were enough. And the baby. There was bound to be talk of the baby, I realised. Richard should have been happy enough with these facts.

He had obviously decided he had allowed enough time for the last announcement to land, and he began talking again. 'And if Dolly gets bored of London, there is always plenty of work to do back here, as you can all imagine.' He gestured at the fields around him and frowned in a stagey way. It was not amusing, but some of the guests laughed faintly, and those who resisted instead fidgeted in their seats or sipped their drinks in acknowledgement of his efforts at humour.

Vita and Rollo were drinking their champagne and watching Richard disinterestedly. They were both leaning back in their chairs with their eyes half-closed, although it was impossible to tell if this was due to the sun, the speaker or simply the length of the party. Richard looked across admiringly at Dolly, who was now arm in arm with both her father and her grandmother. 'We are thrilled for Dolly and very proud, although we will miss her terribly. Please, raise your glasses to Dolly.'

There was a general hum of approval, and Dolly stepped forward to stand next to Richard.

'Thank you, Granddad. And all of you.' She was the gracious bride I had imagined earlier, benevolent and serene. 'I would like to make a toast, if I may.' She paused demurely to look at Richard for permission and he, thrilled, nodded in encouragement. She bit her lip uncertainly before holding up her own glass. 'To my daddy and his lovely wife . . .' She paused here to share a meaningful glance with the woman who was standing, swollen, at the side of the King, '. . . And, of course, the big news – the new baby! To my brother or sister, and our growing family of Forresters!'

The guests all stood to raise their glasses in a toast, and the King, who did not normally speak at all during these speeches, stepped forward. 'To my daughter, the working woman!' he said, in a loud and carrying voice. And I realised why he did not make the speeches. Bunny and Richard, of course, knew better than most people that their son's appeal was too distracting for a shared platform. When the King continued, his eyes were on his daughter and not on the entranced crowd. 'To Dolly's new life in London!'

I became very small, perched as I was on the narrow, hard seat. I was suddenly intensely aware of my bones, my elbows pressing into my own ribs and my protruding ankle bones flat against either side of the chair legs. The Forresters all congregated at the front of the marquee together, with Dolly shining at the centre. The whole family seemed to be growing to fill the garden, joyfully expanding while I shrank.

I could not speak for some time. Rollo left the table to join a group of middle-aged men who were drunkenly playing croquet on the edge of the party, and Vita, too, went off into the crowd. Eventually, I rose and went to find Vita, who was in giggly conversation with a passing waiter.

'Vita,' I said, 'when did Dolly decide she wasn't going back to school? Why didn't you tell me? You are taking her away to live in London? Without even talking to me?' I had expected to cry when I finally spoke, but, instead, my entire body felt dry and tight, as if incapable of producing a single tear. It seemed as if there were dust floating inside me rather than blood and fluid. That, since Dolly's announcement, I had become only wood, dust, sand, hair, and bones inside skin. I had been remade, new, of everything that could choke you. And I had to speak through this dehydrated version of a real person.

Vita had a cigarette in her mouth and her eyes were closed as if in deep concentration. She smoked in the way some people drink tea, with that almost erotic surrender, with closed eyes and short, little gasps of pleasure. Interrupted, she took the cigarette from her mouth in an abrupt movement and waved away the smoke; her lips were a little paler now, but still red.

She opened one eye below the stiff red netting of her hat. 'Are you *very* cross, darling? We only spoke about it – yesterday? It was Dolly's idea; I was surprised, in fact. And you know me, I'm simply not interested in domestic arrangements, am I?' She inhaled deeply on her cigarette and opened her other eye slowly, blinking as if emerging reluctantly from a pleasant dream. After a moment's silence, she exhaled and closed both eyes again, while white smoke gently wreathed her face. I did not want to admire the way that the lashes of her closed eyes shadowed her cheekbones. She opened her eyes and flicked her cigarette on to the pristine lawn, watching it suspiciously as it died on the grass. She rose from her chair and briskly smoothed down her red dress, unsmiling. 'Not at all.'

'That is not an answer,' I said. 'You! You should give me an answer. Why would you take her to London? And without talking to me about it.'

Vita moved so close to me that I could smell her smoky breath before she spoke, and the burned sweetness of it made me blink and step back. Undeterred, she moved closer again. 'Look, darling,' she began in a low voice.

'Look, we both know you can't do what I can for Dolly. You're simply not . . .' She paused and smiled briefly. '. . . Not *equipped*, are you? So, the best thing you can do now is to be graceful about it. Smile and wave us off and be glad that she's getting the chances you can't give her.'

I stepped back again. 'She can't go. You should have spoken . . .'

As I was talking, Rollo had appeared at Vita's side. Placing one arm easily along her back, he asked, 'Everything OK?'

Vita leaned into him, collapsing slightly as if in exhaustion. 'Sunday is upset about Dolly deciding to leave.'

'Oh, of course she is. Of course you are, Sunday. It's awful when they move out, isn't it? My mother cried for days every time one of us went back—'

'Rollo,' I interrupted, 'this is not like you going away to school. Or university. Dolly is sixteen and you made these plans without even speaking to me.'

'He didn't actually,' Vita said. 'I did; Dolly and I did. And she is thrilled about it, as you saw. As I said, darling, the best thing for you is to accept this. You can come and visit as soon as we are settled.' She smiled and said lightly, 'It's up to you how long that takes. It's really up to you. It can be easy and nice, or it can be' – she wrinkled her lovely nose and exhaled sadly – 'difficult.'

'I don't want this,' I said. And then realised the phrasing of my objection somehow made it sound as if this, their plan with Dolly, was already in motion, spreading as silently as smoke across the pretty garden. And at the same time, my ability to speak was retreating again, the words I wanted slipping away from me as if I had never had language at all.

Rollo had removed his arm from Vita's back and was straightening his glasses. 'Vee, do we need to talk about this more? Perhaps we—'

Vita took his arm. 'We can talk as much as you both like. But get us another drink first, Rols.' She pointed vaguely towards the bar, and he obediently went away in that direction. She stayed silent for a moment with her eyes on her husband as he walked away. Finally, she exhaled deeply, then spoke. 'I've told you, Sunday. It's up to you how difficult you want to make this.' She smiled brightly, still looking towards Rollo and not at me. 'Let's keep it friendly. It's better for visits, isn't it?'

And I watched her move across the lawn to him at the bar and put an arm around his middle. She said something to him, and he laughed and wagged a finger at her in mock disapproval. Then she made a toast, with a teasing gesture, and he played along, raising his glass back at her and smiling. I could still see the appeal they both held, could see them as they must appear to Dolly, and I knew, if I had not already known, that I was lost.

By half past six, most of the guests had begun to leave, which was quite right. *This is the correct time for exiting a garden party that began at 3 p.m.*, Edith Ogilvy has assured me each year. *Those that start at 4 p.m. ought to finish at 7.30 p.m.* Dolly, the King and his parents lined up by the side gate, saying their goodbyes. The King's wife had already gone into the house, showily holding on to her stomach. I imagined her taking off her shoes and lying prettily on Bunny's sofa, ready to be discovered by the King when he went inside. As the garden began to clear, I looked away from Vita and Rollo, who were still relaxed and squinting into the low sun. It was uncomfortable to look at people who would not wear sunglasses in that brightness. I felt as if I were being forced to absorb the light along with them.

Eventually, Vita got to her feet and Rollo immediately followed, standing up and noisily finding his car keys in his pocket. She came over and held out a hand to me, which I did not take, but she remained beside me, apparently unperturbed. If I had not needed to get home and into darkness after an afternoon of uninterrupted brightness, I would have found alternative transport.

'Come on, Wife, I will take you home. Dolly is staying here tonight, isn't she?' she said. As we walked towards the gate, she continued: 'Will you come on Friday for a last dinner with us?'

I remained silent. But I found that, for the first time, I was not looking forward to a Friday supper with Vita, Rollo and Dolly. I would prefer to be at home, already dressed in pyjamas, and walking around my garden, checking on my plants. I no longer wanted to spend an evening next door, wearing smart clothes, and eating complicated food.

We walked down the garden to thank Bunny and Richard, and to say goodbye to Dolly. They were still in the peculiarly formal row at the gate, thanking each guest as they departed. I hesitated before joining the line. *A queue! To speak to my own daughter!* Rollo must have felt my reluctance, because he, unusually, went ahead of Vita and me. His rigid adherence to etiquette meant he typically danced around behind us, closing doors and seeing us to our seats, treating our movements like those of unpredictable children. For once, I followed him, and then submitted to perfunctory kisses from Richard and then Bunny. Even the King kissed me goodbye. I think it was the momentum of a procession of goodbyes rather than an expression of care.

When I walked away from him, he nodded and said, '*Sunday.*' His tone was abrupt, as if in dismissal rather than recall.

But I stopped anyway. 'Yes, what?' I had been surprised to hear his wife say 'Pardon?' And not 'What?' to one of the waiters earlier. I wondered what the King would think of that. Would he correct her vocabulary, as he frequently had done with me during our short marriage? He and his mother, and Edith's book, too, had schooled me to say 'what' and not 'pardon', which was banned, along with 'settee', 'toilet', 'serviette', 'lounge', and so many other words. I tried it out myself, loudly, thrilled by my little transgression: 'Pardon? Pardon?'

'It's just a way of saying goodbye. Saying someone's name like that. *Sunday*. That's all. Isn't that in your book?' He sighed deeply and looked away from me, smiling when he saw it was Vita in her pretty red hat who was the next guest in line to be thanked and kissed. I saw him unconsciously squeeze his hands open and closed as if in anticipation of holding her.

'*Arrivederci*,' I said. 'That's a way of saying goodbye.'

When I reached my daughter in the line, we both spoke at the same time, and I immediately fell silent, allowing her to speak first. Her cheeks were flushed with high dots of colour and her eyes shone. She looked like someone with a fever.

'What do you think, Mummy?' she said. 'About my news?'

'I'm worried. When did you decide all this? What has happened, Dolly?'

But she was already looking behind me, towards Vita,

who would be greeting her next, and her reply was insubstantial. 'I've been thinking about it for a while . . . a real experience . . . love working . . . wanted to surprise you . . . Knew you'd be thrilled . . .'

I thought of Vita's frequent touch on my arm, the reassuring weight of her firm hand. I reached out to pat my daughter's arm in the same way, and she looked uncertainly down at my hand as if to identify it.

'Dolly, have you really decided?' I asked. 'To leave school. To move to London.'

'Yes. I decided a while ago. We didn't tell you before because it's hard for you to go over and over it. Vita thought about it a lot. She wanted to make it easier for you.' And she lightly kissed both my cheeks. 'Thank you so much for coming, Mummy,' she continued. She kept both her arms fixed to her sides as I embraced her, which gave her an uncharacteristic awkwardness. Her gaze was behind me once more, her eyes fixed again on Vita.

'Dolly, come home tomorrow, and we can talk about it,' I said, and she nodded, although it was not clear whether this acknowledgement was for me or Vita.

Rollo walked back to me and held out a beige linen-covered arm. 'Can I escort you to the car, Sunday?' He gestured towards Dolly and his wife, already deep in discussion. Dolly had turned from me towards Vita, so I could not hear their low conversation. Rollo smiled at me, his eyes softening honestly with the expression. 'They could be some time, I'm afraid. Vee adores a long goodbye.'

It was a calming exercise, getting me to the car in the company of the Forresters and their friends. I was eyed as warily as an infant bridesmaid at a society wedding, a concern to onlookers.

When Vita finally got into the passenger seat, I told them both that I was tired, and also that she should not come to my house again uninvited. This was met with a silence that remained with us for the short journey home. When Rollo pulled up in their drive, Vita went indoors immediately and without a word to either of us. She was barefoot and must have left her shoes in the car, for she was not carrying them. Her formal dress, the high, netted hat, along with her naked little feet and the silence of the street, were disconcerting when put together. She looked as though she was emerging from an accident or in the process of sudden flight. Rollo stood on my side of the car; he opened the door for me without looking away from Vita. He, too, was watching her walk away. And perhaps he also felt something of the oddness I felt, shared my certainty that something was not right, for he did not say goodnight with the usual formal kisses that were as quick as pinches. Instead, he embraced me, resting his cheek against the side of my head and gently displacing my hat a little, as he spoke quietly.

'I do so hate the end of summer,' he breathed into the space next to me, as if addressing someone standing by my side, between us. 'It's that crushing back-to-school feeling.' Then he looked directly at me and said: 'It's not you, darling. It's Vee, I'm afraid. She doesn't think these things through. It might all change again by tomorrow.'

As he straightened up again, I patted his arm. The thin linen fabric felt damp and hot beneath my hand; he must have been terribly uncomfortable. When I was almost at my front door, he shouted something at me, and I turned. He was still standing at his car, as if he were too tired to go indoors, and he looked smaller and more crumpled than I had ever seen him. He took off his glasses and wiped them with his shirt while looking at me. They no longer seemed an endearing part of him, as they so recently had, but more a sinister piece of costume, a ploy to make him appear vulnerable and boyish where he was neither.

There was something unnatural, almost alarming, about Rollo being in any kind of disarray. Phyllis was burgled once, a long time ago. It happened while she slept on upstairs, alone and untroubled. She told me that the most difficult part of the whole experience had been waking to the unfamiliar chaos in her organised little study, of which she had previously been so proud and so particular. It felt, she said, as though she were a ghost, walking through her home after her own death. Her hands had shaken as she spent weeks reordering all her papers, and she had not known if it was fear or fury that made her tremble. I imagined Rollo looking at himself as Phyllis had looked through the disorder of her home, putting himself back together, smoothing out the creases of his suit and his forehead, touching his sad little face. The process of repair would itself cost him something, though, as it had cost Phyllis. A small but visible mark would remain, irreparable.

'What?' I shouted back at him.

He called out again, louder this time. 'I said, good-night, Sunday!'

'Goodbye, Rollo.' And I knew, somehow, that it was the last time I would ever see him.

The garden party was the beginning of an end. At least, it was the beginning for me. For Dolly, Vita and Rollo, though, the conclusion of that summer must have been ticking slowly and noisily away for some time.

The following day, I woke with a painful wisdom tooth. On the Monday, I took the day off work, knowing that David would manage on his own. I booked a dentist's appointment for the afternoon. After breakfast, I did laundry and performed other undemanding domestic jobs, still dressed in my pyjamas. When the telephone rang, I failed to get to it before the caller hung up. The shrillness of it had pierced the quiet of my house, and I was still feeling interrupted when the doorbell rang half an hour later. I opened the door to Dolly's grandparents, who stood there characteristically stiff-backed and brisk. Bunny was holding keys, which I recognised by the small, pink-haired troll doll, which hung from the keyring. It belonged to my daughter.

'Oh! You're in. Now, we don't want any nastiness,' warned Bunny, as if she had found herself unexpectedly in the centre of a fight. 'We are just going to get Dolly's things, and then we're going.'

'Hello, Bunny. Hello, Richard,' I said, trying to catch up with them. Richard nodded, but Bunny was still eyeing me warily, as if I were something interesting and unpredictable. 'Would you like a drink?' I asked. 'Why do you want Dolly's things?' I stood back, politely. 'Would you like to come in?' They remained silent. 'Where's Dolly?' I asked. I was entirely lost, but the feeling was not unfamiliar to me, and I waited for reason to catch up with the conversation, as it generally does.

'Richard. You go upstairs and pack her bedroom.' Dutifully, he jogged up our narrow stairs with two large, heavy-looking suitcases that bounced loudly on each step. 'Now, Sunday. No nonsense, please.' Bunny held up both her hands theatrically, palms outwards, as though playfully warding off a child's unthreatening blows. She was speaking slowly and carefully. 'I am going up to help Richard. I would like you to bring me whatever you can think of that Dolly might also need.'

'Where is she?' I could not tell what was happening. Was she in hospital, injured? What facts were they keeping from me? 'Will you take me to her?' I reached out to Bunny and unselfconsciously grabbed at her bare arm as if I was falling.

Bunny stepped neatly backwards, and my hand grabbed at nothing, unbalancing me, so I placed a palm against the wall to steady myself. Bunny did not move, but shouted, 'Richard!' As she called for him, she continued to stare at me in her unblinking and watchful way. She repeated herself, louder this time and even more shrilly. Richard appeared at the foot of the stairs and walked down slowly.

'Look, Bunny, I haven't even started packing. I think you should do it. It's all . . . girls' things, isn't it?' He spoke crossly, as if Dolly's gender were an unexpected complication.

'Richard,' I said, my hand still flat against the wall as if it were stuck there. Bunny stared as if afraid to move her gaze away from me. 'Please tell me what's happening. Is Dolly hurt? Is she still at yours?'

When he finally spoke, it was not in his own cheerful and questioning way. Instead, it was with the deliberately slow voice that he used with distressed and difficult animals on the farm.

'Dolly is not coming back, Sunday. Do you understand? She is going to live with us until she goes to London.' His palms were raised as if to indicate that he was not armed, was not going to fight with me. In Sicily, at a different time, I could reasonably have fought him simply if he stood during a seated confrontation. He led me into the kitchen and guided me to a chair. I sat down, and he placed a glass of water in front of me, as if my reaction had been caused by thirst. Bunny was watching from the hall, and when he joined her again, I could hear her whispering excitedly, although I could not hear what she was saying.

I might kill her, I thought. She is a small woman, and it would not have been difficult to do. By the time I had decided against this, I heard them both upstairs in Dolly's room. After some time, they appeared again in the hallway. I watched them warily from the kitchen table. Bunny was struggling nervously with the lock, an actress playing at escaping capture. Richard held the suitcases tightly, as if I might steal them, and his exaggeratedly resigned air reminded me of a debt collector I had once seen in a bad film. Bunny flinched with fresh excitement when she saw me.

'Now, Sunday. Remember what I said? No nonsense, please.' Her voice was high, and her cheeks were flushed with something like pleasure. Her body quivered visibly with expectation; I thought that just then, she could have been played to produce music.

I moved past them and raised my arm over hers. Bunny gasped loudly and drew back at the gesture, while I flicked the lock up in one easy movement. Richard tried to position himself between me and his wife, but the bulkiness of the cases and the narrowness of the hallway prevented him from doing so. Bunny, still thrilled with excitement, scuttled out of the house, with Richard following her more slowly, a case in each hand. I would not speak to them, would not please Bunny with further questions, and I would not allow them to see me standing there as they drove away. Instead, I went up the stairs and got into Dolly's bed.

The beating pain of my wisdom tooth meant I had to keep the dentist's appointment that afternoon. The kindly receptionist assumed my tears and distress were tooth-related and insisted I was treated before my allotted time and the other waiting patients.

That evening, with an anaesthetised mouth that was not yet fully under my control, I called Bunny and Richard's number. After only a few rings, Dolly answered. Her voice sounded untroubled, but when she heard my voice, she immediately hung up. I subsequently called back several times, and each time, Richard told me that Dolly did not want to talk to me, and that I was not to call again. The fifth time I called, the line was engaged, and it remained that way for the rest of the night. Catching sight of myself in the hall mirror during another attempted call, I was briefly distracted by my reflection; by the swollen eyes, the blood that had dried in grim lines around my mouth and chin, by the blue-black bruising across parts of my face that the dentist's slow and gentle hands had not touched. I looked as though I had been brutally attacked, and the appropriateness of this made my gory reflection reassuring rather than disturbing. It had been an assault of some years rather than a few moments, and the assailants were people I loved.

When I eventually slept, the post-operative painkillers brought confused dreams: Richard and Bunny, dancing closely in their garden party outfits, glided past us. *Don't make a fuss, Sunday. Forresters don't like a fuss.* My sister was there, too; she wore her swimsuit and an expression of intense interest. She was blue-skinned and dry-haired, and examining something in Vita's out-stretched hand. Rollo, without his glasses, watched them both indulgently while smoking a cigarette. I leaned in to

279

see what they were looking at, and Vita held it out to me with a smile. It was a blue evil-eye charm on a long chain, and I distinctly felt the cool roundness of it in my hand before I woke. On waking, my thoughts immediately went to Dolly. Had I done this to her? Did I watch over her too much or not enough? I trusted my child, always, more than I had myself. Perhaps that was how I lost her.

Without Dolly to come home for, I spent longer days in the greenhouses and my hands were never empty or still. I was in permanent, greedy contact with the pleasing textures, the smooth leaves, the oily earth, and the cool metal of the counter surfaces. And all these satisfied like a hunger met. With my hands muted by soil, I am pure calm. It buzzes happily on my fingers, the only sound around me. Hours pass without notice, and I do not stop for a break or for lunch unless David is there to remind me. I am a well-designed machine. This is the other world access, the sublime gift for which I would willingly pay with all that I cannot do and every face I cannot read. It would be an easy sacrifice if the choice were ever given: this visceral ecstasy or the art of social interaction and fleeting conversation. I imagine this offer, if it were made, would be posed by an immaculate man, someone like Rollo, persuasive and proper. My transformation would require drugs of a complex kind that would lessen my intensity but impair my focus, and therapies that would focus on normalisation above self-expression. I would disappear inside, my true nature trapped behind an orderly appearance of myself.

The bliss of sensory experience at a precisely set level is a rare gift, though, and I accept the price of it. I am instantly made whole when my environment is carved into manageable pieces. The greenhouse reveals itself politely to me in small slices of information. It is this morphine-like comfort that I live for, the knowledge that this is accessible to me every day. If loud noise and artificial light do not pain you, you cannot know the sublime relief of silence, of dullness. I intimately know both states; I have learned to live through the chaos and wait for the reward of stillness, knowing it will eventually come for me.

Some weeks after the garden party, I returned from work to find two front door keys on the otherwise bare kitchen table. Dolly's bedroom initially looked unaltered. How-ever, a check of her now-empty wardrobe and drawers confirmed that she had been back to retrieve the clothes that her grandparents had left behind. My only suitcase, a little-used wedding gift, had also disappeared. She had not taken any of the sentimental items – the gifts and the photographs – that I believed she would want. This, too, added to my conviction that she would be returning to live at home again soon. But the next day, Bunny came into the greenhouse. I had not seen her since she had come to my house for Dolly's things, and she had refused to update me on any aspect of my daughter's welfare whenever I called. David had just left to work outside, and I was finishing my lunch alone while I planned how best to reorganise a line of seedlings that were not settling in. It was a satisfying little problem that I was immersed in privately solving, a warm bath that I was not yet ready to get out of. Bunny walked in, and then looked around interestedly, as though surprised to find herself here, as though she had taken a wrong turning. I said nothing, but I watched her as I continued to slowly eat my sandwich, the conjured water around me rapidly dropping in temperature and appeal.

'Sunday. Hello.' She spoke slowly and deliberately, as though carefully starting an engine, and then subsequently spoke in a rush, eager to get through the question. 'I wondered if you had heard from Dolly recently?'

I found I was standing up.

'Where is she? I thought she was with you?' I said, ridiculously, as if Dolly would have remained positioned in one place, like a book or a vase. As if Bunny and I were quarrelling over the safekeeping of a simple and replaceable possession.

'She said she was going to see Vita two days ago. Not in London, but next to you. For lunch. She had an appointment with my hairdresser afterwards, but apparently she didn't go. I don't know where she is right now. Could she be at yours?'

'She doesn't have a key,' I said, remembering the two keys on the table, identical and shining.

'I've been to Vita's twice and they weren't there. I wondered if you had seen their car outside?'

I considered this. I had not seen their car for some time, and I had watched out for them. I had put the absence down to the different hours we kept.

I shook my head. 'I don't think so.'

'A friend of mine called Tom, and he told her that Vita and Rols left his house two days ago.' And I knew from the quick and dismissive way she pronounced Vita's name, and the soft, thoughtful way in which she said 'Rols', that Vita was the one she did not care for. It made sense to me that the mother of the King would fall, too, for Rollo's easy charm, yet be alarmed by the same quality in a woman. 'They have left Tom's for good, he says.

They have gone back to London. But Dolly never said goodbye.'

She paused and then spoke again. 'We had been talking about her staying on with us. To work on the farm instead of going to London. I thought she was going to stay. But she didn't need to go away like this . . . it's . . . Does she have many things at yours?' she asked.

'Nothing she cares about. Did she take everything she had at yours? All her clothes?' I asked.

Bunny considered this, 'Yes, she did. But—'

'There is your goodbye,' I told her. It did not make me feel better that she was now standing where I had stood.

I got the next bus home and walked up the path to Vita's house thirty minutes later, not knowing what I was looking for or hoping to find. I knocked on her door, went through the open side gate and into the garden. And it was Tom's house again. There was no sign they had ever been there. When I peered through the French doors and the windows, the grand paintings had all gone and, from the walls where they had hung, small children smiled hopefully back at me instead. There was a small scratching noise in the little shed near the house. I assumed a cat had somehow got trapped in there, but when I opened the door, I saw it was actually Beast. His lovely coat had developed a yellow-grey tinge, and he looked already thinner. There was no food visible in the shed, although there was a large bowl with a little water in it. I was unsure if he had been abandoned deliberately or believed lost.

I remembered Vita carrying him around her house and garden, so casually that it seemed as if she had forgotten he was even there. He, too, relaxed happily in her hold, his short legs and round head bobbing along in surrender when she moved around. I thought of her placing the little dog carefully in my arms, and of her laughing fondly at him on Friday nights in her garden as he sat on her lap and gazed up at her. She openly fed him bits of her dinner from the table, even though she furiously told the rest of us off if we did the same. Of all Vita's behaviour that summer, her apparent desertion of Beast was the one that spoke of maliciousness. It is an act that I cannot easily connect to simple self-interest. He is my dog now, and I have persuaded myself that this is what she intended when she put him into the shed on the day they left and closed the door on him.

It was easy to imagine Vita and Rollo slipping effortlessly into another new life. Lives that would be unfailingly comfortable; glamorous, even. Most of us have our vulnerabilities, those things we love that make us fragile. But not those two. It is not a security I envy.

When I think of Rollo, it is not the glamour of his smile, his lovely suits and his funny stories to which I return. I think, instead, of how he looked standing on his drive after the garden party for Dolly. He was tired and hot, the linen jacket and trousers all lined and hanging crookedly. He knew that he would be leaving Tom's house soon, and he knew, too, that they were taking Dolly with them, that she was never coming back to me. That he had made some arrangement with his wife to keep her happy, which involved Dolly living in their home and being kept expensively by them. It was another concession, similar to that he had made in leaving London after Vita took Annabel's baby. Perhaps he regularly had to remake new lives for his wife and himself. His face was sweaty and disappointed; he was uncomfortable and overdressed. That is Rollo.

I can still picture Vita, laughing as she dances barefoot on Rollo's polished brogues in her yellow dress, or red-lipped under her veiled hat in the sunshine. And I remember him arriving in the garden on those summer evenings, his arms full of Harrods boxes and his face bright and excited. Always, though, they are smiling, though I can see, now, that their eyes are not. I am unlike Vita and Rollo, unlike the Forresters, who believe love is a performance and something to be sold to an audience. And I am not Dolly, who believes that the showy affection between the King and his wife is proof of devotion.

Since my daughter was born, I have fallen asleep each night to images of her in my mind, and I wake every morning to the same thought: *Dolly!* It is how I can continue to live, now, without her, because my love for her remains constant; it is as fat as a beloved pet and receives the same frequent attention. It is more, certainly, than conjuring polite and pleasing lies for onlookers.

My feeling for my sister never recoiled from her recklessness or her endless secrets, but persist far beyond her death, as independent as a clock. After Dolores died, my mother could not give up on the lake. She continued to watch it, from a growing distance and with a feeling of unease. This unflinching connection to the lake became something to which she resigned herself, regardless of what it did to her. Ma was Walter's greatest love, and hers was the lake; each sustained their solitary devotion without asking for reciprocation. And I am more their daughter than I once believed.

I have learned that fire waits patiently and prettily inside little bird-hearts everywhere. That it behaves like light, but it burns. It burns even beneath the water and inside our homes. These fires, though, do not happen yearly and after the harvest, although they will draw you close in the same insistent way. They are not the Sicilian farmer's intense and transformative journey across an agricultural field, not *bruccia la terra*, but flames started by beloved people who want things that you do not want. When these people get the things that they want, it may just hurt you. It is not intentional, not often, but it will hurt as if it were. It will hurt like fire that lives on your skin, and it will mark you for ever in the same way. I have chosen to accept this rather than to make myself forget. So I do not have to feel the shame my mother felt for continuing to love her lake. So I can still love them.

Epilogue

1991

I immediately know I will keep the letter from Dolly, although it is brief and factual. It is worded neither as a request nor as an invitation. There is no address or telephone number to which I can respond. She recommends the brunch at a café in Lancaster, the city close to her father's farm, and announces that she will be there on a Saturday in two weeks' time. It is not quite an invitation, but more as though she is letting me know her own plans on a particular day. I read the letter through several times before deciding that I am welcome to go to the café too. When I see Bunny and Richard at work, I do not mention that I have heard from Dolly, just as they do not tell me when they visit her. We used to play a game about the King in his absence, and now we do the same with his daughter. I know when they have seen her; I do not need to be told, because when they return, they are smiling and generous and full of happy secrets. I know my child is well because they hold their knowledge of her possessively to themselves. They are shinier and lighter after these visits. They do not leak concern in worried looks and hissed whispers in the way that they would if she were troubled. She is my beloved child; I do not need the lists of her wins and achievements to share with acquaintances, as they do. I only need to see her to know if she is content. If I can see her face, I will know. I ache for the sight of her as she does not for me. She is not mine, but I am, painfully, hers.

From the café window, I see my daughter some way down the road opposite. I immediately and involuntarily raise my arms at the sight of her. I experience happiness and excitement viscerally now because I no longer hold on tightly to the compulsions and tics inside; these must be expressed to become feelings. My arms can raise and float up as they choose to, and my hands can clench and tap until they are satisfied. I do not have a mother, a husband, or even an Edith Ogilvy to please any more. I no longer resist the urges to tap, to touch, or to wave my hands, as these people insisted I should, but allow them instead to travel through me uninterrupted. I believe this surrender has, curiously, made me more still, because such twitches only multiply when they are stored up inside.

Dolly is shaking an umbrella, and I watch with fascination as she rolls it up. I marvel at the perfection of her woman's hands now just as I did when they were the fat little hands of a baby, busy and satisfied, and grabbing at nothing but air. She is marvellous. She squints towards the café as if against bright sunlight, but the day, in fact, is overcast, with intermittent bursts of heavy rain that flash and then disappear, the temper of an infant too tired to sustain his bad mood. It is unclear whether she can see me past the customers seated at the window. I am a pale-eyed, pale-haired woman dressed in grey; it is easy enough to believe she has not noticed me, despite my expansive gesturing, which I know did not go unremarked at neighbouring tables. She remains out on the street, looking towards the café, and I find myself getting to my feet, as if pulled by some invisible thread, like Rollo rising politely from the table at those Friday night dinners.

Dolly's fawn-coloured coat, tan boots and bag are smart and carefully co-ordinated. Her hair is shiny and neatly cut just above her shoulders, and her expression is soft and untroubled. There is a patterned silk scarf expertly arranged around the collar of her coat. I imagine the home of such a person: a carefully but comfortably furnished apartment, with walls painted in calming tones and just the occasional contemporary painting or oversized ornament to avoid resembling the home of her neighbours, whom she often visits for coffee or a glass of wine. Perhaps there would be a boyfriend, a regular visitor who would bring her breakfast in bed on Saturday mornings. He would not be embarrassed by any of her perceived eccentricities, by any of her interests or behaviours, but would instead value them. He would encourage her to see friends and to attend the non-compulsory work meetings that would secure her future promotions, even if she then missed his sister's birthday dinner or the new film that he would instead wait to see with her at a later date. He would listen and never silence her when she said unexpected things, expressed odd opinions. If she spoke out of turn in company, he would not see it as such. He would not kick imperceptibly at the bones of her feet under tables to remind her who he was. He would not attempt to reshape her, would not wish to do so even if he could.

She turns and walks away from the café, but her step

is slow and unhurried, as though she is early for an appointment and simply passing the time until she ought to arrive. She moves like the youngest of the Fraser girls who grew up opposite us, like the one who skipped down the street and invited distraction into her path. But she will never become that girl, who grew up to stay at home and care for her ailing mother.

If she stops, I think, if she stops or if she looks back now, she will come to me. I do not breathe when she turns round on the pavement and looks directly at me where I stand. Her gaze is easy and unconcerned, as if she has known all this time where I am and had simply been attending to something routine before returning to me. As if we have spent only moments and not years apart.

What is it to be beloved? To be like Dolly, with her surety that she will be met, always, with gratitude and love? And Vita too. If a wounded person ever failed to receive Vita with adoration, indifference would direct her pretty smile as she moved on, her eyes firmly fixed ahead. I acquired a little of Vita and Rollo during my summer with them. I know this myself, although I cannot say if others would see the change in me. A piece of their noise and their humour, something of their presence, has remained with me. It is their superficiality of feeling I have been unable to cultivate. I am grateful, now, for that stubbornness of my feeling, the triumph of love that remains even when seemingly unreturned. This is the opposite of their studied nonchalance, and it is joy.

I am disappointed when Dolly refuses my offer to get her a drink, or something to eat. It seems like the refusal of something more, perhaps an indication that she does not plan to stay long. But after a moment, she puts her hand over my yellow milkshake and slides it possessively towards her.

She sips through the straw, looking up at me as she does so. 'Yum,' she says. 'I'm going to get one of these. I'll get us cheese on toast, too. It's really good here. I don't know what they do to it, but it's great.'

I cannot look away as she moves to the counter to speak with the waitress, a girl of a similar age to her. They laugh together at something and the girl points in my direction, her eyebrows raised in enquiry.

'Over there,' Dolly agrees. The girl asks a question and Dolly smiles, says, 'Yes, my mother.' She listens while the girl speaks again, then looks back at me thoughtfully before replying. 'We are, aren't we?' she says slowly.

'Do you know her?' I ask as she sits down again.

'Sort of, I suppose. I live close by, so I come here often.' She drops her chin in an approximation of shyness and looks up at me. 'I still can't cook. Not even as much as you.' This reference to us having shared failings and shared memories puts me at ease. It somehow conveys that we can acknowledge who we were to each other, who she remains to me.

I want to ask questions until I know every moment between her leaving and then coming to this café, but it is too much, and I look at her instead, studying her face.

'How is the greenhouse?' she asks. 'Grandma said you are introducing new . . .' She pauses as if wondering how to refer to the plants I work with, before settling on, 'Things.'

'Yes, work is good. And David is still there. He's getting married, did you know?'

Dolly shakes her head. 'I did not. Grandma didn't say.'

'Well, the wedding is next weekend. I'm doing the flowers, and he's—'

Dolly looks towards the counter, where the waitress is assembling a tray. 'Is that our order?' she wonders out loud. She smiles reassuringly at me as if I have voiced concern about a perceived delay. 'I bet it is ours. They're usually super-quick in here.' The waitress approaches our table, and Dolly says, 'Here it is! Told you.' When the girl puts the tray down, Dolly takes her glass and then the two plates and arranges them carefully around us. She has ordered glasses of water, too and she places these before us both. 'There,' she says eagerly. 'Isn't it nice?'

'Yes,' I say. It is so unlike Dolly to take pleasure in this simple meal, in our being together in an ordinary café, that I laugh.

'What?' she says, smiling.

'I'm surprised by you,' I say. 'And happy. I am so happy to see your face. Your lovely face.'

Dolly talks while she eats her cheese on toast, and most of mine, too, and then she goes to the counter again, ordering us both coffee, and then immediately returning to cancel one of them when she remembers I don't take hot drinks.

'I can't drink two coffees, you know,' she tells me cheerfully when she sits down again, as if the double order had been my idea. She has a flat and a boyfriend, she says, and she describes both in terms as ideal as those I had imagined for her moments before. She is working as a land agent specialising in farm and estate sales. 'The clients can't believe that I know as much about farming as I do – that always goes down well. And I can always talk to Daddy about the things I don't know. I'm really good at it, at selling, you know. Rols always said I would be.'

'I'm sure you are. How long have you been working there?' I ask. 'Is it recent?'

'Almost eighteen months,' she says. 'I went to London when I . . . left. And it was really fun, at first, but then Vee and Rols got friendly with a couple on our street. I never knew what they saw in them. And it became very complicated very quickly, so I left them all to it. I came up here, to Daddy's farm. And he knows the owner of the estate agency, so he got me—'

'What was complicated?' I ask.

'Do you want to know about them?' she says, looking at me thoughtfully. 'I wasn't sure if you would. Vita said you wouldn't speak to her. After the party. And when she called you.'

'I never saw her after the party. And she didn't call. I want to know everything that has happened to you,' I reply. 'Why did you leave them? What happened?'

'Katie, the woman, had three little girls, all close together: twins, and then another baby just before we moved in. She's only a few years older than me, and she spent a lot of time at ours with the children. And Vee loved it at first, having the babies around, but then, after a few months, she started to lose patience with it. With the mess and the crying and the . . . reality of it all.' Dolly exhales and tilts her head conspiratorially, as if we are teachers discussing an errant, but harmless, young student. 'You know what she's like.' She takes a sip of her coffee and places it back on the saucer with an air of finality, as if that is the end of her explanation.

'But why did you leave then? Did they keep coming over?'

'Oh, well, no. Oh!' She starts slightly, as if remembering I don't know the rest of the story. 'So, Vee told Katie she couldn't visit so much and was very blunt about it. But we kept getting home, Vita and me, to find Katie there with Rols. And then Katie was having another baby. Another one!' She raises her eyebrows and smiles indulgently. 'She already had three children under three. Can you imagine, she didn't even—'

'But why did you leave?' I persist.

'Because it was Rollo's,' Dolly says patiently, as though this is obvious.

'What was Rollo's?'

'The baby. It was Rollo's baby. I just told you that.'

'He left Vita?' I could not imagine either of them without the other.

'Not at first. Well, he didn't really want to leave, and Vita tried . . . But it was impossible. Finally, he moved in with Katie and the girls.'

'Poor Vita,' I say. 'He lives on the same street as her? With the baby?' I could not imagine that even Vita's icy graciousness could adequately arm her for such an environment.

'No, not for long. The husband, Katie's husband, was furious. Furious!' she repeats, as if personally exasperated by his response. 'He agreed to a divorce in return for the house and minimal support payments. And that's what he got. You know how Rols can't stand any *unpleasantness*.' She pronounces the last word slowly, as though mocking the indirectness of it, the obfuscation becoming somehow Rollo's and not her own. 'He gave Vita their house and pretty much everything else, too. Which wasn't as much as you might expect. But I think he thought he could still make it up to her, somehow. He couldn't, of course. So, he and Katie left quietly. Vee said they moved to a teeny-tiny house miles from London.' She lingers over the vowels in 'teeny-tiny', which shapes her mouth into a brief smile. 'With four children.'

I pictured Rollo and the woman who was not Vita, banished from London to live with all those small children and on a significantly reduced budget. I think of him grimly attending the endless school events and the weekly children's parties, his new life full of unruly noise and colour, but devoid of the privileges and pleasures he once enjoyed. Parental tedium and the girls' childish grubbiness would direct him to dress as an ordinary man and not in beautiful suits with soft and polished shoes. Those things he once wore every day, and with an easy pride, would gradually be relinquished as relics of his former and more picturesque existence.

'But what about Vita?' I ask.

'Depends who you ask.' Dolly shrugs, removing her hand from mine to pick up her cup. 'She took up with' – she pauses to take the final sip of her coffee, and then places it back on the table at a distance from her – 'her divorce solicitor. As far as I knew. But, last Christmas, Granddad heard a very grand friend of his in Scotland was marrying a Vita. A glamorous divorcée from London without children. He hasn't met her yet, but there aren't many Vitas around, are there?'

'No,' I agree. 'There are not.'

Dolly carefully writes down her telephone number and address. She reads it all back out loud to herself with an endearing frown of concentration before handing it to me. I fold the paper and tuck it carefully into my wallet as she watches with approval.

I stay in the café for some time after she has gone. Then I move towards the square, where a crowd of people – families, couples, and the occasional lone figure like me – all stand hypnotised. Their gazes are all fixed on a street performer, a small woman dressed in gold.

Her clothes are tight-fitting, and her skin is painted the same metallic colour as the fabric, so that it is impossible to tell what parts of her are clothed and what is exposed. She dances balletically and there is a fixed smile on her little gold face. As she dances, she moves towards and then sternly away from the crowd. I shuffle closer, wanting to look at her. The people, too, lean towards her and then step back as she approaches them once more. Their collective movement is as natural as the horizontal breaking of a wave. When I finally get to the front of the crowd, the dancer lurches conclusively towards us all, with her gold arms raised and her gold fists clenched. The people step neatly back together, silently choreographed by their shared ability to predict what will happen next. I alone am motionless, riveted in position and unashamed with wonder.

I know, since I have come to understand the nature of bird-hearts, since Vita, that the unexpected and beautiful will not always hurt when it finally reaches you. That sometimes it will be lit as brightly as fire and yet not burn. The dancer's arms complete their circular motion above her head. Her hands open and their weightless contents spare the watching crowd, who have stepped back as one and so remain immaculate and untouched. The dancer's fistfuls of secrets are released over me alone; it all comes down on my clothes, my skin, as light and silent as snow. It is glitter and I am gold.

Acknowledgements

Firstly, thanks to Amy Sackville for her wisdom, encouragement, and thesis supervision, all of which made writing my first book seem possible. Patricia Debney, thank you for the inspiring teaching and unwavering support. Thanks also to all at Lutyens and Rubinstein, especially my agent, Jenny Hewson, for her insight and guidance. Mary-Anne Harrington of Tinder Press made editing this book a total joy, and thanks to the whole publishing team, in particular Ellie Freedman and Alara Delfosse.

Thank you to my girls, Kitty and Betsy, and my boys too – no longer tiny, but still all perfection. And Steven, thank you always and for everything, including the sea.

VIKTORIA LLOYD-BARLOW holds a PhD in creative writing from the University of Kent and has extensive personal, professional, and academic experience relating to autism. Like her protagonist, Sunday Forrester, in *All the Little Bird-Hearts*, Lloyd-Barlow is autistic. She has presented her doctoral research internationally, most recently speaking at Harvard University on autism and literary narrative. Lloyd-Barlow lives with her husband and children on the coast of northeast Kent.